A TRAITOR'S TEARS

Fiona Buckley

CRÈME de la CRIME

This first world edition published 2013
in Great Britain and 2014 in the USA by
Crème de la Crime, an imprint of
SEVERN HOUSE PUBLISHERS LTD of
19 Cedar Road, Sutton, Surrey, England, SM2 5DA.

Trade paperback edition first published
in Great Britain and the USA 2014 by
SEVERN HOUSE PUBLISHERS LTD

British Library Cataloguing in Publication Data

Buckley, Fiona
  A traitor's tears. – (An Ursula Blanchard Elizabethan
  mystery; 12)
  1. Blanchard, Ursula (Fictitious character)–Fiction.
  2. Murder–Investigation–England–Surrey–Fiction.
  3. Great Britain–History–Elizabeth, 1558-1603–
  Fiction. 4. Detective and mystery stories.
  I. Title II. Series
  823.9'14-dc23

ISBN-13: 978-1-78029-057-7 (cased)
ISBN-13: 978-1-78029-543-5 (trade paper)

Except where actual h
described for the story
publication are fictitic
is purely coincidental.

All Severn House title

Severn House Publish
the leading internatior
are printed on FSC ce:

l,

MIX
Paper from
responsible sources
FSC
www.fsc.org FSC® C013056

Typeset by Palimpsest Book Production Ltd.,
Falkirk, Stirlingshire, Scotland.
Printed and bound in Great Britain by
TJ International, Padstow, Cornwall.

This book is dedicated to my family in Kent:
Pat and David, Derek and Val

ONE

Tower Hill

It is possible to dislike someone quite heartily, without actually wishing them dead, let alone murdered. When in the July of 1573, a group of ladies walking in a sunny garden came suddenly upon a flowerbed with a corpse lying in the middle of it, the horror was not less because one of the sauntering group had every reason to detest the victim.

I was that one and the sight burned itself into my brain. It was the contrast that added the final edge to the shock; the contrast between the couch of bright gillyflowers on which the poor thing lay, and the hard glitter of the silver dagger hilt that jutted from its heart. The blade had been driven in viciously, all the way to that hilt, and the blood had spread in a wide stain across the cream silk bodice and run down to darken the pretty pink blooms below. I can see it now, and I still recoil from it.

But I am getting ahead of myself. The events of 1573, which caused so much trouble to me and to people I cared for, didn't begin in that garden in July. They began more than a year before, on 2 June 1572, on Tower Hill in London, when Thomas Howard, 4th Duke of Norfolk, met his end.

No one could say he hadn't courted it. He had harboured wild dreams of marrying Mary Stuart, the dethroned former Queen of the Scots, and becoming her consort if ever she regained the Scottish crown or – as she and her many supporters hoped – she managed to snatch the English one from the head of our own Queen Elizabeth. Norfolk had become involved in two successive plots concocted by a Florentine banker called Roberto Ridolfi. He was forgiven the first time. He was Elizabeth's cousin and she had a family feeling for him. But when he became entangled in a second such conspiracy, even Elizabeth's patience ran out, and besides, her advisers, especially her Lord Treasurer Sir William Cecil (by then Lord Burghley) and Francis Walsingham, who was her Ambassador to France but had come back briefly to help with the crisis of this new Ridolfi plot, would not agree to let him live.

She couldn't execute Ridolfi, who was safely abroad, and she refused vehemently to execute Mary Stuart, though Mary had known about the plot. Dethroned or not, Mary was an anointed queen and her person was sacrosanct. But when it came to signing Norfolk's death warrant, Elizabeth had no choice.

She didn't want to witness his death yet she seemed to need to know what happened, to be able to picture it, not for pleasure but, I think, because in some way she wanted to feel she hadn't abandoned her cousin but had tried to be with him at the end, if only in her imagination.

There were others, at court, who could have been witnesses on her behalf, but instead, she chose to call me from my quiet home at Hawkswood in Surrey, to attend the execution and report on it to her. It sounds like a curious choice, but it was not as strange as it may seem. Although it wasn't widely talked about or all that widely known, I was her half-sister. Her father, King Henry VIII, had had a roving eye. Elizabeth trusted me and I had carried out a number of secret assignments for her. But as a result of such an assignment, it was partly due to me that Norfolk's latest attempt at treason was foiled and her feelings about that were mixed, a tangle of gratitude and bitterness. I knew that perfectly well. She knew I would give her an accurate account but perhaps she also wanted me to see for myself exactly what I had done. I think so. I wasn't so very surprised when, at the end of May, her summons to London arrived.

I wasn't so very pleased, either.

'I don't want to go,' I said, standing in the small snug room that had once been a private parlour for me and my dear late husband, Hugh. 'I don't want to see Norfolk die. I can't!'

I then discovered that the three principal members of my household who were with me at the time were unanimously embattled against me.

Roger Brockley, my reliable manservant, who had been my

resourceful companion in many times of danger, had a high forehead, lightly strewn with pale gold freckles, a receding hairline and very steady grey-blue eyes. At the moment, he was looking at me as one might look at a small child who was being difficult.

My tirewoman – who was Roger's wife although I still called her Dale as I had done before they married, when she was Fran Dale – had slightly prominent blue eyes and a scatter of pockmarks from a childhood attack of smallpox. The pocks became more noticeable if she was tired or frightened, and they were noticeable now. The idea that I might refuse a request from Elizabeth clearly alarmed her.

Also, I thought, looking at her with compassion, she wanted to agree with Brockley, whatever his opinion might be. They had recently been at odds with each other, and I was the reason. Dale was not a highly intelligent woman, but she had moments of perception and when she had become jealous of the friendship between Roger Brockley and me, it was not quite unjustified. He and I were not, never had been and never would be lovers, but we had come near it once and, more recently, during a time of shared danger, had formed a mental bond which was rare. Dale had sensed it, and that had caused trouble.

The third member of the trio was my gentlewoman Sybil Jester. Sybil had an interesting face, which looked as though it had been slightly compressed between chin and scalp, so that all her features were just a little splayed. The result, though unusual, was quite attractive but when she was worried or displeased, she would frown and then her somewhat elongated eyebrows drew together like a storm cloud. Glancing at her now, I could almost hear the thunder rumble.

I surveyed the three of them in exasperation. I felt outnumbered.

Brockley cleared his throat. 'It isn't wise to ignore the queen's requests, madam. Besides, I think that she has need of you. This will be a bitter business for her.'

'Roger's right, ma'am,' said Dale nervously. 'Saying no to the queen . . . it wouldn't be safe!'

Sybil said, 'I agree. But we'll all come with you. We'll soon be home again, and then it will all be over.'

'Oh!' I said exasperatedly. 'If only I could be let alone and allowed to stay *here*! With my little Harry.'

'If you're away at court for a while,' said Sybil, 'it might help the gossip to die down. I'm tired of it. Last time I went to Guildford – you remember, I went to buy linen from the warehouse there – some other customers came in and one of them must have recognized me, because . . . well, I overheard a comment. And it's not the first time things like that have happened. They've happened twice in Woking. I know where it starts from, too.'

'So do I,' I said. 'Jane Cobbold. Well, I knew it would be like this. It will die down on its own, eventually. I just have to see it through. Running away won't help. *I want to stay here with Harry.*'

I knew I sounded petulant.

Harry was my baby son, born the previous February, a good twelve months after my husband's death and the cause, therefore, of much ill-natured gossip, largely inspired by my conventionally minded acquaintance, Jane Cobbold of Cobbold Hall, near Woking. She was all the more offended because she wasn't allowed to ostracize me. Her husband, Anthony Cobbold, believed in cultivating people who were in high places or had relatives there.

He was proud to be a friend of the county sheriff, Sir Edward Heron; he had lately made friends with one Roland Wyse, who at the moment was working for Lord Burghley; and he also knew that the queen was my sister. He clearly hadn't been able to silence Jane's gossip-mongering, but he had compelled her to maintain social contacts with me – had indeed quarrelled with her on the subject. Their butler was the cousin of my chief cook, John Hawthorn. We had heard all about it.

Jane was not, obviously, mistaken when she went about saying that Harry couldn't be my late husband's son, but her assumption that during a visit to the Continent the previous year I had misbehaved myself as no lady, certainly not a recent widow, ought to do, was wrong. It hadn't been like that at all.

Now, though, her spiteful tongue was a nuisance, even worse than I had expected. It was true that a brief absence due to being invited to Elizabeth's court *might* do me some good. And could I, really, say no to the queen?

I felt my resistance falter. I couldn't refuse the queen. I would have to go to Tower Hill and watch Norfolk's execution, and that was that.

The door of the parlour opened and our little gathering was increased by one. Gladys Morgan had joined us, uninvited, but that was typical. Gladys was an aged Welshwoman who had attached herself to my household years ago, after we had rescued her from a charge of witchcraft. We had had to do it again since, for Gladys was just the kind to attract that sort of suspicion.

I had long since insisted that she should wash with reason-able regularity, but she detested it and in any case, she seemed to have a body odour whether she washed or not. Her teeth consisted of a few brown fangs, her laugh was a disagreeable cackle and her temper was short. She had a repertoire of blasphemous curses which in days gone by she had regularly hurled at people who annoyed her. She had done that much less since it nearly brought her to the scaffold, but it could still happen occasionally. She was also very skilled with herbal medicines, and nothing irritates a physician more than a woman who concocts more efficient potions than he does. Vicars and doctors had been among her accusers the last time she was arrested for witchcraft.

But Gladys had been part of our lives for a long time and we were used to her ways. That she should walk without knocking into the midst of our discussion neither surprised or annoyed us.

'This is to do with that letter from the court, ain't it?' she said, hobbling across the room and seating herself in a patch of sunlight. She had become very lame that year. 'Saw the seal, I did. From Lord Burghley. He wants you for something, mistress?'

'The queen wants me,' I said. 'To witness Norfolk's death on her behalf.'

'And told Lord Burghley to summon you on *her* behalf,' said Gladys, and snorted. 'Lord Burghley. Same man as he was when he was just Sir William Cecil. All these fancy titles!

Folk don't change their natures. Whenever Cecil wanted you for anything in the past, or the queen either, it always led to trouble. Didn't it, now?'

'Not this time,' I said. 'Why should it? I don't want to go though I'm beginning to think that I'll have to. But it won't be anything worse than unpleasant.'

'You wait and see,' said Gladys ominously.

'No,' I said. 'This time *you'll* see.'

We were both right, in a way. Trouble did follow, but for once it wasn't because of any ulterior motive on the part of either Cecil or the queen. Quite by accident, they placed me where I would witness the beginning of the disaster, without at that time understanding what I had seen.

Gladys said, 'Don't want me to come along, do you? Don't feel like travelling, these days.'

'I shouldn't think you ever want to see London again,' I said, remembering her narrow escape at Tyburn. 'Very well! I'll do as the queen bids me. I'll take Sybil with me, and Dale and Brockley, of course. But I'll only ask Brockley to come with me to Tower Hill. If you will, Brockley. You've been a soldier.'

'Of course, madam,' said Brockley.

It was several hours' ride from Hawkswood in west Surrey to London, allowing for refreshment breaks at inns, for us and the horses. We set out early. There were five of us: myself, Sybil, Brockley, with Dale – who was no keen horsewoman – on his pillion, and John Ryder, the courier who had carried Lord Burghley's summons to me. He had not heard my protests and near rebellion because at the time, thirsty after his ride, he had been taking a tankard of ale with my steward, Adam Wilder. It was just as well. Ryder, grey-bearded and fatherly, was an old friend but I knew he would have sided with the others. He and Brockley had known each other long ago, when both of them were soldiers. It was bad enough to have Brockley looking at me as though I were a tiresome little girl; I wouldn't have liked to have John Ryder doing the same thing. I had immense respect for him. He had joined us on our last adventure, which had taken us into dangerous Spain. But for him, we might not have got out safely.

Not that he didn't understand what a sad business this execution was. He said as much to me as we journeyed. 'There'll be tears shed for that foolish man Thomas Howard of Norfolk tomorrow. I understand that because his family pleaded for him, he's been given a decent lodging in the Tower; he's not in a dungeon. There hasn't been an execution on Tower Hill for so long that the old scaffold wasn't fit for use when they went to make it ready, and it had to be rebuilt. It's a shame it's for Thomas Howard. He's been more silly than wicked, in my view.'

The queen was at Whitehall. I had seen all the queen's palaces in my thirty-eight years and Whitehall wasn't my favourite; it was too confusing. It was not so much a coherent building as a small-scale town, with numerous separate or nearly separate buildings, amid a maze of courtyards and little enclosed gardens. However, we were expected. Ryder was passed straight in to announce our arrival and we only had a short wait before one of the senior officials known as White Staves, with the white stick that was his badge of office under his arm, appeared to greet us, followed by three menservants and two grooms. Our horses were led away except for Ryder's. He belonged to Cecil's household and intended to return there for the night, since it wasn't far away.

Brockley, whose past career included being a groom as well as a soldier, would normally have gone to see for himself that our horses were properly cared for, but at court, he knew he need not worry. He came with Dale and me as we followed the White Stave to our own quarters.

Our lodging turned out to be three rooms at the top of a building that I remembered from the past as guest accommodation. They were comfortable if small, and there were attendants to bring us hot washing water and towels. Supper would be in three hours' time, we learned, and would be taken in the main dining hall across an open courtyard. At Whitehall, guests sometimes had to brave bad weather if they wanted to eat.

At dinner, the Brockleys were directed to a lower place but Sybil and I were together close to the top table. My position at court was never closely defined, even though court protocol was always stiff and over the years had grown stiffer. I had once been a Lady of the Bedchamber but was not so any longer; I was the queen's half-sister but not openly acknowledged; I had also at times been an espionage agent for her, but few people were supposed to know that. I had no claim to a place at the top table; nor could I be thrust down towards the salt, let alone below it. Every time I came to court, whoever planned the seating must have to worry over where, exactly, to put me. It amused me.

The queen was absent, presumably taking supper in private. Looking towards a table parallel with the one where Sybil and I were placed, I saw, in an equivalent position to ourselves, someone I knew. It was Anthony Cobbold's friend Roland Wyse, who was now one of Cecil's assistants, though I didn't know why, since he had originally been attached to Francis Walsingham. It puzzled me that he was not in France, where Walsingham now was.

I knew Wyse fairly well, since we had met last year during the process of unravelling the plot which tomorrow would bring Norfolk to the block. He had errands in Surrey sometimes and he usually seized the chance of calling both on Anthony Cobbold and myself. I rather wished he wouldn't for he was much given to boastful accounts of life at court, and would talk at length about his ambitions and his hopes for future advancement, and I found this tedious.

He was capable of charity; I had seen him giving alms to somebody in need which was a point in his favour, yet I could not like him and neither could Brockley. Wyse had sandy hair and a snub-nosed face that at first sight looked boyish, until you noticed his pugnacious jawline and the coldness of his stone-coloured eyes. Brockley had once said that Wyse looked like an assassin. He noticed me and bowed in my direction. I bowed back.

Seated at the top table were a number of dignitaries, and among them, to my surprise, was Sir Robert Dudley, Earl of Leicester, who I knew usually took meals in his own apartments. He was a man for rich and colourful clothing but today, though his velvet doublet was rich enough, if rather too hot for a June evening, it was dark blue.

I realized suddenly how muted was the atmosphere in the

dining hall. It was usually lively with talk and very often musicians would play while the diners ate, but not this evening. Voices were quiet and not only Leicester had chosen a sombre outfit. I myself had instinctively chosen a dark brown dress, lightened only by a cream kirtle, while Sybil was in black and white. The impending execution was affecting everyone, I thought, and perhaps Dudley was here because in such circumstances, people draw together.

I could understand it. Norfolk was in his prime, and he had been popular. He had been married three times, though none of his wives were long-lived. His marriages had brought him three sons and two daughters, and three stepdaughters to whom I knew he had been a conscientious guardian. His third wife had died five years ago and it was after that that his romantic fantasies about Mary Stuart had begun. John Ryder had been right, I thought, to call him foolish rather than wicked.

His death was timed for the morrow, at eight o'clock in the morning. We rose shortly after daybreak. John Ryder was coming to escort me, but as I had said, back in Hawkswood, Brockley would come with me as well. Dale and Sybil would stay in our lodgings.

As I prepared to set out, I looked at myself in a mirror and noticed how the years were changing me. My hair was still dark and glossy, but my eyes, which were hazel, had little lines round them and a wary expression. This morning, they also looked large and dark, and my face – it was triangular, not unlike the queen's in shape – was pale. Sybil, coming into the room to see if I were ready to go to breakfast, said: 'Ursula, you look tired. Did you sleep badly?'

'Not too well,' I admitted, 'though I wanted to sleep. The long ride yesterday was tiring. I don't think I've quite regained my strength after having Harry, even though it was much easier than I expected.' I had had trouble in childbirth on previous occasions, and until Harry arrived, my married daughter Meg was my only surviving offspring.

'You hate all this,' Sybil said. 'We all do. But one *can't* refuse the queen.'

'No, I know. I hate being back at court, too,' I told her.

Sybil, who rather enjoyed the contact with glamour that

such visits brought, looked surprised. 'You hate being at court? But why?'

I thought about it, visualizing Hawkswood, that quiet, grey stone manor house with its big, light hall, its two pleasant parlours, its terrace and the rose garden that Hugh had so much loved, and wishing myself back there, with all my heart. Life at Hawkswood was . . .

'At home,' I said, 'life is simple. Everyone knows who they are and what they have to do each day. We're like a family, even if most of us aren't related to each other. At court, everyone's watching everyone else. They're sensitive about where they're seated in the dining hall, or who goes first and who goes last when coming into the queen's presence. They eye each other, wondering if so and so, who smiles at them so nicely, is really scheming to oust them from whatever position they're in. Roland Wyse aches to be granted a title and appointed to the Privy Council; I know he does. I've heard him say so. People at court become subtle, cunning, suspicious, and when I'm here for any length of time, I find myself beginning to think like them, seeing the world through their eyes and I don't like it.'

'I never thought of it that way!' said Sybil, much astonished.

'No, you just see the dresses and the jewellery and the sunshine on the River Thames!'

'Not today,' said Sybil gravely.

John Ryder arrived to accompany us when we set out but in fact, it was a big group that left Whitehall. We rode, as it was some distance to Tower Hill. Roland Wyse was there, on a showy chestnut gelding. Robert Dudley of Leicester was not, and there was no sign either of Lord Burghley. Neither, I knew, greatly cared for gruesome spectacles. There were, however, many ladies and gallants who had chosen to attend, though they were surely not obliged to do so. Some would have come to sorrow, perhaps to give Norfolk some kind of support. But others, those who didn't know him well, were probably just there to gawp at the scene. I shivered, thinking about it. My stomach was churning.

To keep my mind off the immediate future, I brought my

horse alongside John Ryder and asked him why Roland Wyse
was in London with Lord Burghley and not in Paris with
Walsingham. Since Ryder himself belonged to Burghley's
entourage, he was likely to know.

He did, and laughed. 'He's still officially one of Walsingham's
assistants but he's been seconded to Burghley till Walsingham
comes home for good. Rumour has it that Walsingham wants
a rest from Wyse's pushy ways. I think he lends Wyse to other
departments, or sends him on errands away from the court
whenever he gets the chance!'

I nodded. I knew all about Wyse's pushy ways.

'My lord Burghley uses him sometimes for the courier work
I used to do,' Ryder said. 'I still do some short journeys but
the longer ones are too wearing nowadays. I'm getting older!
Wyse is welcome to those.'

'Does he mind?' I asked. 'Being sent back to England to
run errands for Lord Burghley?'

Ryder shrugged. 'Can't tell. But one impression I do have
is that if Walsingham doesn't really like him, he doesn't like
Walsingham, either.'

I had some sympathy with that. I knew that Walsingham
was a valuable and most loyal servant to the queen, but he was
also a stark, stern man who on the few occasions when I had
met him had made me ill at ease. I had even heard rumours
that the queen herself didn't care for him either, though she
trusted him. The two things aren't the same.

As we rode through London we noticed that many people,
on foot, were going in the same direction. 'By the look of
things, half the city means to be in at the death,' Brockley
muttered, coming up on my other side.

It was a beautiful morning with brilliant sunshine, though
London, of course, was as smelly as ever, with chimney smoke
and horse droppings, food cooking in kitchens with open
windows, middens beginning to steam in the warmth. But all
such things, sunlight and smells alike, were part of living. Life
was pulsing everywhere. It was no day for anyone to die.

Tower Hill was beyond the Tower of London itself, just
outside its walls. There were barriers to keep the crowds back
from the scaffold, which was a high platform, with the block

in the middle and thick straw all around it. My stomach churned more than ever. I knew why the straw was there. It was to absorb the blood.

Grooms were waiting to take our horses. They led them away – probably, I thought, to some convenient stabling or hitching posts. I was sure that the grooms didn't intend to miss the spectacle through having to hold horses' bridles. We continued on foot. Most of the crowd had to stand but members of the court had the privilege of seats and there were benches ready for us. They were closer to the scaffold than I could have wished. We were going to have an unpleasantly good view.

It was quarter to eight when we sat down. I was between Brockley and Ryder. Glancing to my right, I saw that Roland Wyse was a few yards away and at that moment, a man I didn't recognize pushed his way along the row of benches and took a seat next to him. The stranger, who was dressed in black, with a style of hat that didn't look quite English, hadn't been with us on the ride to the Tower and probably wasn't from the court. Perhaps Wyse had arranged his seat in advance for they embraced as they met, as friends do, and then sat talking with an air of intimacy.

I looked away, not wanting to be caught staring, and found myself looking instead at a group of younger people, men and girls, all in black. The girls were tearful and, after a moment, I identified one of them and realized that the group consisted of Norfolk's children and stepdaughters. Ryder had noticed them, too. 'I suppose they're here so that Norfolk will see friendly faces at the last,' he said. 'I wonder, does it really help a man, to see his family grieving?'

I shook my head, not knowing the answer.

There was a pause, tense, like the air before a thunderstorm. Then, in the distance, trumpets blared and we heard a slow drumbeat. The sad procession appeared, calling forth a murmur from the throng, half excited, half distressed. The trumpeters walked first, as heralds, clearing the way with noisy blasts, since the crowd was spilling in all directions. The drummers followed, sounding a regular, muted roll like the tread of heavy and inexorable feet. It pounded at one's nerves.

After the drummers came a man who, Ryder told us, was the constable of the Tower. Behind him were guards with halberds and, in the midst of them, a small forlorn figure in doublet and hose but without a ruff, was Norfolk. A chaplain walked beside him, reading from a prayer book and behind them was a man in the dark gown of a clerk.

I looked up at the horrible straw-bedded platform and saw that the headsman had arrived, masked and dressed in skin-tight sable. He held his long-handled axe at his side, not attempting to conceal it.

Silence fell as the guards took up positions round the scaffold, except that I could hear sobbing from Norfolk's family. The guards had their backs to the block, and were watching the crowd in case of trouble. Of all the people present, they would be the only ones who wouldn't witness the end.

The constable came to Norfolk's side and motioned to him to climb the wooden steps to the platform. He did so, looking, as he climbed, smaller and more forlorn than ever. The chaplain and the clerk followed him, and I realized that in a corner of the platform, incongruously, there was a small table where paper, held down by stone weights, an inkpot and a quill pen in a holder were set ready. The clerk at once went to dip the quill in the ink. I wondered what he was about and then understood, because as Norfolk turned round, took hold of the surrounding railing, and began to speak, the clerk began to write. He was recording Norfolk's final words.

I was near enough to see how white Norfolk was, and I could see that behind him, the chaplain, still clutching his prayer book, looked just as bad. It was difficult to hear, for voices carry poorly in the open air and Norfolk's was trembling, anyway. But I made out some of his words.

He said that he had only met Signor Ridolfi face to face once, and nothing had been said against the queen. I lost much of the next few sentences but thought he was saying that they had only talked of money matters. There was something about Ridolfi appreciating the tranquillity of England. A murmur broke out at that and I stiffened, too. There would have been little left of that tranquillity if any of Ridolfi's schemes had reached fruition. He would have loosed a Spanish army on us, dragging the Inquisition in its wake. Norfolk's next few words, though, did in a way admit as much, for he seemed to be saying that in his opinion, Ridolfi was ready for any wicked design. Then he said that God would witness that he, Norfolk, was a good Protestant and loyal to the queen.

In the silence following his speech, he turned away, taking off his doublet. He handed it to the clerk, who put it over his arm, gathered up the paper he had been writing on, and then scurried down the steps to get out of the way. The headsman knelt and Norfolk gave him a purse. It was customary but I thought it must be a bitter thing, having to pay the man who was about to kill you. Presumably to make sure he did his best to make a quick job of it.

The headsman stood up. Norfolk knelt at the block. The chaplain, who now looked as though he might collapse at any moment, read something aloud from the prayer book, but his voice was so faint that I couldn't follow any of his words at all. The axe swung up and its polished blade glittered in that lovely morning sunshine. It swung down with speed and force and blood spurted up, splashing the headsman. He was presumably used to it but I flinched and drew back as though it had splashed me as well.

Norfolk's crouched body seemed to fold on itself and sink into a heap. The headsman leant down, picked up something round which dripped with red, and held it up by its blood-dabbled hair, as he declared: 'So perish all enemies of the queen!'

I swallowed hard, trying to contain a surge of nausea. Beside me, both Brockley and Ryder had gone rigid. I glanced towards Wyse, wondering how he had reacted and saw, to my astonishment, that Roland Wyse, of the pugnacious jaw and the chilly eyes, was in tears, and the friend at his side was anxiously patting his back, trying to give comfort.

As I watched, Wyse turned his face into his companion's doublet and, judging from the heaving of his shoulders, had abandoned himself to the most desolate weeping.

TWO
Gifts from a Queen

The summons to the queen came soon after our return to Whitehall. Indeed, I had barely taken off my hat, before a page came to fetch me. He led me to the queen's private apartments and showed me through an outer chamber where a number of her ladies were stitching while one of them read aloud from a book of verse, and on into a small room that Elizabeth used as a study and for practising music. It had a mullioned window with glass panes leaded in a pleasing pattern, open this warm June day, so that birdsong came in from outside. The room was furnished with a spinet and a writing desk, a set of bookshelves, and a carved oak settle which just now was occupied by a mysterious object hidden under a silk drape.

Elizabeth was waiting for me on a cushioned window seat. She was simply dressed, by her standards, in a long loose peach-coloured gown with neither ruff nor farthingale, but most people would have thought the damask of the gown, the profusion of pearls – rope, earrings, the edging of her headdress and the glimmering bunches on the ends of her girdle – were highly elaborate. She smiled at me as I curtsied and, as I rose, I smiled back, but I was nervous.

As the years went on, my royal half-sister had become increasingly royal and therefore increasingly intimidating. She was not yet forty and every now and then there was renewed talk of marriage plans for her. At present, it was rumoured that an alliance with a French prince was being discussed. Looking at her now, however, I could not imagine her joined in marriage to anyone. Her face was shield-shaped and she used it as a shield, hiding her thoughts behind it; the jewels and fine fabrics were armour too, holding her aloof from others. I couldn't visualize a man ever finding his way past them.

'So, Ursula,' she said. 'What happened this morning?'

I told her, briefly and also truthfully. She nodded. 'So he tried, at the end, to excuse himself, to say he had never plotted treason with Ridolfi. I thought he would. But he died with dignity.'

'Yes, ma'am. Yes, he did.'

'Of that, I am glad. He was my cousin. It is a sad burden, having to pass such a sentence on a member of one's own family.' She did not add, *And you helped to put me in that position*, but I heard the trace of resentment in her voice. It was only a trace, though, and it vanished as she said: 'A burden, but inevitable if I and the realm are to stay safe. Thank you, Ursula. This morning must have been an ordeal for you, too. You are well? How is your small son? My little nephew!'

'He thrives, ma'am. A young Hawkswood maidservant, Tessie, has been appointed as his nurse and is caring for him while I'm away.'

'I hear you have called him Harry. After my father?'

'Partly that, ma'am. But it is of course a popular name.'

'So it is. And now, I take it, you will wish to return to your home at Hawkswood. What of your other house, Withysham, that I gave to you so many years ago?'

'That flourishes, too, ma'am. I visited it earlier this year.'

'I do hear a good deal about you,' Elizabeth said. 'As you know, I take an interest in your welfare. There are those who send word to Burghley now and then.'

'Yes, ma'am,' I said. I knew of Burghley's discreet surveillance and tried not to be irritated by it, knowing that it was for my good.

'In places close to Hawkswood, I hear there has been unkind gossip about Harry,' Elizabeth remarked. 'It was to be expected. Withysham, being in Sussex, perhaps gave you a chance of escaping from it.'

'Yes, ma'am,' I said, none too truthfully, for I had an uncle and aunt near Withysham, whose comments about Harry had been even more scathing than Jane Cobbold's gossip, and for less reason. I had been frank with them, for from the start I had determined that Harry should grow up knowing who he was, and accepted as who he was, with no deception. I had hoped that since my uncle and aunt still held, though discreetly, by the Catholic faith, they of all people ought to have been understanding about Harry. I had been disappointed.

But then, they had never liked me. They took my mother in when she came home from King Henry's court, disgraced and with child and refusing to name its father, and when I was born, they had given me a home as well. But it hadn't been a happy one. My mother died when I was sixteen, and when I was twenty, I ran away to marry my first husband, Gerald Blanchard, which had further enraged Uncle Herbert and Aunt Tabitha, since he was supposed to be betrothed to one of their daughters.

My marital situation was an odd one. After Gerald's death from smallpox, I had married Matthew de la Roche, who was half-French by blood and all French in his ways. I had lived with him in France for a time, though I left my little daughter by Gerald in England, as I didn't want her to grow up a Papist. I had married Matthew by Catholic rites and under a degree of duress, yet I was in love with him and he with me. But he was forever getting involved in plots against Elizabeth and there was never any real peace between us.

When I was on a visit to England because Meg had need of me, I heard that Matthew had died, of plague. Some time after that, I married Hugh, my very dear Hugh, who was much older than I was, but as good and kind a companion as anyone could ask for. And then I learned that Matthew was not dead; that the queen and Cecil had lied to me, to keep me in England, and that he had been told the same lie about me. Elizabeth said that she had also annulled our marriage, on the grounds that the rite was unlawful and there had been duress. But in Catholic eyes, the marriage had been legal in its form and the duress questionable, since for a long time I had lived as Matthew's wife, of my own free will.

After Hugh's death, I had had occasion to visit the Continent. I had met Matthew again and he had rescued me from a dangerous situation. For a short time, we came together and Harry was the result. I had hoped that in the eyes of my Catholic uncle and aunt, Harry would be legitimate, but they hadn't taken that view at all and, between their virtuous condemnation of my morals and the merciless tongue of Jane Cobbold, my plan to face down gossip and rear my son without apology as Harry de la Roche was turning out very difficult. I had set myself a hard field to plough.

'You will win through,' said Elizabeth, who knew all about the circumstances leading to Harry's arrival. 'You have a gift for that. And I have a gift for your little son. I promised a fine christening present for him – do you remember? I have kept my word. Come.' She slid off the window seat and shook out her skirts. 'My ladies helped in the making. They can all embroider skilfully. I have it here.'

It was the object on the settle. Elizabeth drew back the drapery and revealed a child's cot. It was made of exquisitely carved walnut, with a canopy that could be set up to protect its occupant from over-hot sunshine. The canopy was of blue silk with little animals and birds embroidered on it in gold. There were pillows with embroidered covers, sheets with edgings to match, a soft woollen blanket and a sealskin coverlet.

'It takes to pieces,' Elizabeth said. 'It will need a packhorse to itself, but John Ryder will go with you, and bring the packhorse back.'

'It's a royal gift!' I said.

Before I left Whitehall, Elizabeth also presented me with a small purse of money, which I used before starting for home, by visiting a cloth warehouse and buying a roll of lightweight worsted. It was a new type of cloth which I had already found ideal for making summer-weight cloaks and everyday dresses. I talked to the merchant across a counter in a congested room where the walls were covered all the way up to the ceiling by shelves full of fabric rolls. The higher shelves were only accessible from ladders. He said I was lucky that he actually had some worsted available.

'It's hard to get. I've had to bring some in from abroad. The Guild of Weavers that make the old heavy cloth have been creating a to-do and saying this new stuff is affecting their business, and they've somehow got a regulation made about how many worsted weaving looms can be allowed in the

country. I know all about it because one of the Guild officials
is my brother-in-law and often dines with me.'

The merchant grinned. He was a small, bald man, with bright
grey-green eyes in a wrinkled face. 'Since he *is* a relative, in a
way, I took the liberty of telling him not to be a noddy. If folk
want this new kind of cloth, I said, they'll clamour till they get
it. Your weaving shed's big enough to take an extra loom or
two! Apply for a licence and put in a couple of worsted looms.
King Canute couldn't turn the tide back and nor can you. But
he wouldn't have it. Nice man, in his way, and good to my
sister, but when it comes to business he can't see past the end
of his nose.'

Turning round, he stepped nimbly on to a ladder, went up
three steps and heaved a roll of cloth down to the counter
below, where it landed with a thud. Stepping down again, he
unrolled a length for my inspection.

'This is good hardwearing cloth, if it being brown is all
right with you. It'll take a black or dark blue dye if you want
. . .'

I bought it and watched while he put a length of twine round
it, and put it in a hamper. Then he came out of the warehouse
with me and Brockley helped him to add it to the load on the
extra packhorse. Sybil and I – and Dale, too – would have new
dresses and cloaks out of that, and making them would keep
us busy for a while.

The pause at the warehouse had delayed our start and it was
late in the evening when the chimneys of Hawkswood at last
came into view. We had been sighted, and found a welcome
waiting for us in the courtyard. As we rode in, our two half-
mastiffs, Hero and Hector, bounded joyfully towards us and there
were our three grooms, and Tessie with Harry in her arms, and
beside her was our tall grey-haired steward Adam Wilder,
beaming, and there was Gladys, with the leer that with her
did duty as a smile.

From an upstairs window, two of our maids, Phoebe and
Netta, waved dusters to us and in the kitchen doorway stood
John Hawthorn, the cook, big and impressive, arms akimbo,
and there behind him were his assistants, Joan and Ben Flood,
respectively clutching a long wooden spoon and a rolling pin.

Savoury supper smells drifted past them to add to the greeting and my stomach rumbled.

'It's good to be home,' I said to Sybil.

It was slightly less good when, as soon as we were indoors and had changed and come down to the big hall to eat the supper that smelt so appetising, Wilder presented me with a letter bearing the Cobbold seal.

'It came yesterday, madam.'

'Thank you, Wilder.' I broke the seal and undid the little scroll. It was an invitation to dine with the Cobbolds the following week. Anthony Cobbold understood, because of a chance meeting with Adam Wilder in Woking, that I had been to court but was likely to be home by then and it had been so long since I last visited. Please would I bring charming Mistress Jester and, of course, my two good servants the Brockleys. Master Cobbold awaited my reply with impatience.

'I'm invited – or bidden – to Cobbold Hall for dinner next week,' I said to Wilder.

'I guessed as much, madam. John Hawthorn saw his cousin, the one who works at Cobbold Hall, only yesterday.' Wilder smiled. 'You have been in London with the queen, you see. Master Cobbold will surely want to hear your news.'

'He'll hope that Her Majesty's power and influence will have rubbed off on me and that some of it will miraculously rub off on him!' I said candidly. 'I don't suppose Jane Cobbold is overjoyed.'

'I daresay she does her husband's bidding,' Wilder said mildly.

'Just about,' said Brockley, who had just come in from the stable, where he had been rubbing his horse down. 'Thin ice over very cold water, if you ask me.'

'I'll have to accept,' I said, with regret.

THREE
Spiteful Tongues

S ince my return to England the previous year, I had not dined with the Cobbolds, though I had met them twice at the home of Christina Ferris, their younger daughter, who had resolutely remained friendly to me. On a few occasions too, Anthony had made informal visits to Hawkswood, bringing a stiff and reluctant Jane with him.

Faced with this unwanted invitation, I too was reluctant, but as with the summons to see Norfolk die, I decided to make the best of it. Maintaining social contacts with my neighbours was a necessary part of my strategy for making myself and Harry acceptable.

Therefore, I and my companions dressed well for the visit, put smiles on our faces, and got out the old coach that had belonged to Hugh, so that Dale and Sybil and I could travel in style. Our usual coachman, Arthur Watts, who was also our head groom, had no more wish to visit Cobbold Hall than I had, and was happy enough to let Brockley take the reins for the day, so Brockley, dressed in his best black suit, did the driving.

Cobbold Hall was a pleasant house. It was smaller than Hawkswood, with fewer rooms, most of them less spacious than mine, but all comfortably furnished, and the grounds were quite extensive. There were formal gardens close to the house and further out were a shrubbery, an orchard, a vegetable garden, a park which included an extensive oak wood, three or four outlying cottages with their own gardens, and then a couple of smallholdings.

The path to the house led past one of the cottages, which was occupied by a solitary, middle-aged man called Jack Jarvis, who represented one of Jane Cobbold's charities. Jane might be, and was, thoroughly narrow-minded, regarding me as immoral and unwomanly, but she had her virtues nonetheless and she was generous to the poor. Jack Jarvis had fallen on hard times when the common land, where he had once grazed sheep, was enclosed for a landlord's benefit and anyone who wished to graze their animals there was thereafter charged for the privilege. Jarvis could not afford the charge and lost his livelihood.

The cottage and its garden had at that time been unoccupied and neglected. Jane Cobbold had persuaded Anthony to let Jarvis have the place for a modest rent, on the understanding that he would tidy it up and support himself by growing vegetables and keeping poultry.

Jarvis had done fairly well. I had heard – via John Hawthorn and his Cobbold Hall cousin – that the Lion Inn in Woking habitually bought not only vegetables, but also eggs and fowls for the table from him, and that he also regularly took his produce to market in Woking and rarely brought any of it back unsold.

The weather was sunny, and when we rode past he was working in his garden. He came to the gate to doff his battered straw hat to us. He was not a prepossessing individual, being skinny and scruffy, with large red ears poking through the lank grey hair that hung to his shoulders. The left ear had a white scar across it, as though he had been in a knife fight at some time. But he was mannerly enough, and I gave him a couple of coins, which he accepted without any false protests.

When I offered him a small gift as well, he accepted that too, with alacrity. Knowing that we might encounter him, I had brought him a belt of good polished leather, with a little ornamental chasing on the steel buckle. I think I did it as a means of hinting to Jane Cobbold that I, too, was a charitable lady, but when I saw how worn and old was the belt he was wearing, I was glad I had thought of it. He waved his awful straw headpiece to us as we rode on our way, and Brockley said: 'Next time, madam, I recommend bringing him a hat.'

'If there is a next time,' I said. 'I expect Master Cobbold had hard work to talk his wife into inviting us even just this once.'

Anthony came out to welcome us in person. He was a tall,

saturnine man, his dark eyes deep set under black, winged eyebrows, and Sybil always said he looked so demonic that he made her nervous. In fact, he was a pleasant and peace-loving man. Brockley, as always when possible, went with the grooms to see that the horses were properly cared for while Dale came into the house with Sybil and me, walking correctly just behind us.

We were led into the parlour, where Jane awaited us. She rose as we entered, and I saw that she too had made the best of things and dressed for the occasion, though her efforts hadn't been entirely successful. Jane had never been a very good-looking woman and she had put on weight since I last saw her, with the result that she was now almost ugly. Extra flesh had blurred the bone structure of her face and her elegantly embroidered sleeves, close-fitting from elbow to wrist, were strained into creases by the plump arms inside them. The rings that adorned her short, fat fingers looked too tight for comfort. She spoke a few formal words of welcome and remarked on the warmth of the day. We took seats, Dale choosing a low stool at a little distance from the rest of us. Wine was brought in by John Hawthorn's cousin, and conversation commenced.

Everyone was on their best behaviour. We began by discussing matters agricultural. Anthony Cobbold said they were having trouble this year in getting hold of the men who usually sheared their sheep. A neighbouring farm had increased the size of its flock and the men were having to stay there for longer than in previous years. However, it had been possible to cut the hay on the home farm in good time, and the yield had been satisfactory.

I responded by saying that on the Hawkswood home farm, haymaking was in progress and seemed promising. I hoped the good weather would hold.

'I never look forward to haymaking!' Jane said. 'It causes trouble indoors, believe it or not. Every year, one of my maids, as soon as haymaking time comes round, begins to sneeze and *sneeze*. I can't allow her to work in the kitchens or serve food until the end of August.'

The conversation moved on to the subject of food. Jane

gave us an anecdote about a new recipe which her cook had tried and which had gone disastrously wrong. She made a long story of it; Jane was apt to be voluble. 'We won't be offering you that for dinner, I assure you,' she said, reaching the end at last.

I replied with a similar anecdote; Sybil, whose deceased husband had kept a pie shop in Cambridge, guided the talk towards flavourings for various types of meat. Jane broke in with recommendations of her own. I slipped in a few inoffensive comments. It was all more than a little stilted and I found it a welcome diversion when Hawthorn's cousin (John Hawthorn only ever called him *my cousin*, while the Cobbolds addressed him as Hawthorn and to this day I don't know what his Christian name was) came to announce that dinner was served. We went into the next room, where a table was set and dishes were being placed upon it by several servants, none of whom was the girl with the sneezes.

There was freshly made bread, a cold fennel soup with almonds and ginger to flavour it, roast pork with an apple dressing and accompanying dishes of peas and fried beans, bread pudding with cinnamon in it, and spiced wine custard. There were suitable wines. The talk continued along its careful channels, like a well-regulated river.

The Cobbolds had two married daughters, Alison and Christina. I asked after them. Both were well, Jane said, and both had visited Cobbold Hall recently. The elder girl had made them the grandparents of twin boys, which was delightful.

Anthony nodded and said that although Christina had originally married against his wishes, he was now getting to like her husband. 'Our two families were on bad terms for generations and it was time to put an end to it. When it came to the point, I found it much easier than I expected. Christina has just told us that she expects her first child soon. I hope for a little granddaughter.'

I expressed congratulations and Sybil praised the apple dressing with the pork. Jane thanked her. Anthony spoke of the excellent cuisine at the Lion in Woking and how pleased they were that their tenant Jack Jarvis now contributed to it.

Jane agreed and said that Jarvis was proving a satisfactory tenant. Talking about good and bad tenants took us safely through second helpings of roast pork.

We were broaching the bread pudding and the spiced wine custard when Anthony observed that he had seen me recently, riding a horse he hadn't seen before. 'You used to have a dapple grey, did you not, Mistress Stannard? Have you sold her?'

'That was Roundel. No, I still have her, but she is out at grass as she has a foal. The black mare you saw me on is called Jewel. I bought her recently. She is a most comfortable ride.'

'Ah. So last year, when you were away so long, you let Roundel be used for breeding.'

'Yes, that's right. I put my instructions in a letter I sent to Adam Wilder.'

'The foal is sweet,' said Sybil sentimentally. 'It's the dearest thing I ever beheld.'

We could talk of the Cobbold grandsons and Roundel's foal but no one asked how my little boy was thriving. I didn't mention him, either.

Dessert came to an end. There was an odd hiatus, because servants should by now have been coming into the room to clear away the used dishes and offer a last round of wine, but there was no sign of them. Anthony began to frown. Jane murmured, 'Where has everyone got to, I wonder?' and rose to her feet, presumably to enquire into the delay.

Before she reached the door, however, it was thrust open and there in the doorway stood Brockley. The sight of him brought us all to our feet. His receding hair was tangled and speckled with blood. A vivid red patch on his left cheekbone would soon darken into an ugly bruise and he was holding a reddened napkin to his nose. There were scarlet streaks all down his smart black doublet.

There was a horrified silence. Then Jane exclaimed: 'What is the meaning of this? How dare you break in on us in this unseemly fashion? Mistress Stannard, is this the way your manservant behaves?'

Dale, gasping, 'Roger! You're hurt!' started towards him.

Brockley wiped his nose with an angry movement, and said:
'I beg your pardon, Master Cobbold, Mistress Cobbold, and
you, madam. I beg all your pardons. But a man has a right to
defend himself and his employers, too. Master Cobbold, I have
punched your spitboy on the jaw and he is now unconscious
on your kitchen floor, and the uncommonly rude individual,
who calls himself your assistant cook, is sitting on a stool,
doubled up and moaning. I punched *him* in the stomach.'

'Brockley!' I said, horrified. Dale was now beside him,
examining the state of his nose.

'This is *disgraceful*!' Jane cried. 'Mistress Stannard, can
you not keep your manservant in order?'

'They said things, madam,' said Brockley, ignoring Jane
and addressing me. 'Unforgiveable things. It's all right, Fran.
I think it's almost stopped bleeding now. I won't repeat them,
madam, but they were about yourself.' He turned to Anthony.
'Master Cobbold, you should warn your servants to guard their
tongues, especially when the people they are talking about are
actually under this roof. I never wanted the matter to turn into
a fight. I spoke up when ugly insinuations were made to me,
and your assistant cook sneered at me and struck me in the
face. I struck back and the spitboy joined in. It was two to
one and I was the one – though I trust I gave a good account
of myself. Your chief cook did nothing to control his sub-
ordinates. In fact, he stood by, laughing. Madam, I am sorry
for this intrusion, but if I may advise, I think we should go
home. You have been insulted here and it won't do.'

'Dear God!' said Anthony.

Jane, scarlet with mortification, said: 'This is what happens
when we invite questionable people here.'

'That is enough!' said Anthony. Whereupon Jane burst into
tears and ran out of the room.

I said, 'Your pardon, Master Cobbold. But I think Brockley
is right. We should leave.'

We took ourselves off. I remember apologizing to Anthony and
remonstrating with Brockley, though not very drastically
because, after all, what had he done wrong? He had spoken up
for me when someone talked of me in an offensive way, and

hit back when he was attacked. I couldn't blame him for that.

Anthony seemed to understand. He assured me that he realized how Brockley and I felt and promised to speak to his kitchen staff in the sternest terms. He bitterly regretted that basic laws of hospitality had been broken in his house. He did not mention Jane, who didn't reappear.

Brockley's nose had by then quite stopped bleeding and he was able to help the grooms to harness our horses. Dale and Sybil were silent and shocked. When Brockley came to say that the coach was ready, Anthony saw us into it and through the window had a few last, quiet words for me.

'I meant well,' he said. 'Jane is so . . . virtuous. Such a good woman. But anything can go too far, even virtue. I thought . . . travellers tell of far-off places where everything seems strange to them, the animals, the birds, the plants, the houses. But to the people who live there, these things aren't strange at all. They see them every day and they're used to them. I thought, perhaps if Jane sees you often enough, in time she'll grow accustomed to you again, as she used to be . . . Well, it didn't work. I am sorry. But if eventually I invite you here again, please don't be afraid to come. Please *don't*. Nothing like this will ever happen again, I swear it.'

'All right, Master Cobbold,' I said, and through the coach window, I gave him my hand. 'It wasn't your fault,' I said. 'I know that. Goodbye.'

I was shaken, though, and badly. It seemed that my reputation in the district was in worse tatters than I had ever foreseen. Would I ever live down the untimely birth of Harry? One thing seemed certain. Incidents like this wouldn't help. Once home, I had a private word with Brockley.

'Brockley, this sort of thing just must not be repeated. Even if you do hear me harshly spoken of, please don't get into fights on my account. In fact,' I said, militantly, 'I forbid it! If there's another such occasion, then kindly go deaf.'

'I'll try, madam,' said Brockley reluctantly.

He kept his word for quite a long time, though according to John Hawthorn (who remained in regular touch with his cousin), this was as much as anything because he had indeed given a good account of himself in the Cobbold kitchen. The news got about and no one was particularly anxious to provoke someone with such a ready fist. Spiteful tongues might wag and no doubt did, but not where Brockley could hear them.

As for me, I thought it best to stay at home, out of sight, and let time do its healing work. The autumn passed. We held a quiet Christmas feast. In the new year, Brockley went to Woking to buy salt and candles and some other necessities. He came back with a black eye.

'Well, I'm sorry, madam, but there's a groom at the Lion who always gives me sideways looks when I go there and this time there was a new young lad working with him and you know how it is – old hands like to impress youngsters. He pointed me out to the lad as . . . er . . .'

'Go on, Brockley.'

'A fellow who thinks a mighty lot of himself, though he works for . . . I *can't* go on, madam. And I couldn't go deaf. It was just too much, too insulting. I told him to stop his vile talk. I said he didn't know what he was saying, that he didn't understand the circumstances and shouldn't be passing judgement on things he knew nothing about. That made him angry. He said I was calling him a wantwit, and he wasn't one, and with that . . . he took a swing at me. So what could I do?'

'Hit back,' I said resignedly. 'How is he now? And the lad?'

'The boy just stood there gaping. I left the groom lying in the straw, nursing his ribs. I pulled him away from the horse he'd been wisping, though. I didn't want him trodden on or kicked.'

'Very well, Brockley. But you're not to go to Woking again for a while. Or Guildford either, I think. Hawthorn can do the errands – he likes doing them, anyway. If he's too busy, Ben can go, or our new man, Alfred.'

We had taken on a new man as a general help because we needed one. Hugh had always looked after the rose garden himself and often lent a hand in the adjoining knot garden too. I had little spare time and lacked his skill. Roundel's new foal, and my purchase of Jewel, meant that the stable work had increased as well. Alfred had presented himself when Wilder had our requirements cried in Guildford, and he seemed to be good both with horses and gardens. He was in his mid-twenties, the youngest son of a farmer some distance away, and had left home because when his elder brothers married, there was no longer room for him. He was therefore a newcomer to the district and didn't know much about me. He took me as he found me: a widow with a small son to bring up. He was quiet-spoken, with a tendency to surliness if he was criticized in any way, but he seemed honest and he was certainly industrious.

But after a month or two, somebody must have enlightened him about the respective dates of Hugh's death and Harry's birth. I chanced to be in the great hall, which had a side window overlooking the courtyard, when I heard his voice out there, announcing, apparently to Brockley, that he'd now found out just what kind of household he had accidentally entered.

I went to the window, which was partly open. Alfred was enlarging on his discoveries and his opinion of them. I also saw Brockley seize him by his shirt collar, run him across the yard and plunge his head into the water trough. I didn't call out in protest. I had with my own ears heard myself described as a whore. I found that I approved wholeheartedly of what Brockley had done about it.

Alfred was off the premises the same day. I told him, as Brockley had told the groom at the Lion, that he did not know the circumstances, that Harry's father had once been my husband, that in Catholic eyes he still was, that he had rescued me from being thrown to the mercies of the Inquisition, and that we had briefly come together again afterwards. I said that I would be happy if Alfred would put these points to anyone he heard speaking ill of me in future. I also declared that after what I had heard him say, I could not go on employing him. I gave him a written reference, describing his honesty and industry, and handed him a month's money. And then sent him off, looking chastened up to a point, but also *very* surly.

There would, I supposed wearily, be further incidents. I sighed, thinking that I only wanted a quiet life.

It was an optimistic hope. Fate was laying out the pieces on her chessboard, and the first pawns had already been moved. In the August after the death of Norfolk, on the Eve of St

Bartholomew, there had been a massacre in France. Thousands of French Protestants, who were known as Huguenots, had been murdered. Through England then ran a wave of loathing for the Catholic faith, which had very likely helped to injure my reputation, wiping out any sympathy I might otherwise have won. *Mistress Stannard has a son by a former husband who's a Catholic. Shame on her!*

And then, in the spring of 1573, a further new piece came into the arena. Francis Walsingham, that stark and determined Protestant, who had for so long been Elizabeth's ambassador in France, came home.

FOUR

The Season of Abundance

'**Y**ou are sure you want the sand-coloured one?' said Christina Ferris, deftly slipping a needle into the back of the white kid glove that she was embroidering. 'He has a sweet nature but a ferocious appetite. He'll eat anything! What will you call him?' she added, with laughter in her dark eyes. 'Must it begin with an H? Herod?'

'Certainly not!' I looked across the stretch of grass to where a trio of half-grown dogs, respectively black, brown and sandy yellow, were gambolling together. 'Just because we called our dogs Hero and Hector,' I said, 'doesn't mean we can't have a different sort of name for this one. We'll probably call him Sandy. We won't mind his good appetite. It will make him grow quickly.'

Christina called to the animals and they came bounding towards us. I held out a hand to the sandy one and he responded at once, as if he had recognized me as his future owner. I stroked his smooth golden head. He was only half-mastiff and would never be as big as a pure-bred, but he would be quite big enough, as the size of his paws, which were like overstuffed cushions, made plain. He was still growing to fit them.

'We'll send him over to you at the end of the week if it's not convenient to take him now,' Christina said. 'I'm sorry about Hector. He was a lovely dog. You'll miss him.'

It was four days since our second groom, Simon, who also looked after the dogs, had come to tell me that on the previous day, our beautiful Hector hadn't wanted his food or been willing to come out of his kennel, and that this morning, he had been found dead. We would need a replacement, I said, and remembered that the last time I saw Christina Ferris, she had told me that one of their mastiff bitches had a new litter.

'Not pure bred,' she had told me ruefully. 'Ruby got out at

just the wrong time, ran off, and got together with a sheepdog! But the puppies will be handsome enough. I hope we'll find takers for them.'

Now, lacking Hector, I had ridden over to Christina's home, White Towers, to ask if any of the litter were still available. Hero and Hector were only half-mastiff; another crossbred suited me well enough.

All three young dogs were still available. Christina showed them to me and then suggested that we should sit out in the July sunshine. She brought her sewing with her. Then, with her head bent over it so that she need not look at me, she confided that she was pleased to see me as there was something she wished to discuss with me. When I heard what it was, I shook my head vehemently and said: 'No, Christina. No, really,' and turned the conversation back to the dogs. But now, as we sat petting them, she returned to the attack.

'I wish you'd change your mind about this afternoon. It will be quite informal – it hasn't been arranged in advance.'

'I daresay! You and Thomas started planning it the moment you saw me arriving!'

'It's a glorious day. We can admire the Cobbold Hall gardens. They are a picture this year. And perhaps things will begin to smooth over for you. Surely you want that? I certainly do. I don't like having my mother at odds with my friends. Thomas feels the same. We don't like feuds. Look at the trouble the old quarrel between my family and the Ferrises used to cause. Thank God that's all over!'

'That's all very well,' I said. 'But . . .'

'Oh, dear Mistress Stannard! It's over a year since Brockley had that fight in my mother's kitchens. No one at the hall will say anything unkind about you now. I heard all about it, you know. My father was furious.'

'I hope no one lost their place over it,' I said. 'The trouble was . . .' I stopped, feeling awkward.

'The trouble was,' said Christina roundly, 'that my mother's servants were only repeating her opinions. But Father says he has forbidden her to utter them ever again in the servants' hearing. He didn't dismiss anyone, but he did make it clear to them all that they must watch their manners in future.' She put in another couple of stitches and added: 'How odd. This is the first time we've talked about this, though we've met from time to time since it happened. I felt too embarrassed to mention it.'

'I rather hoped you knew nothing about it!' I said. 'That's why I never mentioned it either. Only now . . .'

I didn't add that even if Jane was now entirely silent on the subject of myself, the unpleasant gossip which had in the past year got Brockley into another fight and lost Alfred his place, could probably be traced back to her. Christina's suggestion that I should accompany her to Cobbold Hall on a spur of the moment visit after dinner, and pretend that last year's debacle had never happened, was kindly meant, but it made my spine stiffen.

Christina, however, said in a firm voice: 'There are plenty of other things to talk about besides your little Harry. My little Anne, for instance! And if *anyone* says anything – anything hurtful – I shall start talking about the Massacre of St Bartholomew's Eve and Francis Walsingham's new anti-Catholic policy! That will drive every other subject of conversation out of sight. It always does. I still shudder when I remember our vicar telling us about the Massacre. I can't imagine what it can have been like. The terror those poor people must have felt! *Children* were murdered, because of what their parents believed! I can hardly bear to think of it. But I *will* think of it, and talk about it, if I have to. I won't let anybody upset you. My father won't stand for it, either.'

We were silent for a few moments. Somewhere, a blackbird called. It was such a beautiful morning and the garden where we were sharing a bench was beautiful, too. It had been enlarged since Christina and her husband, Thomas Ferris, had taken charge of it.

They had made many changes at White Towers since Thomas had inherited it. Once, it had been crammed with massive and elaborate furniture but much of this had been replaced by smaller things, in walnut instead of dark oak, and there were bright hangings in place of sombre ones. Thomas's mother, who still lived there, had welcomed the changes. When her husband was alive, she had had precious little say in anything. The whole house, now, had an air of peaceful contentment.

Perhaps, I thought, we *could* carry that with us to Cobbold Hall, and have a polite, peaceful visit. Preferably without discussing the French massacre, which might well distract Jane from me, but would hardly encourage an air of serenity.

It was still a frequent talking point, because of its effect on our own country. Francis Walsingham, now back at court, was fiercely determined not to allow Catholic influence to increase in England, and he had learned that Catholic priests from France were slipping into our realm in secret, to do what they called spreading the word and Walsingham called spreading sedition, and to gather funds, presumably in the hope of financing future plots. He had made it illegal for Catholics to seek converts, a move which had considerably strengthened his hand. The matter would outrank the subject of my little Harry, in any company.

'Anyway, it's time I showed my parents how my little Anne is growing,' Christina said, pressing on. 'She's well grown for seven months and Father was so delighted to have a granddaughter. We can all coo over her like a choir singing in tune. She's going to have a good complexion, if only she can avoid the smallpox.'

Christina herself had not avoided it, but the marks on her face were not as obvious now as they were immediately after the illness and she had learned some useful tricks. She dusted her skin with a powder made of ground up eggshells, and trained her beech-nut brown hair forward in front of her cap, to make a fringe over her pitted forehead. Her lovely dark eyes had been unharmed.

Thomas Ferris, who had been in love with her before her illness, stayed in love with her afterwards, as if her scars did not exist, and finally married her against her father's wishes. He had once remarked to me that, in a way, he was grateful for the scars, because they would have made it that much harder for Anthony Cobbold to find her someone else. 'They gave him a good excuse to forgive us,' he told me.

'Mistress Stannard,' Christina said persistently, considering her work with her head on one side, 'I *wish* you'd say you'll come. Please. It could well be a first step towards putting everything right.'

I said obliquely: 'Well, I haven't got Harry with me, which is fortunate because, no, I couldn't possibly take him to Cobbold Hall. Or Brockley either. Luckily, I brought Joseph as my groom today. Being our youngest groom, he doesn't get many outings and anyway, Brockley's doing an errand to Woking. According to Hawthorn, we're running out of salt and pepper – again! I tell him he uses them too much, and then he tells me that I wouldn't enjoy my meals so much if he didn't!'

Brockley had lately resumed going on errands to Woking and Guildford and, so far, nothing untoward had happened, which seemed hopeful. Perhaps a visit to Cobbold Hall would be safe.

'Then you *will* come?' Christina said, pouncing. She stuck a needle into her work and put her reel of thread into her workbox.

She was obviously determined. 'All right. But only for a very short visit. *Very* short.'

Thomas Ferris, whom I remembered as a youth under his father's thumb, but had now turned into a broad-shouldered young man with an air of consequence, suitable to a landowner with a wife and child, had come out of the house and was striding briskly towards us. 'Thomas!' Christina called. 'Mistress Stannard has said yes!'

It was a pleasant two-mile ride to Cobbold Hall, through narrow lanes fringed by hedgerows tangled with dogrose and honeysuckle, and banks submerged in tides of long grass and foaming cow parsley and starred with clover, dandelion, campion, St John's wort, the mauve-pink of valerian and the vivid blue of bellflowers. It was the season of abundance.

For most of the way, it was possible, just, for two to ride side by side so I rode with Christina, while Thomas, behind us, was alongside the quiet mule on which sat little Anne's nurse with the child in her arms. Joseph brought up the rear. Christina and I talked about my Harry and her Anne while we enjoyed the warmth of the sun on our faces.

It was impossible not to feel eased by such a golden afternoon. Jewel, moving gently beneath me, seemed contented, too. All would be well, I said to myself. There would be talk of harmless things. I would not stay long, and perhaps the unhappy breach between me and Jane would indeed begin to heal. Hadn't I been striving for that all along?

This agreeable tranquillity was somewhat disturbed when, arriving at Cobbold Hall and glancing through the archway to the stableyard, we could see a tall black horse being groomed out of doors. I was sure it wasn't a Cobbold horse. So was Christina.

'Maybe there are guests,' she said doubtfully. 'I don't recognize that black horse. Oh, dear. We may have chosen a bad day.'

'Well, we're here now and we can't very well just turn round and ride away again,' said Thomas in practical tones. 'Anyway, here comes our host. Good day to you, Father-in-Law.'

Anthony had appeared at the front door, waving away the butler who had opened it. He came down the steps towards us, looking pleased. 'This is an agreeable surprise. Christina, my dear, why didn't you let us know you were coming today? You could have come earlier and dined with us.' He came to help me dismount. 'Mistress Stannard, I am truly glad to see you here. It's been too long.' Then he cleared his throat and added in a low voice: 'There is nothing to worry about. I assure you.'

He turned from me to embrace Christina and exclaim over the healthy looks of his granddaughter, while Thomas beamed on all of them. Grooms took our horses and they and Joseph went off with them to the stableyard while the rest of us found ourselves being steered up the steps and into the house.

'But it seems as though you already have visitors,' Thomas said as we went into the parlour. 'I hope we're not going to put you out.'

'By no means.' Anthony went to the table, where there was a trayload of glasses and wine flasks. 'There are clean glasses here,' said Anthony. 'Let me help you to wine. We did have two guests at dinner but one of them has already left. Sir Edward Heron came to dine today and Roland Wyse was here as well because he had come into Surrey with some message or other for Heron, from Francis Walsingham's office – he's in Walsingham's department again now. He caught up with

Sir Edward here and joined us for the meal. But then he said he couldn't stay but must set off back to London, and took his leave. He seemed to be in a hurry. He was in quite a panic because he hadn't been able to find Sir Edward at once – as if he felt he might be blamed for it, though it wasn't his fault in the least.'

'From various things I've heard, I expect working for Francis Walsingham is demanding,' Thomas remarked.

'I daresay. Wyse did seem harassed. Maybe he had to set out at short notice, because he was riding alone. He usually has a couple of men with him as an escort,' said Anthony.

'I've met Roland Wyse,' Thomas remarked. 'Indeed, I met him here, Father-in-Law, only last month, did I not? He had an escort then. But I suspected it was there to show off his importance. I can't say I took to him.'

'Whyever not?' said Anthony in surprise.

'Just because I think he shows off. I can believe he wouldn't like anyone to think he couldn't carry out an errand on time! I've gathered from that cottager, Jack Jarvis, that Wyse always gives him alms when he comes this way. Jarvis is grateful but if you ask me, it's just another way of making sure he shows up well.'

I looked at Thomas in surprise, for he wasn't usually waspish. It seemed clear that the dislike he had taken to Roland Wyse had been not only instant, but intense. I said nothing, however, because Anthony looked annoyed and I didn't want to annoy him further. Even though, privately, I rather agreed with Thomas.

'Personally,' Anthony said testily, 'I find Mr Wyse rather good company. He is very much a man of today, of course. He insists on being called Mr instead of Master, in the modern fashion. But there's no harm in that. He always tips the groom who looks after his horse. I think that's a virtue and shouldn't be a cause for criticism.'

'Well, well. You may be right,' said Thomas pacifically, having caught Christina's eye.

We had just finished our wine, when Sir Edward Heron came into the parlour. He had a letter in his hand, which he was reading as he pushed the door open. He folded it when he saw

us, and bowed politely. He was a tall, lean man who actually
bore a resemblance to his surname, because of his long legs
and neck, his sharp aquiline nose which really did have a faintly
yellowish tinge, and the keenness of his grey eyes. Sir Edward
Heron was a man of integrity but he was also a fanatical
Protestant who believed in and loathed witchcraft to a dangerous
degree. He had accused me of it once. However, his presence
might help to ensure that Jane, when we met, would be polite.
She wouldn't want to display bad manners before the Sheriff
of the County. I wondered where she was, having seen no
sign of her as yet.

'Roland Wyse was chasing me round Surrey with this,' he
said, flicking the letter at us. 'And making a great to-do about
it though the matter isn't that urgent. There are a couple of
prisoners in Lewes gaol, French priests suspected of attempting
to convert honest Protestants, who Francis Walsingham wants
brought to London. They were arrested in Surrey. We only
keep short-term prisoners in Guildford Castle these days; the
rest go to Lewes.'

'Francis Walsingham is still hot in pursuit of priestly
invaders, then,' Thomas said.

'Very much so.' Heron folded the letter away in his doublet
and sat down on the nearest seat. 'And rightly. These intruders
are dangerous. Probably more dangerous than the schemes
laid by romantic Florentine bankers and ambitious noblemen
dreaming of becoming royal consorts. These young priests are
trained in the arts of seducing others and talking money out
of them, and creating networks. Though,' he added, 'they might
be less of a menace if Mary Stuart's lifetime could be cut
short!'

'I doubt if the queen will ever agree to that,' Anthony said.

I found this subject no pleasanter than the French massacre.
I said to Anthony: 'We should pay our respects to Mistress
Jane. Where is she?'

'She went out after dinner,' he said. 'To see that cottager,
Jarvis. I saw her come back a little while ago but she went
straight into the garden – I think to check on the weeding the
gardeners have been doing. She's still there. She keeps
the gardeners very much in order, you know. They regard her

as a slave-driver; I've overheard one of them saying so. He
didn't know I'd heard, of course. I didn't mention it. He may
have had a point.'

It occurred to me that if Anthony Cobbold really had taken
his wife to task for encouraging her servants to be rude to
mine, it was a rare event. He probably didn't like giving orders
to Jane. The fact that the old, and at one time very bitter, feud
between the Cobbold and Ferris families had now died away
completely, no doubt owed something to Anthony's essentially
peaceable nature.

'Christina and I ought to go out into the garden to find her,'
I said. *And get it over.* 'Christina?'

'Of course.' Christina, who had been rocking Anne on her
knee, rose, handing her daughter to the nurse. 'Mary, you
come with us and bring Anne with you. It's a lovely afternoon
for a saunter out of doors.'

If Jane had been slave-driving the gardeners, the result
justified her for the garden was a delight. It was L-shaped,
extending round two sides of the house, and though it was a
knot garden, it wasn't rigidly patterned. The beds were laid
out in a casual way, as though someone had shaken them like
dice and then cast them on the ground to fall where they
would. The effect was charming, and just now, the place was
at its best, for here, too, it was the season of abundance.

On the sides away from the house, the garden was bounded
by walls of weathered brick that supported climbing roses and
an espaliered pear tree. Soft, grassy paths wound here and
there, low hedges of box and lavender sweetened the air. There
was one whole bed of heartsease in a variety of colours: yellow,
purple and velvety red. A big triangular patch was full of
sunflowers and hollyhocks. There was a display of marigolds
in a riotous tangle that spilt on to the pathway, wallflowers in
a glorious mix of yellows and dark reds, and framing them,
by way of contrast, the slim blue spires of larkspur. There
wasn't a weed to be seen as far as I could tell and the grass
paths had been scythed to a perfect smoothness.

'I wonder where Mother has got to?' Christina remarked.

We had been walking at the side of the house, moving
towards the rear of it. We turned the corner into the other arm

of the L. Here there were beds of scented herbs as well as flowers and a few evergreen bushes, and in a far corner, there was a gap in the wall and a path leading away into the inviting green shade of a shrubbery. The path we were on led past another well-weeded bed of heartsease, skirted one of the bushes and brought us to a patch of deep pink gillyflowers.

We stopped short. Christina uttered a shriek and threw herself on her knees beside the flowerbed, and the nurse, her eyes wide with horror, turned Anne's face into her shoulder so that the child shouldn't see. I stood rigid, a hand jammed against my mouth to hold back a shriek of my own, unable to believe what was before my eyes.

We had found Jane. She lay on her back among the gilly-flowers and a silver dagger hilt jutted from her heart. It had an engraved pattern of curving lines, interlinked as in a plait, and it sparkled in the sun. Her blood had spilled round it, drying on the cream silk of her dress, running down to darken the pink blooms of her flowery deathbed.

Pale in death, her too-plump features might have been moulded in uncooked dough. Her left hand had been flung out, palm up, and the sleeve from which it protruded was, once again, tautly creased by the short fat arm within. When I saw her at that disastrous dinner party, I had thought she was beginning to look ugly. Now, she just looked pitiful.

She was quite dead.

FIVE

Summons to Court

'They've taken Roger away!' Dale screamed. 'Ma'am, those sergeants have taken my husband away! They're taking him to Lewes. Where's Lewes? I've never heard of it! Will I ever see him again? Oh, God, they'll hang him, I know they will, ma'am, can't you do something? They've taken Roger away!'

'I tried to argue with them,' I said wretchedly. 'I said to them, the inquest jury only brought in a verdict of murder by someone unknown. But they wouldn't listen. They said they had orders. Dale – Fran – I'm sorry . . .'

'They've taken *Roger*!' Dale shrieked, and threw herself down on the floor of the hall and pounded it with her fists.

Coaxing, crooning as to a child, I somehow pulled her back on to her feet and shouted for assistance. Sybil and Gladys came running, their faces frightened.

'We saw!' said Sybil. 'We were in the kitchen. We heard those two men – from the sheriff's office, weren't they? – ride in. We went to the door and we saw them dismounting and heard them asking where Brockley was, and then Brockley came out of the hall door and they seized hold of him and the young groom Joseph went rushing off to fetch you . . .'

'We saw you run from the garden,' said Gladys, 'and Dale was there all of a sudden, pleading and crying. You tried to argue with them but they took no heed of either of you. Faces like stones they had, and they took Roger Brockley off with them, on that spare horse they brought, white as the moon in the sky, he was, horrible!'

'They'll kill him!' Dale wailed. 'And all for nothing! He never harmed that Cobbold woman! That dagger – I didn't see it but you told me what it was like, ma'am, and Roger never had such a thing, never. I'd have known! It wasn't his! He didn't do it!'

'Gladys,' I said, 'do you have any of your calming valerian and camomile draught made up ready? If not, make some! Quickly. And put it into warmed wine and bring it up to Dale's room.'

'They've taken Roger!' Dale moaned, sobbing in my arms.

'I know, Dale, dear. I know. But we'll get him back, you'll see. Now come upstairs. I'm putting you to bed. Gladys will bring you a potion to soothe you. Then we'll plan what to do.'

'We know it's a mistake,' said Sybil reassuringly. 'We all know that, and we'll get the authorities to know it as well. You'll see.'

'He had fights because of the things the Cobbold woman said and they've no one else they can fasten it on and what *can* anyone do?' The tears streamed down Dale's face. 'They've taken my Roger away and we've never really made it up after we had that great quarrel . . .'

'Never mind that now,' I said. 'We have to think about how to help him, not worry about bygone arguments. Come along.'

Somehow, between us, Sybil and I persuaded her upstairs and settled her in bed. Gladys followed with her herbal potion. Gladys could be and often was utterly maddening but in times of crisis, she showed her worth. Most of her troubles had come about because she was old and ugly, had been at times ill-used on account of this, resented it, and said so, roundly. She was sound at heart.

Dale turned her head away from the potion at first but somehow we coaxed her into swallowing it and got her to lie back on her pillow. I gave the empty glass to Gladys to take away and she went out of the room but came back almost at once.

'Met Wilder on the stairs, mistress – he says Sir Edward Heron's here asking for you.'

'I'll stay with Dale,' said Sybil.

Dale heaved herself upright and said: 'It was him who decided Roger was guilty. The jury didn't! I'm getting up! I'll tell him . . .'

'You won't tell him anything!' I said. 'I'll go down and talk to him myself. Sybil, stay with Dale and don't let her out of this room. Dale, if you don't lie down and do as I bid you, I . . . I'll have to lock you in! Gladys, go and tell Wilder I'm coming!'

I went downstairs on shaking legs.

It had all happened so fast. That morning, we had all awakened to an ordinary day. After breakfast, I had gone into the rose garden with Tessie and Harry. Harry was vigorously engaged in trying to toddle more efficiently and Tessie kept a careful eye on him while I cut away dead blooms and thought of Hugh and how much he had loved his roses. Then Joseph, our youngest groom, came running to say that there were sergeants in the courtyard, and they'd come to arrest Brockley.

'Take Harry indoors!' I barked at Tessie and then I picked up my skirts and fairly raced to the courtyard, to find that they had already got Brockley on to a horse, and had tied his hands. Dale was there, weeping and imploring. Brockley himself was silent but, as Gladys had said, horribly white.

The sergeants told me that he was being arrested for the murder of Jane Cobbold and was being taken to Lewes until the assizes. They rode off, leading him. I led Dale back into the hall, where she collapsed in hysteria, and engrossed in looking after her, I had scarcely had time to take in what all this meant to me. But it was coming home to me now.

Brockley, despite the suspicions that Dale had once had, had never been my lover but throughout his many years in my service, he had been my friend and in times of danger, my ally. If anything happened to Brockley, my heart would break as completely as Dale's would. And, as I knew perfectly well, it would all be because he had fought in defence of my good name. There was no other reason to accuse him of this killing. He would – he might – die because he cared for me enough to use his fists on my behalf.

Halfway downstairs, just before the turn that would bring me in sight of the entrance vestibule below, I stopped short, feeling faint. I couldn't bear it. If Brockley came to harm because of his friendship for me, then Dale would blame me and she would be right. She would not forgive me. I would lose her, too.

Black spots whirled before my eyes and I sat down on the stairs and put my head between my knees. Gradually, the spots faded. I stood up, warily, holding on to the banister, telling myself to stop this. This was no time for me to have the vapours. Hideous though the situation was, I must deal with it, not retreat into a swoon. The world steadied. I went slowly on, round the turn and saw Wilder awaiting me in the vestibule.

'Madam, I have asked Sir Edward to wait in the hall.'

'Thank you. I'll see him there.' With a great effort I managed to speak calmly.

Sir Edward was pacing round the hall when I entered. He turned to face me and bowed. I looked at him fearfully.

'Mrs Stannard.' Like Roland Wyse, Heron always used the short modern forms of address.

'Sir Edward. Please sit down.' I did so myself, glad to take the weight off my uncertain legs. 'What brings you here?'

'I felt that, since my men this morning arrested your manservant Roger Brockley for the stabbing of Mrs Jane Cobbold, I should at least call on you to explain why. I believe you hold Mr Brockley in some esteem, and of course, in view of your relationship to the crown, you are owed some courtesy.'

He had once come within inches of having me arrested for witchcraft. Possibly, I was on his conscience. I folded my hands in my lap, kept my back straight and said with as much composure as possible: 'I would certainly like an explanation, Sir Edward. I know perfectly well that Roger Brockley did *not* murder Jane Cobbold and I would very much like to know why anyone supposes that he did.'

'I am aware,' said Heron, 'that he has repeatedly been in fights because of gossip concerning you, Mrs Stannard, and the child you have borne out of wedlock.' He spoke with distaste. 'I am also aware – I make it my business to be very aware of what goes on in my county – that the source of some of that gossip was probably Mrs Cobbold, who admittedly was something of a scandalmonger. I may say that I have learned of the circumstances surrounding the, er, arrival of your little son and I realize that the matter is less scandalous than Mrs Cobbold wished to believe. However, that is beside the point just now. The point is that she was the source of gossip, and your man Brockley objected to it, and said so, at times with violence.

'On the afternoon of Mrs Cobbold's death, the man Brockley was seen in Woking, which is not far from Cobbold Hall. He could easily have gone to the hall and been there at the right time. In any case, no one else could possibly have done it.'

'Except that someone else most decidedly did do it,' I said. 'Have no other possibilities been considered? What about that dagger? The hilt looked costly. Can nothing be learned from that? I can tell you that it doesn't belong to Brockley. If he possessed such a dagger, I would have seen it. So would Dale.'

'That dagger,' said Sir Edward, 'isn't what it seems. The patterned hilt is actually common bronze, made in a standard mould, and then washed over with a thin skin of silver. It's one of hundreds. They're made by a smith in London and half the smart young men about town have them. They're popular with the ones who want to make a show but can't afford solid silver or jewels. The blades are good steel, though, and very sharp; most of whatever value those daggers have lies in the blade. I sent you and the other women out of the room before I pulled the thing out of the wound. It had gone in to the hilt and the sharpness was the reason why.'

I shuddered. I had been thankful enough to be shooed away after the body had been brought indoors. I had seen violent death before, more than once, but I would never grow used to it. I was shaking with shock, as much as Christina and the nursemaid Mary were. Christina sent for some wine, and the three of us drank it as we sat shivering in the parlour. The only one who remained obliviously serene was the baby Anne, who had fallen asleep in Mary's arms.

I said again: 'Brockley never had such a dagger!'

'Are you so sure? He carries one, does he not? But I don't suppose he often takes it out of its sheath. He could have bought a new one the last time he went to London but has never had occasion to use or display it, and you might never have seen it.'

'Dale would know and she says—'

'Your woman? Of course she would say it wasn't his.' Sir Edward was dismissive. 'She's his wife. Other names besides Brockley's have been suggested, of course. Anthony Cobbold, who seems to share your good opinion of Roger Brockley, had some to offer – at least, he did when he had had time to pull himself together. He was more shattered even than Christina, their daughter.'

'I know,' I said. 'I saw.'

I remembered how Christina, kneeling by her mother, had wailed that Jane was dead, *dead*, and how she had then cried out that she must fetch her father and Sir Edward, and had sprung to her feet and run off to do so. She brought them back within minutes. When they had joined us beside Jane Cobbold's body, she began to weep, but her father had stood looking down at his wife's body, his body as rigid as a statue and his face so blank with shock and disbelief that it seemed wiped clean of all emotion. He said nothing at all. After a few moments, he turned away and walked off, back to the house, blunderingly, as though he couldn't see clearly where he was going.

'You'll remember,' Heron said, 'that when we had got the poor lady back to the house, we found Mr Cobbold just sitting in the parlour, grey in the face and near to collapse. His daughter called his valet, who persuaded him to lie down.'

'Yes, so I recall.'

'But later, after I had given you permission to go home and you had left, he came downstairs again and it was then that he offered his ideas, which I did indeed consider. I assure you, Mrs Stannard, that I have studied all possibilities with care.'

'What – who – who were they?' I asked.

'The two gardeners who had been weeding the flowerbeds that very day, and a cottager called Jack Jarvis. But none of them can have done it. They exonerate each other, and both I and Mr Cobbold can to some extent bear out the accounts they give.'

'Can you tell me about them?' I asked.

'If you wish. Mr Cobbold suggested the gardeners at first – he said they didn't like his wife. He had more than once heard them complain about her. *But* . . . well, firstly, to take things in order, I took dinner at Cobbold Hall, and Mr Roland Wyse was there as well. He left for London straight after the meal, and a little while later, Mrs Cobbold went out to call on Jarvis, the cottager, about ten minutes away on foot. She was going to ask him to supply the hall with some eggs. Jarvis is by way of being one of Mrs Cobbold's charities, having fallen on hard times which were not his fault, or so he claims.'

'I know him,' I said. 'I've given him charitable gifts myself.'

'Mr Cobbold said that his wife had been generous to him, and took an interest in his welfare. But Mr Cobbold also described him as scruffy to look at and never averse to taking a handout. The men I sent to question him confirm the scruffiness, though they couldn't speak for the handouts. But it occurred to Mr Cobbold that perhaps this man had asked for extra charity, more than Mrs Cobbold felt she could give, and become angry when refused. However, that theory wouldn't do, as I reminded him.'

He paused, apparently looking back into his memory. 'Wouldn't do?' I prompted.

'No. It wouldn't. After dinner, when Mrs Cobbold had left, Anthony and I sat talking in the parlour, by the window. Now I come to the gardeners. We could see them weeding. We also saw them finish their task, pick up some tools and a ladder they must have laid ready, and leave the garden. Mr Cobbold remarked they were probably going to deal with a tree that was becoming dangerous because of a partly broken branch that might fall on to a path – the track between the Hall and Jarvis's cottage. He'd given orders to see to it. I have inspected the tree myself and seen where the dangerous branch was cut. To get at it, the men would have had to climb quite high. They would have had a good view of Jarvis's cottage, and much of the path between it and the hall. You understand?'

'Yes. Please go on.'

'So the gardeners set off to attend to the tree. They agree that that is what they did. And they say that once up their ladder, they saw Mrs Cobbold starting to walk back to her home after visiting Jarvis. They also say that Jarvis then came out into his vegetable patch and started work there. Now, you see? The gardeners saw Jarvis in his garden, and he saw them up their tree. They say he didn't follow her or anything of that kind. She reached home safely but shortly after that, she was found dead in her own garden. All that time, Jarvis and the gardeners were within sight of each other. There was trouble with the broken branch, which was awkward to get at. It took the men quite a while.'

I was working it out for myself. 'So Mrs Cobbold came back and went into her own garden, while Jarvis and the gardeners were all about half a mile away, close to the cottage?'

'Yes. Mr Cobbold and I saw his wife come into the garden and examine the weeded beds – I suppose to see if the work had been done properly. When I called it to his mind, he remembered well enough. I remember, too. I was with him, after all.'

I was silent a moment, puzzling. 'There's no link between Jarvis and the gardeners, is there? They're not all related to each other, or anything like that?'

'Collusion? No. One of the gardeners has been at Cobbold Hall for years. He lives in Woking. The other is a lad from the village of Priors Ford, who only came to work for the Cobbolds a couple of months ago. Jarvis has had the cottage for a couple of years and isn't known to have any relatives at all. Certainly not the gardeners. Mr Cobbold was definite about that.'

'I see,' I said bleakly.

'You, of course, arrived with the Ferrises and had been with them since the morning. Otherwise,' said Sir Edward disquietingly, 'we might have considered you as well, since you were the subject of Mrs Cobbold's gossip. A woman could have done it – the dagger blade *was* good. With such a keen edge, it wouldn't need a man's strength to drive it home. But you are obviously not a possibility, unless the Ferrises were in it too, which is hardly likely, since Mrs Ferris is Mrs Cobbold's daughter. Ha ha.'

I had never heard him laugh before. That sudden harsh bray took me aback. He had a cruel sense of humour, I thought.

'And so,' he said, 'we come to Roger Brockley. Who else is there?'

'Was Brockley seen anywhere near Cobbold Hall itself?' I demanded.

He shook his head. 'No. Only in Woking. But that's near enough.'

'I sent him there to buy salt and pepper. And Woking is

nowhere near enough,' I snapped. 'It's all of two miles. If he wasn't seen near Cobbold Hall, or on the road between it and Woking, you have no case against him.' I stood up. Anger had come to my aid, taking the quiver out of my leg muscles, bracing my spine. 'I shall approach Lord Burghley, whom I know well and who is a lawyer, for advice. I will not have my servants falsely accused!'

'I doubt very much if this accusation is false,' said Sir Edward Heron calmly. 'The gardeners can't have done it and nor can Jack Jarvis. Roger Brockley had every reason to detest the lady. He could have heard fresh gossip in Woking, come to the hall to protest to her, met her in the garden, been outraged by something she said, and struck her down in a fit of momentary fury.'

'Only,' I said coldly, 'he didn't.'

'Loyalty between servant and lady is of course a virtue,' said Sir Edward politely. 'But it can be carried too far.'

I didn't offer him any refreshment. I bade him good day, gave him a sketch of a curtsey, and walked out of the hall. I found Wilder hovering outside. 'See him off the premises,' I said, and went on upstairs, back to Dale and Sybil.

I couldn't leave instantly to seek Lord Burghley's advice, because Dale was too upset to travel and I wanted her with me. While I waited, I tried to make plans, with difficulty because to make a journey of any length without Brockley in attendance felt so strange, and Dale burst into tears every time she was reminded that he couldn't be with us.

I finally decided to take Arthur Watts, our gnarled and gnome-like but very reliable head groom. Dale could ride on his pillion. Sybil could stay at Hawkswood and act as my deputy.

'There may be visitors to receive,' I said to her distractedly.

There might – oh, please God – there might be a messenger from Sir Edward Heron to say that Brockley had been released; his arrest was all a mistake. Or there could be visits from friends who had heard the news, coming to offer help or condolences.

Dale was better the next day and we had begun to pack, when the first of the possible callers arrived. Wilder came up to the bedchamber where we were filling saddlebags, to announce that Master Anthony Cobbold was here to see me and was waiting in the Little Parlour.

The Little Parlour was the room in which Sybil and the Brockleys had so firmly told me that I must obey the queen and attend Norfolk's execution. It had once been very much a private place for Hugh and me. In those days, visitors were taken into the hall or the bigger parlour, which nowadays we often called the East Room. During my absence abroad just after Hugh's death, Sybil had taken to calling it that, because it was at the eastern end of the house, and the name had stuck. And now, visitors – unless they were official, as Heron had been – were usually shown into the Little Parlour to await me.

'Anthony Cobbold?' I said. 'What can he want with me?' I didn't in the least wish to see him. I pitied him in his loss but that same loss was doing dreadful injury to Brockley and to all of us at Hawkswood. I had stayed away from Jane's funeral. I couldn't imagine what had brought her husband to Hawkswood.

For a moment, I considered refusing to see him but it would be discourteous to send my guest away, even if he had come uninvited.

So with Dale at my heels, I went downstairs. I found Master Cobbold, all in black, standing uneasily by the window, twisting a velvet cap between his hands and obviously embarrassed.

'Mistress Stannard!'

'Do sit down,' I said automatically. I seated myself and signed to Dale to do the same. 'Have you been offered any refreshment?'

'Yes . . . but I said no. Thank you. Mistress Stannard, I can hardly suppose I'm welcome here but I had to come . . .' Tall and swarthy as ever, he looked like Beelzebub in a hangdog mood. 'I'm so *sorry*! I couldn't stop Sir Edward from . . . Of course I know that Roger Brockley wouldn't have harmed my wife. Even he had reason to be angry with her and I suppose he had, and so had you, but I've known

you both for years and I am as sure as I can be that there's
been a terrible mistake!'

'*Please* sit down!' I said, and this time there was some
warmth in my voice. He did as I asked, and I said: 'Brockley
has been arrested. If you know of anything that may help him
– or if you can suggest anyone else who might have been
responsible – please tell me. If you noticed any strangers on
your land, or anything else that might help to uncover the
truth, please, please tell me!'

'I didn't,' said Anthony sadly. 'It was a perfectly ordinary
day. There was nothing – *nothing*. I saw no strangers at any
time that day. Do you suppose I haven't been all over it in
my mind, again and again? I can't think of a single thing that
might be of use. I did have ideas that I told to Sir Edward,
but he proved them all to be impossible.'

'He has said that to me. He's been here.' Awkwardly, I
added: 'Please don't think that I don't feel for you and for
Jane, too! And I do ask you to take some wine.' Without
waiting for an answer, I picked up the little bell that always
stood on the Little Parlour's one small table, and rang it. Wilder
appeared immediately and had probably been nearby. I
requested wine for three.

'You had reason to feel bitterness against my wife,' Anthony
said heavily, as Wilder disappeared. 'I know that. Jane was a
good woman, perhaps too good. She did not understand the . . .
difficulties of your life. She herself never had many difficulties
to face. For me, the fact that Her Majesty the Queen accepts
you and your son and recognizes you as relations of hers is
enough for me. But . . .'

His voice tailed off, helplessly. It seemed as though he didn't
quite know what he had come to Hawkswood to say. Wilder
came back with the wine, poured for us all and then withdrew.
Dale, who had as usual taken a stool at a little distance from
me, wrapped her hands round her glass as though she were
trying to warm them on it. Anthony glanced at her and said:
'Mistress Brockley, I know this is a wretched time for you. I
am sorry for you and for your husband. I can only hope that
things can be put right and that you will soon have your
husband home.'

'He didn't do it,' said Dale miserably. 'I know he didn't.'

'I do have one idea,' Anthony said. 'It seems to be impossible, but I suppose the gardeners could be lying for some reason though I don't know what. Maybe they were bribed. They've been questioned hard – I must give Sir Edward credit for that – and they swore they hadn't been but I still wonder. In my opinion, that tenant of mine, Jack Jarvis, is the man. We don't know much about him, but he had a grudge against the world, I can tell you that. It wasn't his fault that he lost his livelihood when the land where he used to graze his sheep was enclosed; that's true enough. But I always felt that because of that, he hated everyone, even Jane, who was so kind to him. That could have been it, you know. He always took charity just a little too willingly.'

I nodded, having felt the same thing.

Anthony sipped his wine. 'He sometimes asked Jane for things, you know, things that I thought he could have provided for himself. He did quite well, selling eggs and vegetables and fowls for the table. But he has asked my wife to provide him with new garden tools, and two or three times said could he have a bag of corn for the hens, things like that, and a couple of months ago, he asked if she could buy him a donkey! And she did. Jane was so *very* generous, so *very* charitable.'

He sounded heartbreakingly proud of her. 'She always said that charity was a virtue she was in a position to practise and that she was glad to do so. I admired her for that.' His voice broke. 'Sometimes I can't bear it, knowing she isn't there. I keep expecting her to open a door and walk into the room I'm in . . . then I realize that she never will and it's dreadful. The world seems so empty. If I speak, if any of the servants speak, the house seems to echo!' There were tears in his eyes. 'But do you see? Jarvis was beginning to ask for bigger, more costly things. He might have gone too far, asked her for something that she felt was a little too much, so that she said no . . . and then he became angry. I think the killer was Jarvis.'

'The dagger,' I said. 'I understand it wasn't valuable but it was quite ornate. Did you ever see such a thing in his possession? Brockley never had such a dagger. I'd have known, and certainly Dale here would – wouldn't you, Dale?'

'Yes, ma'am. I would indeed.'

'If Jarvis had one, I never saw it but what of that? Maybe he did,' said Anthony. 'But there's one other thing, and *that's* the real reason why I feel so sure that Jarvis was the killer. It's what I came here to tell you, only these days I seem to be so confused. I should have explained at once, instead of waffling. Jarvis has disappeared.'

'Disappeared?' I said, startled.

'Went the day before yesterday, the day of the funeral. I didn't go to the graveside myself; the vicar said it wasn't proper for spouses to do that. But everyone who was there came to the house afterwards and Jack Jarvis wasn't among them and when I asked about him, no one had seen him. I couldn't understand it, thinking how good Jane had been to him. Then Master Poole – you don't know him; he rents a smallholding from me and he was at the funeral – he came up to me and said that Jarvis had called on him the day before, in the afternoon, and said he was obliged to go away for a while, and asked if Poole could take care of his chickens for him!

'So yesterday I went to Jarvis's cottage, and sure enough, it's all shut up, and the chickens were gone. I rode over to Poole's place and found that he'd collected them and taken them home. He said it was easier to look after them if he didn't have to keep going over to the cottage. It's my belief,' said Anthony, 'that Jarvis has run away, afraid of being accused. And I think that whatever my gardeners may say, he killed my wife.'

I stared at him. 'Why didn't Master Poole come to you at once and warn you that Jarvis was planning to run away? Didn't he realize how it looked?'

'Poole said that Jarvis was on his donkey, with a pack on his back and said he was setting off at once. He supposed that Jarvis had had a message from someone – a family crisis, perhaps. He doesn't know Jarvis well and he isn't very quick-minded,' explained Anthony. 'He knew he would see me the next day and he imagined that Jarvis had told me, anyway.'

'Does Sir Edward know about this?' I asked.

'Yes, I went myself to tell him. But he seems inclined to

discount it. I said, he questioned the gardeners hard, but they both tell the same tale, about seeing Jarvis in his garden at the time when Jane must have been . . .' He swallowed. Then he said: 'Heron believes the gardeners, and he is obviously sure Roger Brockley is his man. Sir Edward tends to get fixed ideas and doesn't like them disturbed.'

'Quite,' I said. 'I have, er, experienced this side of Sir Edward Heron myself.'

'Mistress Stannard, I wanted you to know. About Jarvis, I mean. I thought . . . you have powerful friends and a great knowledge of . . . of life. I hoped you might think of something you could do, or someone who could help. I want my wife's murderer to be caught, but I want it to be the real murderer, not Brockley. I can't believe it's Brockley. I know him well enough to feel convinced of that.'

I said, 'I'm glad you came.' I looked at Dale's woebegone face and gave her an encouraging smile. 'I leave for London tomorrow, Master Cobbold, and I'm going to see Lord Burghley. He knows the law, all its ins and outs. And he owes me favours. If anyone can help, he can. I feel that Brockley's arrest has summoned me to court as well – in a different sense. Dale and I were packing when you rode in. When I ask my lord for help, the fact that Jarvis has vanished could be a very useful piece of extra evidence on Brockley's side. Thank you for bringing it to me.'

Afterwards, I said to Dale: 'Do you know, I came within an inch of refusing to see him, and just sending him away! Why do churchmen so often say that curiosity is a sin? It can be an admirable virtue!'

SIX

A Name for a Dead Stranger

When we did finally set off for London, it was without knowing where we might find Lord Burghley. He was usually with the court but Elizabeth was forever on the move between her string of palaces along the Thames, from Greenwich to Hampton Court. I didn't know where she was at that moment.

I therefore began by taking us to the Cecils' house in the Strand, where Burghley's wife, the dignified and intellectual Mildred Cecil, greeted me and Dale without surprise. 'We know all about it, Ursula,' she said. 'As you know, my husband keeps himself informed of the events in your life.'

I nodded. The informant had probably been Dr Fletcher, the Hawkswood vicar. It was mainly Fletcher, on Cecil's behalf, who kept a quiet, benign eye on me, and had done so for years.

'William and I wondered if you would come to him,' Lady Mildred said. 'He's with the queen at Richmond just now. You are in time to see him – just. Her Majesty hasn't yet set off on her summer progress. He'll go with her, of course.'

Cecil had gone to Richmond by river, in his own barge, but there was a smaller one that his wife used for her own purposes. 'The tide will be right in half an hour,' she said. 'You dined on the road, I take it? Good. Then you just have time to change into a suitable gown for the court. I suggest you use my barge and the team of rowers I make up from our menservants. Our steward Thomas Mellot can go with you.'

I smiled. Mellot was as elegant and haughty as any prince and would certainly make an impressive escort. Mildred Cecil smiled back. 'He'll smooth your path to Lord Burghley,' she said.

'Will it need smoothing?' I asked.

'The court has changed in the year since you last visited it,' Lady Burghley said.

I left Arthur Watts behind, looking after our horses, and embarked with Dale and Mellot. It was a splendid afternoon. On land, it was hot, but out on the river it was delightfully fresh and the sunshine sparkled so brightly on the water that our oars seemed to drip molten gold. We would have enjoyed the journey, if only Dale and I had not been so anxious. We sat tensely under Lady Burghley's white canopy, wishing the barge could travel faster, and were very glad to see the turrets of Richmond Palace appear ahead of us.

I liked Richmond, for it was light and graceful, most of it four or five storeys tall, with slim windows and wind chimes that sang softly to us across the river. From some angles, the palace looked like a collection of slender towers, and it was surrounded by gardens where herbs and vegetables were grown as well as flowers, and by orchards that in spring were filled with blossom and in September were laden with fruit. Much of the food served at the tables of Richmond Palace was grown on the premises and taken fresh-picked to the several kitchens.

Usually, the very sight of it gave me pleasure. This time, I hardly noticed its charm; it was just a place where I might find help for Brockley. I could hardly wait to step ashore.

The guards at the river landing were new. None of them had ever seen me before and none of them recognized my name, either. I doubt if I would ever have got past their crossed pikes if it hadn't been for the presence of Thomas Mellot, and for the Burghley arms displayed on the side of the barge. The shield, which had six divisions, rearing lions on either side, an elaborate crest and a Latin motto, which in English meant *One heart, one way*, in clear bold lettering, would have impressed even raw guards who didn't recognize it, and these men were not quite as uninformed as that. They knew Mellot, too. One of them went to consult a superior somewhere within, and came back to say that yes, anyone who arrived with such obvious Burghley credentials could be admitted and taken to him.

'It used to be easier,' I said to Mellot as an usher led us through the palace.

'The Ridolfi plot, and the way the Duke of Norfolk was entangled in it, upset Her Majesty a good deal, I believe,' he said. 'There are stricter rules now about who can and cannot enter any palace where she is.' He dropped his voice so that the usher couldn't hear him, and added: 'She has grown distrustful. Norfolk was her cousin. If you have a source of peril within your own family, then who *can* you trust?' He went on: 'This is my private opinion; I do not repeat what my master says. But I shouldn't wonder if he thinks the same.'

It was a long walk through galleries and passages to the suite that Cecil used as offices when he was at Richmond. Its main room was octagonal and spacious with slender beams criss-crossing a high ceiling and paintings of angels and cherubs between the beams. While we were walking through the palace, the sun had gone in but silvery reflected light from the river still came through the tall windows to ripple over the beams and the paintings and the elegant linen-fold panelling on the walls.

It was a place of work, however. Cecil was there at his desk, studying a reference book while two clerks with ink-stained fingers were copying documents at a long table. And beside Cecil, leaning over his shoulder and pointing to a passage in the book, was Francis Walsingham.

They both looked up as I was announced, and to my surprise, the look of anxious care that Cecil's long, bearded face usually wore, broke into a delighted smile, while Walsingham's dark countenance also brightened, though I noticed that his eyes seemed sunken, as though he were unwell. Cecil rose and hurried round the desk to take my hand, while Walsingham muttered something to the usher, who at once dragged out chairs that had been set against the wall, and put them in a semi-circle.

'Ursula!' said Cecil. 'My dear Mistress Stannard. You are manna from heaven.'

'Am I?' According to his wife, Cecil had half-expected me to seek him out, but I hadn't been sure that he would be pleased about it. This near effusiveness took me aback.

'Take seats, all of you! You too, Mellot. I suppose my wife sent you as escort to Mistress Stannard.' Cecil suffered greatly from gout and his usual walking stick was propped against his chair, but just now, he seemed to be free of pain – indeed, almost vivacious. 'Very wise of her; I can always trust Mildred to do the right thing.' He nodded a dismissal to the usher, and then said: 'Dale, are you well?'

'I . . .' Dale began, and stopped, confused at being addressed directly.

'I know all about it.' Cecil glanced towards the door, which the usher had closed behind him as he went out. 'No doubt my wife explained that I partly expected you and Mistress Stannard to come to me. I know that your husband has been arrested for the murder of Jane Cobbold. I imagine that you seek my help.'

'Yes. We're turning to you because you know us all and because of your knowledge of the law.' I didn't add *and because of the risks Brockley and I have taken for you and the queen, and because I am her sister.* There was no need. He'd hear the words I hadn't spoken. 'I take it that Dr Fletcher informed you?' I said.

'Yes, but Sir Edward Heron got in first. He felt he should report the matter to me, in view of your link to the queen.'

'That didn't stop him from taking Brockley in,' I said acidly.

'He thought it his duty. Really, Ursula,' said Cecil in a positively rallying tone, 'can you not pay a visit to a neighbour and go for a walk in the garden without stumbling over a body in a flowerbed? It's the sort of thing that causes talk.'

Walsingham let out a bark of laughter. I didn't know him well, but I had always found him intimidating. Tall, dark and invariably dressed in black, he was even more saturnine than Anthony Cobbold and, in his case, his looks reflected his nature, which Anthony's did not. Walsingham did not mind attending interrogations in the dungeons of the Tower. It was said that at home he was an affectionate family man, but I found it difficult to imagine him down on all fours, playing with his children as I sometimes played with Harry, and still more difficult to imagine what he was like in bed. I would as soon have snuggled up to Old Man Death himself, with his skull face and the scythe under the mattress.

I believed the rumours that the queen disliked him as much

as she valued him. I corresponded sometimes with friends who were at court and, according to them, she sometimes threw things at him.

'Mistress Cobbold's death has been a disaster for us,' I said, not responding to his amusement. 'And we *know* that Brockley didn't do it. There is a Cobbold tenant, Jack Jarvis, who was suspected at first, and who has now disappeared . . .'

'We know that,' Cecil said. 'Anthony Cobbold reported his disappearance to Heron, who sent us word of that, too.'

'Though it is possible,' said Walsingham, 'that he has been found. But we can't be sure.'

I looked bemused and so did Dale. Mellot also raised surprised eyebrows. Cecil said, 'Well, Francis. It's your story. So tell it.'

'When I left France earlier this year,' Walsingham said, 'I had some unfinished business. I had ordered a set of new furniture, that should have been ready to travel to England with me, but was not. It has only just been completed, and had to be sent from France. I was informed of the ship that was to bring it and sent some of my men to Dover with a wagon, to collect it. Yesterday, on the way home along the Dover Road, not far outside London, they came upon a dead man at the roadside. He had been stabbed. He was dressed for riding and there were a horse's hoofmarks – but no horse.'

'You think it's Jarvis? He didn't own a horse, only a donkey. He apparently left his home riding it,' I said.

'Indeed? There was no donkey around, either. My men examined the body to see if there was anything to tell who the man was. There wasn't, but they did find a sealed letter stowed in an inner pocket of his jacket. They broke the seal and found that the letter was in cipher. That was no help in identifying its carrier, but letters in cipher are highly suspicious and because of that, they put the body on top of their wagonload of furniture and delivered it here before taking the furniture on to my house. At the moment, the corpse is in a side chapel here in this palace, and I have clerks trying to decode the letter, though not, as yet, with any success.

'But,' said Walsingham portentously, 'one of the men in the group had recently accompanied Roland Wyse on a journey into Surrey. He takes messages to Sir Edward Heron at times. He did that on my lord Burghley's behalf while I was still away in France; now he does the same for me. When he's in Surrey, he usually takes the opportunity to visit Anthony Cobbold, who is a friend of his. He has met Jack Jarvis and so, of course, have his companions. This man says he thinks the body is that of Jarvis. Only he isn't sure because he didn't know Jarvis well enough. By the time the body was brought here, we had learned that Jarvis had disappeared from his cottage, so, yes, the corpse could be his. You knew him quite well. That is why we're pleased to see you. If the dead man is Jarvis, you may be able to identify him.'

'What about Roland Wyse himself?' I said. 'He would know. I suppose he's one of those working on the cipher. Isn't he your best codebreaker?'

'Wyse isn't here. He's in Norfolk on compassionate leave,' said Walsingham. 'That's where he comes from – his home is somewhere near Kenninghall, quite close to what used to be the Duke of Norfolk's country house, I believe. I don't know exactly. Wyse had word that his mother was gravely ill and asked permission to visit her. I let him go. I approve of dutiful sons. But he may be gone for some time and we can't wait for him. The weather's too warm.'

'I was about to send someone into Surrey at a gallop, to fetch Anthony Cobbold,' Cecil said. 'But as I said when you arrived, Ursula, you have come to us like manna to the Israelites.'

Walsingham rose to his feet. 'Come this way, Mistress Stannard.'

He did not say please. Nor did he ask if I minded being asked to identify a corpse that might well be several days old. The sun had been agreeably warm for all that time. He just said *come this way*.

I never did come to like Francis Walsingham.

But I went with him obediently. On the way, he did relieve my mind a little, by saying: 'My men thought the corpse was a recent one – I mean, that it had only been dead for a short time. In that case, the killing only took place yesterday. This won't be too unpleasant.'

Nor was it. The tiny side chapel leading off from a bigger one was made of white stone and lay on the northern side of the palace. It was fairly cool and the poor thing on the trestle table in front of the little altar was more pathetic than horrible.

There was a guard on duty at the entrance to the little chapel, who came in with us and drew back the white linen cloth in which the dead man had been covered. Whatever the pains and terrors of his killing had been, his face was quiet. But the straw hat that still adorned his grey head was dirty, with broken ends of straw sticking out here and there, and the hair, which someone had smoothed on either side of his face, was greasy and limp and his mouth had fallen in, showing where, over the years, he had lost teeth. He looked as if life had used him harshly and it seemed a shame that death, coming to him with such violence, had continued the hammering.

I studied him, though, with care as well as pity. The big ears jutting through the hair looked familiar, although they were no longer red. I recognized the scar on the left ear, however. I drew the cloth back further. Beneath it, he was still dressed as he presumably was when he was found, in a brown jacket and an open-necked shirt, once white though now somewhat grubby. Over the heart, there was a slit, and a dark red-brown stain, that made me shudder. The jacket was open and I could see the belt that held up his breeches. It was of good polished leather with a chased decoration on the steel buckle. I put the cloth back, covering body and face once more.

'It's Jarvis,' I said. 'I know for sure by the scar on the left ear, and by that belt that he's wearing. I gave it to him myself, last year, when I was visiting the Cobbolds. I did give him small things sometimes, useful things, a kind of practical almsgiving.'

'You're certain?' Walsingham said.

'Yes, quite certain.'

'Very well.'

We left the place, the guard resuming his position by its entrance. I went with Walsingham across the main chapel and then back into the labyrinth of rooms and passages that were the interior of Richmond Palace, to rejoin Cecil and the others.

'Yes,' said Walsingham tersely as we came in. 'It is Jarvis. A sorry sight. Excuse me!' He stepped quickly across the

room and disappeared through a small inner door. I looked at
Cecil in surprise. 'What . . .?'

'He hasn't been well since his return from France,' said
Cecil. 'Some affliction of the bowels. Through there is a privy.
Be seated.'

I did so. 'There's no doubt,' I said, and explained again
about the scar and the belt. Cecil nodded and then we waited
until Walsingham reappeared. Then the two of them looked
at each other thoughtfully, as though they were exchanging
silent messages.

At last, Walsingham said: 'Mistress Stannard seems quite
sure of her facts. So there's no dispute now over who the man
is. But what was he doing on the Dover road, with a cipher
message in his jacket? Was the Jack Jarvis that you knew in
Surrey, Mistress Stannard, the kind of man who might deal
in such things?'

'I wouldn't think so,' I said. 'I don't even know if he could
write. He used to make a living by keeping sheep, near Guildford,
I think. Then the land he used for grazing was enclosed and he
couldn't afford the new grazing fees. I believe that Mistress
Cobbold made some enquiries about him before she persuaded
her husband to let him have the cottage. At the cottage, he grew
vegetables and kept chickens.'

'Heron's report said that he left his cottage the day before
Mistress Cobbold's funeral,' said Walsingham. 'Would that be
correct?'

I cast my mind back to what Anthony Cobbold had told me
and then said yes. 'That would be the seventh of July.'

'And yesterday was the tenth, and my men think he was
killed that same day, not so very long before they found him.'
Walsingham sat down by the clerks' table and drummed his
fingers on it. 'Two clear days in between, during which he
acquired a cipher letter and presumably an errand to go with
it. He was surely on his way to deliver that message to someone.
I wish we could read it but so far it seems to have defeated
my people. Someone,' said Walsingham, 'gave him the letter.
Probably exchanged his donkey for a horse as well, though
whoever killed him no doubt stole the horse. But who wrote
that letter and where was Jarvis taking it?'

'Let's take it point by point,' said Cecil. 'Firstly, the man Jarvis occupied a cottage that Jane Cobbold had provided. Secondly, within days of Jane Cobbold being mysteriously murdered, Jarvis disappears. It looked then as though he feared to be accused. Thirdly, he now turns up dead, far from home, with a cipher letter – that's suspicious in itself – on him. And fourthly, he met his death by a stab to the heart just as Mistress Cobbold did, except that this time, the killer didn't leave the dagger behind. What does all that suggest to you, Ursula?'

Dale and Mellot had both been silent up to now, but at this point, Dale opened her mouth and Mellot, seeing it, put a hand on her shoulder and said quietly: 'Wait. Let your mistress speak.'

Dale choked back an outburst but looked at me with anguish and pleading. I spoke for us both when I replied to Cecil.

'It suggests,' I said, 'a connection between those two deaths. Which further suggests that something very odd is going on at Cobbold Hall. Something that has nothing whatsoever to do with Jane Cobbold's gossiping tongue or Roger Brockley's opinion of it, which supports my belief that Brockley has been wrongly arrested. I came here today to implore your help in getting him released. Murder – stabbing Jane Cobbold – just isn't the sort of thing Brockley could or would ever do. But now there are even better reasons for saying that he's innocent. It seems at least possible that whoever killed Mistress Cobbold also killed Jarvis. Please, can you help?'

'There could simply have been a coincidence,' said Walsingham, 'and Jarvis was attacked by footpads while running away because he was afraid he would be accused of murdering Mistress Cobbold. Whether he really did so or not.'

'In that case,' I said, 'where does the cipher letter come in? And there are two gardeners – not related to each other or to Jarvis – who say that Jarvis couldn't possibly have killed Jane Cobbold. So why should he run away?'

'Perhaps Sir Edward Heron should have those gardeners questioned again,' said Walsingham.

'That could be wise,' Cecil said. 'But the cipher letter is more important. It needs explaining. It certainly doesn't fit in with Brockley as the murderer. I agree with Mistress Stannard that a very definite doubt has been cast on the charge against

Roger Brockley. We may be able to get him released on bail.
Can you put up bail for him, Ursula? Walsingham and I have
to remain neutral, at least on the surface.'

'I'll sell Withysham if I have to,' I said. 'Yes. I can offer
whatever bail Heron demands.'

'The queen gave you Withysham,' Cecil said. 'I'd be sorry
to see you lose it. Make sure that Brockley doesn't flee the
country! We shall send word to Heron recommending that he
consents to bail. We can't go further than that but he'll probably take the recommendation as a command. If so, I daresay
he will be in touch with you very soon after your return to
Hawkswood, to arrange the details.'

'Ma'am,' said Dale appealingly.

Once more, I looked at her. Her eyes beseeched me. I knew
what she was asking. I was already asking it of myself although
I had no more idea than Cecil how I should set about it.

'Ma'am,' said Dale again. '*Please!*'

I said. 'Brockley mustn't just be let out on bail; he must be
cleared. I have a duty towards him and to Dale here. I intend
to seek the truth for myself, independently. I hope you will
not object.'

'I rather thought you would say that,' said Cecil, 'but tread
carefully. Leave some things to us. We shall send an official letter
to Anthony Cobbold, to tell him that his erstwhile tenant is dead.
He'll want to find another, anyway. I'll explain the circumstances
– where Jarvis was found and the fact that he was carrying a
cipher letter. I shall also have Master Cobbold questioned. If he
knows anything to the point, we shall discover it and you'll
be informed. Don't complicate things by approaching Master
Cobbold yourself.'

I asked if I could see the cipher letter and Cecil sent one
of the clerks for it. It consisted of a jumble of letters and was
not, therefore, the type of code I knew about. I had no idea
at all how to tackle it. Cecil's own men were more likely to
succeed and one of these days, Roland Wyse, who had quite
a reputation as a codebreaker, would presumably get back
from Norfolk, and might solve it quite easily.

I would do best, I thought, to leave that task too for the
experts, and contented myself with saying: 'Decoding that

letter might answer all our enquiries. If the code is broken, will you let me know what it says?'

'Certainly,' said Cecil. 'Well, I should think the tide has turned by now, so you can start a journey downstream. I suggest that you and your companions stay the night at my house and set off for home tomorrow morning. We'll see you to the landing stage. Francis?'

'I regret to say,' said Walsingham, getting to his feet, 'that I can't come to the landing stage. My apologies, Mistress Stannard. Farewell.' He then plunged once more through the door to the privy.

'Oh, dear!' I said.

'He's always worse when he's upset,' Cecil told us as he guided us through the labyrinth of Richmond Palace. 'And he's upset now. Just when he needs Roland Wyse's gift for decoding, Roland Wyse isn't here, and yet he was glad enough to give that young man leave to go to Norfolk. Wyse is extremely able but he irritates his colleagues by his thrusting ways.'

'You mean,' I said, 'that if Francis Walsingham can find another codebreaker as gifted as Wyse, then Wyse will be dismissed?'

'Possibly.'

Well, the internal politics of the Secretary of State's department were not my concern. I had other things to deal with, which concerned me more.

SEVEN
The Elusive Beginning

*B*ut *where on earth*, I said to myself as, with Mellot and Dale, I boarded the barge and left Richmond Palace behind, *am I to begin? Dale is trusting me to help Brockley; I want with all my heart to help him, for his sake and mine – as well as for her. But what if I can't?* The whole mystery was like a ball of wool that has been wound so tightly that you can't find the end, which means that you can't use the wool.

Following Cecil's suggestion, we spent the night in London and left for Hawkswood in the morning. Meanwhile, Cecil and Walsingham presumably despatched messengers to Sir Edward Heron and Anthony Cobbold. Once home, I spent three days worrying at the problem of where to begin seeking the truth. Then Sir Edward Heron called on me again.

He came accompanied by a clerk. Their arrival was greeted by high-pitched barks from the new young dog Sandy and a deep baying from Hero, our half-mastiff bitch, by which I knew that whoever had ridden in was not well known to her. Hector, when he was alive, had bayed at everyone but Hero didn't give tongue beyond a welcoming *wuff* when people arrived who were familiar.

With Dale in attendance, I received them in the hall and offered the customary refreshments, which Heron declined on behalf of them both, though he seated himself and asked that his clerk should sit at the table and be provided with writing materials. I sent for these. The clerk, who had brought a box in with him, set it on the table, opened it and removed some sheets of parchment.

'I am here on business, Mrs Stannard.' Heron's chilly eyes bored into me. 'I have to say that it isn't business that pleases me, but a recommendation signed by both Lord Burghley and Francis Walsingham cannot be ignored.'

Cecil had been right. Heron had interpreted their letter as an order.

'I understand,' said Heron, 'that you are willing to put up bail for the man Roger Brockley while I continue my enquiries into the death of Mrs Jane Cobbold. My own personal belief is that in Brockley, I have the right man, but when orders come from such an exalted source, I can do nothing but comply.'

'I am willing to guarantee the bail,' I said. 'What are the terms?'

Heron shifted his feet uneasily. 'I wish that I could discuss these matters with a man. This is not a matter for women.' His frosty glance swept over Dale as well as me and appeared to search the room, as though hoping that something masculine might be found in a shadowy corner.

'But it's I, a woman, who will pay if Roger Brockley runs away,' I pointed out. 'I have no husband to take the responsibility for me. I am sorry, Sir Edward, but you will have to discuss the matter with me.'

'Nothing has been the same in this land since King Henry's son died and the throne passed to his daughters!' said Heron irritably. 'Women should not be in positions of power. I am aware, madam, that Mrs Cobbold disliked you and that you suffered from her tongue, but though I deplore the way she spread scandal about you, I can understand why she did not approve of you. A good deal of your history is known to me and, believe me, it isn't the kind of past I would want for any lady in *my* family.'

'The scandal that Jane Cobbold spread,' I said mildly, 'didn't concern the services I have rendered to Her Majesty. It was entirely to do with my small son, a different matter altogether.'

'Having children is a womanly enough thing to do,' conceded Heron, staring at me down his beak-like nose. 'But it's customary to do so within the bounds of marriage. However, I am not here to discuss that but to arrange the release of the man Brockley. He snapped his fingers at the clerk, who handed him one of the parchments. 'Here is the document you are required to sign. The terms are clearly set out.'

The terms were outrageous. If Brockley did lose his nerve and flee from England, I would certainly have to sell Withysham. Heron enquired whether – and how – I could raise the money and on being told that Withysham would provide it, informed me that until the matter of Brockley's guilt or innocence was resolved, Withysham would be regarded as the property of the state. He added that he had expected something of the sort and turned to the clerk, who at once spread out a clean sheet of parchment, dipped the quill I had provided into the inkpot and proceeded to put this in writing, to Heron's dictation.

I asked Dale, who could read and write very competently, to witness my signatures, and she breathed in with an audible hiss when she read the sum I was to guarantee.

'Hush, Dale,' I said. 'We have to sign.' We did so. 'When can we expect Brockley's return?' I asked as I handed the documents back.

'Within a few days.'

'I shall send a man off to Lewes this very day, with a horse and fresh clothing for him as soon as he is let out. I'll send Simon, our second groom. He's a steady young man.'

Sir Edward nodded. 'You really do take care of your servants, it seems. I will not criticize you for that.'

'Mistress Stannard is the best mistress any servant ever worked for!' Dale could contain herself no longer.

Heron bowed towards her. 'I must admire such loyalty.' He stood up. 'I must take my leave. I am to have the Cobbold Hall gardeners questioned again. It seems possible that the man Jarvis, who I understand has been found dead, may have somehow made them lie to protect him. I doubt it, but I will of course do my duty as ordered.'

'Thank you,' I said.

When he had gone, I turned to Dale. 'You'll have Brockley back soon.'

'For how long, ma'am?' Dale's eyes were still full of worry. 'Unless that man finds someone else to accuse, he won't leave my Roger free for long, I know he won't. He'll *look* for someone else, because he's been told to, but what if he doesn't find anyone? Or doesn't try that hard? I'm trusting you, ma'am.

You're clever at such things. Please, find out the truth, and save Roger!'

'I want to try, Dale. But where I'm to begin . . .'

Dale had a trick, sometimes, of getting to the heart of things. 'Wouldn't it be best, ma'am, to start by going into everything that happened at Cobbold Hall that day? Couldn't you talk to the people who were there? To Master Cobbold?'

'I've been advised not to approach him. You heard Cecil say so. Besides, I've already asked him if he saw or noticed anything helpful but he hadn't. He's clear of suspicion himself because he and Heron were indoors, together, at the time when Jane died. Cecil and Walsingham mean to have him questioned on the subject of Jack Jarvis, in case he knows anything to the point. You heard Lord Burghley say that, as well. I don't think I can go to Anthony myself.'

'Well, what about seeing Mistress Ferris, ma'am? She often visits Cobbold Hall; he'll have talked to her, as like as not, maybe more . . . more freely than he'd talk to you. He might have said something to her – perhaps something that he didn't think was important – but it might be just the little detail we need. I should think those two must have gone over everything again and again – trying to make sense of it all, to understand why such an awful thing should happen to them. You're friendly with her and you haven't seen her since . . . well, since it happened, have you?'

'No, and I wonder if she'll want to see me now!'

'You could call casually, to tell her how Sandy's getting on here.'

That made me laugh, for the first time since Brockley had been snatched away from us. The young dog Sandy was already becoming a character. The grooms usually ate in the kitchen at midday but if it was warm they sometimes took their meal outside to the sunny courtyard where there were a couple of benches. Simon, on one occasion, had put an ale tankard down by his feet while he finished a pie, and then glanced down to find Sandy with his nose in the tankard. Sandy had been very sleepy all that afternoon.

'I could do that,' I agreed. 'I could tell her about Sandy's taste for ale – though perhaps I won't mention how first of all, Hero tried to eat him! Thank goodness she's tolerating him now. And I could tell Mistress Ferris how he got into the house and tore my nice fur slippers to pieces. It might amuse her.'

'I felt shy about calling on you, in the circumstances,' I said to Christina as she led me and Sybil into the parlour at White Towers. 'Dale preferred not to come with us. With Brockley in prison, she's afraid that people will be unfriendly to her. But I did want to see you. There are things I must tell you . . . Oh, *Christina!*'

I had delayed for another three days before coming to White Towers, because like Dale, I doubted my reception. I needed time to summon up enough nerve. I had also dispensed with the usual groom to look after our horses once Sybil and I got there, in case we were turned away at the gate. There was no need to embarrass the servants.

We had been allowed in, but now I had lost my way completely in mid-speech and could only look helplessly at my friend. She was dressed in black and, beneath her pock-marks, her face was pale. She had lost her mother in a terrible fashion and I felt that I had no right to be there, least of all to ask questions of her. Then, moved by the sheer sadness of the mourning gown and the unhappiness in her face, I took a chance and put my arms round her. I feared that she might push me away, but she returned the embrace before gently detaching herself.

'It's all right, Ursula. Truly. I know that Brockley has been seized, but my father doesn't believe it could have been him and I can't believe it, either. It wouldn't be *like* Brockley. Oh, do sit down, both of you.'

We accepted the invitation. The day was cold and wet and we were glad of the velvet cushions on the settles, and the fire in the hearth. 'It makes no sense,' Christina said, picking up a poker and stirring the fire with energy. 'I know that my mother . . .'

She paused at that point, obviously finding it an effort to get the next words out, but after a moment, continued valiantly: 'I know my mother did sometimes, well, gossip about you, not kindly. But my father told her to stop and she did. He talks to me a great deal these days. In fact, he's closer to me than he is to my sister Alison, though she was always the good girl who did as she was told. Isn't it odd? But it's been a blessing for Thomas and me. The old feud between the Ferrises and the Cobbolds might never have existed! But look, if your Brockley was getting into fights over things that were said about you, they were said by other people, not my mother. Perhaps she started the talk, but she'd stopped, long before . . . she was killed. And Brockley is just not the sort of man to injure a lady. Everyone who knows him at all knows that!'

'That makes it easier for me,' I said. 'Easier, I mean, to tell you that arrangements have been made to release him on bail. We expect him home at Hawkswood soon. At least for the time being, while more enquiries are made. I hope they bear fruit. If they don't . . .'

A gusty wind made rain rattle against the windows and I suddenly shivered. Christina saw it. 'Oh, Ursula! And you, Mistress Jester! You've been riding in the rain and I haven't sent for wine or offered you anything hot to eat. One moment.' She was out of the room in a trice, and back again in another trice. Christina's movements were always swift and graceful. After a short time with her, one ceased to notice her pockmarks.

'It's coming,' she said as she returned. 'I am glad that you came – in fact, I had wondered if I should visit you myself, though I wouldn't have chosen a day like this for it. Just listen to that rain!'

'It didn't actually start raining till we were nearly here,' I said. 'We didn't get so very wet. I didn't shiver just now because I felt cold. It was because I'm afraid for Brockley – and Dale is terrified! I want to ask you something.'

'By all means. What sort of thing?'

'I don't wish to approach your father direct. But I want to know, well, everything *you* know – that your father has perhaps told you . . . you said you'd talked . . . Oh, I know I sound incoherent. I'm sorry. I'm trying to say that I want, need, to know all I can about what happened at Cobbold Hall that day, before you and I got there. We arrived after dinner. What happened before it? At the time, your father mentioned things – about Sir Edward Heron and Roland Wyse coming and going – and Sir Edward Heron told me much the same things later, but I don't remember any of it very clearly. Do you know more?'

'Not much more, I fancy, though Father and I have been over and over everything that happened that day. Sir Edward Heron has questioned him at length and my father has had word from someone at court, someone called Francis Walsingham, I think . . .' I nodded. '. . . who says that we have lost our tenant, Jack Jarvis, that he was found dead, miles away from here, on the road from London to Dover! When Sir Edward Heron came to Cobbold Hall to ask questions, he asked if my father could explain that. It seems that Jarvis was carrying a cipher letter of some kind. It hadn't been decoded, at least not then, so no one here knows what it's about.'

A maid came in then with mulled wine and some small, warm cakes. Baking must have been in progress when we arrived. 'I understand,' I said, sipping the hot spiced drink gratefully, 'that the man most likely to be able to crack it is Roland Wyse and he's away in Norfolk just now.'

'Is he? Anyway, nothing of all that made any sense and poor Father knew nothing that could help. He gathered that Heron had been told to find out if there was any possible connection between the Jarvis business, and my mother's death, but there just isn't, or so Father says! Oh, now I'm the one who's wandering, aren't I? You want to know about that day – that morning, before my mother was found . . . Well, let me see.'

She thought for a few moments. Then she said: 'Sir Edward Heron had been asked to dine that day. You know that. He arrived in good time and then I believe that Roland Wyse arrived as well, chasing after him with a letter from court – from the man Walsingham, whoever he is.'

'He's one of the Secretaries of State,' I said.

'As exalted as that!' Christina was impressed. 'Wyse had tried Sir Edward's home and had been directed to us. He shared dinner with us but then he went off again because he said he needed to get back to London as soon as possible. Father said he had an air of being very busy and important.'

'I daresay,' I said. 'That sounds like Master Wyse. I know him fairly well. So does Sybil.' Sybil smiled. 'What next?'

'A little while after dinner,' Christina said, 'my mother went out to call on Jack Jarvis. I understand that my father and Sir Edward stayed in the parlour, talking together.'

'When your mother went out, how long was that after Wyse left?' I asked.

'Oh, a good quarter of an hour, I think, from what Father said. But someone will ask Wyse about that when he gets back to London, surely. Anyway, Mother set off. The cottage is less than half a mile from the house – well, you know that. How on earth Jarvis came to be found murdered, so far from home – Father said it just bewildered him to hear of it. He could *not* make sense of it. It sounds so *unlikely*.'

Christina shook a bewildered head. 'Well, to get back to what I was saying, my mother went to see Jarvis, intending to order some eggs from him. She does – did – that sort of thing. She made a point of buying things from the tenants sometimes, even things Cobbold Hall could supply for itself. She said it was a dignified way of offering charity to people less fortunate than ourselves. Mother was a good woman, Ursula. She *was*! It was just that . . . that she was too good in some ways. She didn't understand people – women – who were different from herself.'

For the first time, her gaze was defensive, as though she were daring me to criticize Jane Cobbold.

'Yes, I understand,' I said pacifically. 'So your mother went to see Jarvis. What then? She came back before we arrived, didn't she?'

'Yes. Father says he and Sir Edward saw her come back – she was on foot. It seems that the gardeners had finished the weeding and had just gone off with their ladder, to deal with a tree near the Jarvis cottage. Father and Sir Edward saw them go, and saw my mother reappear and go straight to where they'd been working to see if they'd followed various instructions she'd given them. But they had left the garden by then. Father said all that to me several times over. He said he'd rather believe the gardeners did it, than believe that Brockley did. But he's come to see that they couldn't have.'

There were tears in her eyes. 'Mother never came indoors. She disappeared round the side of the house and none of us ever saw her alive again. The last words she said to Father were when she was setting off for the cottage. She said she was going to order a dozen eggs from Jarvis. And Father said . . . said . . . Oh, dear God, he's been heartbroken about it. He said he was short with her, and told her she was making too much of a pet of Jarvis. He's been tearing himself to pieces because the last words *he* ever said to *her* were unkind!'

'Please don't, my dear.' It was Sybil, this time, who went to Christina and put her arms round her. 'Hush. Hush.'

Sybil was always a calming influence. Christina quietened and wiped her eyes. Gently, she drew herself back from Sybil. 'What *was* Jarvis doing on the Dover road?' she said. 'And why should he have a cipher letter on him? It's crazy! I suppose it really was him?'

'Yes, it was,' I told her. 'I went to Cecil, to ask his advice – on how to get Brockley released. I was asked to see if I could identify a body, thought to be that of Jarvis. There was a doubt at that stage. I did identify it. It was Jarvis right enough. He'd been stabbed, just the same as . . . well . . .'

'As my mother,' said Christina bravely. Then . . .' I could see her working it out. 'Well, Brockley obviously didn't kill Jarvis! But both Jarvis *and* my mother? Both stabbed, within a few days? There can't be any link and yet there ought to be. You say Brockley is to be freed?'

'For now, as I said. I don't think Sir Edward Heron is at all convinced that your mother's death and Jarvis's are connected. I fancy he can't see how, any more than we can, or your father.'

Sitting stiffly in a corner of a settle, Christina's small black-clad figure seemed to ask for comfort, but she tried to give it instead. 'I shall pray for Brockley,' she said. Gallantly, she smiled. 'Thomas is talking business with our steward,' she said. 'But he'll join us soon. We might collect little Anne from the nursery and walk round the garden. The rain seems to be stopping. Meanwhile, how is that sand-coloured puppy faring at Hawkswood?'

I said, 'I regret to tell you that he mistook my new fur slippers for a couple of rats and killed them very thoroughly.'

It was the lighter note that we needed. It made all three of us laugh.

EIGHT
The Faint Spoor

At Christina's insistence, Sybil and I dined at White Towers. The rain ceased while we were eating, and when we left, late in the afternoon, the sun was out. However, as we neared Hawkswood, we were surprised to see a column of smoke which was not chimney smoke, for we could already see the chimneys. 'What's that?' Sybil asked, sitting up straighter in her saddle. 'It looks as if someone's lit a bonfire.'

'But there was no pruning or lopping to be done today,' I said, puzzled. 'We'd better hurry!'

We touched spurs to our horses and broke into a canter. The gate arch came into view and there indeed was a bonfire, just outside it, being vigorously tended by Joseph with a pitchfork. A gust of wind blew the smoke towards us, bringing with it a vaguely disagreeable smell.

'Joseph!' I called as we came within earshot. 'What are you doing?'

He stepped back and waited for us, leaning on the pitchfork. 'Mistress Stannard! Brockley's home – but he said we were to burn his clothes.'

'Burn his clothes? Is that what the smell is? But . . .'

'He said he was verminous.' Joseph's fresh-skinned face split into a grin. He was young enough to be amused. 'You never saw such a to-do. Brockley and Simon came in two hours since. They'd been riding since dawn – all the way from Lewes! Forty miles, Simon said! Brockley stood out in the courtyard and when Dale ran out to him, he sent her back inside with orders to get water heated for him to have a bath and to bring out two pailfuls to the tackroom as well, quick as she could! And he, Brockley, I mean, wouldn't go indoors till he'd groomed his cob, Mealy, within an inch of its life, and washed all his saddlery in hot water and soap and then rubbed in so much of that neatsfoot oil and beeswax mixture he makes that I reckon he used a week's supply in ten minutes. He went at it like a madman!'

'But now you're burning his *clothes*?' said Sybil, astounded. I said, 'But I sent him fresh ones.'

'Yes, and they're what's on the fire here. He said he'd dumped his old ones in a ditch just outside Lewes! He wore the ones you sent on the ride home but he said they'd got verminous just being on him.' He gave an encouraging jab to the bonfire, which was beginning to sulk. 'When he was done in the stable, he took an old sack from a barn and went indoors and then sent Dale out with the sack, with all these things in it.'

'Sybil!' I said. 'Come with me!'

We clattered through the gate arch at speed. Arthur Watts and Simon hurried from the tackroom to meet us. 'He's home, madam! He's home! He's having a bath!' Simon shouted.

'See to our horses,' I said to Arthur. 'Good to see you back, Simon. Come along, Sybil!'

We used a small downstairs room for baths. The door to it was shut but the voices of Brockley and Dale could be heard inside. Adam Wilder had heard us arrive and joined us. 'He's just let Dale in,' he said. 'He would hardly let her near him before – not until he'd got himself clean. Ah. Here they come.'

The door opened and there was Brockley, dressed in fresh hose, and with a clean, loose-necked shirt on under his best quilted jacket. He was rubbing his hair with a towel. Dale emerged on his heels, with another towel, used and very wet, over her arm. 'Oh, ma'am! Roger's home! Isn't it wonderful?'

'I'm very happy to be here, madam.' Brockley's voice sounded weaker, thinner, than I had ever known it to be before.

'Take him to your room, Dale,' I said. 'Get his hair dry. I'll send up some dinner. Where are the Floods? There you are! Joan, Ben, get something hot ready for these two. Brockley, I am glad to see you – *thankful*! Sir Edward Heron kept his word. We'll talk later. Take him away, Dale.'

He and Dale must have their private reunion first but I badly wanted to talk to him, for I felt anxious about him. Brockley had been in Lewes gaol for only a week but a single glance had told me how much weight he had lost. Sybil said as he and Dale vanished upstairs: 'I don't like that quelled note in his voice, and by the look of him, he hasn't had a square meal for days.'

Gladys had appeared at my side. 'When his meal goes up to him, I'll put a wine posset on the tray for him, with my valerian and camomile mixture in it. He'll likely sleep this afternoon. It'll do him good, indeed. It's what he needs.'

'Thank you, Gladys. Yes, do that.'

The posset must have worked because it was well on in the evening before the Brockleys came in search of me. They found me in the Little Parlour with Sybil.

'We would have come before, ma'am, but Brockley has had a sleep,' Dale said.

'I expect he needed it after that ride from Lewes,' I said, and held out a hand to him. 'How are you feeling now?'

'Better, thank you, madam.'

With a gesture, I invited them to be seated and Sybil smiled at them, but then a curious silence fell. It was an awkward silence, something that had never before happened between the four of us. We knew each other so well. In the end, I broke it by saying directly: 'Was it very terrible, Brockley?'

'I can hardly describe it, madam. The place was filthy, and I was crowded into a big underground room with half a dozen others, all filthy too, and there were fleas and nits. They gave us straw to sleep on and it was changed from time to time but it was always crawling after one night, because most of the prisoners were verminous. I had some money with me but I kept it hidden in case it was grabbed from me. Anyway, how could I send out for food just for me? So I just ate the gruel and bread we were given by the turnkeys. But the worst thing was the fear. Nearly everyone there was on a charge that could mean hanging and everyone was frightened to the point of sickness. Some of them *were* sick, literally, because of the prison food and out of dread. We had buckets . . .'

'Oh, Brockley!' Sybil was horrified and I felt my face become grim. Both she and I knew what it was like to be imprisoned, with only a bucket to deal with personal needs.

'Fran has been a marvel,' Brockley said. 'I think she must have used magic to conjure up that bath I had, she had it ready for me so quickly.' He turned his head to look at Dale and I saw that one good thing had come out of all this. The way he was looking at her now was the way he had often looked at her in the past, before their estrangement, the estrangement I so bitterly regretted because it sprang from Dale's jealousy of me.

It was over. They were again as they had been and they would remain so. I would see to that.

'Well now,' I said, 'we have to decide what to do next. I've been allowed to put up bail for you, Brockley, but Sir Edward Heron has made it clear that he still thinks you're guilty. However, he has had orders to make new enquiries. Meanwhile, I've told Cecil and Walsingham that I mean to make enquiries of my own. Sybil and I started on that this morning. We avoided harassing Anthony Cobbold but we've talked to Christina Ferris, though I don't think we learned much. Sybil, you have a good clear memory. You tell them what we found out.'

'Just the order of events on that morning,' said Sybil, and proceeded to recount them. 'Only we knew most of it already,' she said unhappily, as she finished. We all sat looking at each other in silence, though this time it wasn't awkward but united. United, that is, in feeling defeated.

'We haven't discovered anything useful,' I admitted. 'Heron and Wyse came in the morning and dined. Wyse left, Heron stayed. Mistress Cobbold went to see Jarvis but came back and went straight into the garden. The gardeners had left before she arrived. Later, she was found there, dead. And now Jarvis is dead as well!'

'Jarvis?' said Brockley, and I realized that he didn't know. Simon had gone off to Lewes before I left for London. Quickly, I explained. Brockley scratched his head and said: 'So no one can question him any further, though they can question the gardeners. Maybe they're lying and somehow got Jarvis to back them up . . . I can't seem to think clearly yet. *Someone* came into that garden and killed Mistress Cobbold.'

He paused, puckering his brow as though sustained thought was actually painful. Finally, he said: 'No one saw a stranger lurking about? There's a shrubbery, isn't there? Someone could have hidden there.'

'Wyse hasn't been questioned. What if he noticed something?' said Sybil slowly. 'He can't have done it himself – Christina said he left for London straight after dinner. But he might have seen someone . . . or talked to Jarvis! He'd pass the cottage on his way to the London road, wouldn't he?'

'I've seen him give alms to Jarvis in the past,' I said. 'He might well have stopped at the cottage for a word. That's a point. But Wyse is away in Norfolk now. His mother sent for him, I understand.'

'Do you know where he lives?' asked Brockley.

'Near Kenninghall – where the Duke of Norfolk used to live when he was in the country.'

Suddenly, I was inspired with new hope. Here at last was a new trail to follow. Not a good one, but it was there. It was something to do and it might – it *might* – lead to something useful. 'Brockley, are you thinking that we should talk to him ourselves? We'd have to find him. I don't think Walsingham knows exactly where he lives – we'd have to go straight to Norfolk and enquire for him there. But yes! It could be worth it. It's a faint spoor, so to speak, but it's all we have. Yes, it might be worth it!'

There was another silence, until Brockley said: 'Do I sense the thrill of the chase?' He attempted to smile as he said it, though it was only a shadow of Brockley's rare but broad and infectious grins. It nearly broke my heart to see it.

But I put all the vitality I could into my voice as I said: 'I think you do.'

NINE
Kenninghall

Dale said, rather plaintively: 'But just where is Norfolk? Have we ever been there? And once we do get there, how do we find Kenninghall?'

'We've been to Cambridge,' I replied. 'Norfolk is north-east of there. Finding the Duke of Norfolk's country seat ought to be simple enough and Wyse comes from somewhere near it. There are maps in Hugh's old study. Let's look at them.'

We found a map that was informative. Principal towns were clearly shown and there was more than one possible route. 'Kenninghall's marked,' I said. 'It's just over the southern border of the county. We'd better go by way of Colchester. The road that leads to Norwich would take us too far north. Now, which of us will make the journey?'

We decided that Sybil should stay at Hawkswood, in charge of it as my representative, while the Brockleys accompanied me to Norfolk. We would take our own horses all the way. I would ride Jewel, while Dale would, as she preferred, travel pillion behind Brockley on his sturdy cob, Mealy. Joseph could come with us to help with the horses. He could ride one of the serviceable geldings that we used at times to pull the coach, on the rare occasions when we used it. Rusty and Bronze were both good-tempered animals with plenty of stamina. Joseph chose to ride Rusty. We need not take much luggage. Saddlebags and satchels that we could carry on our backs would do to hold changes of clothing. Dale and I would each wear one small ruff, carry a spare, and dispense altogether with farthingales. The weather was warm again, as it should be in July, but we took felt travelling cloaks. They could be rolled up and pushed into our satchels when we didn't need them.

Harry was upset when he realized that I was going away.

He was growing rapidly and had lately become very
knowing. I hugged him hard, promising to be back soon,
and gave both Tessie and Sybil such a stream of instructions
about keeping him amused and safeguarding his health that
I probably made them feel dazed. He cried when the horses
were brought out for us. I was full of silent rage against
whoever had killed Jane Cobbold, against Jane herself for
so inconsiderately getting herself murdered, and against Sir
Edward Heron for fastening on Brockley. I didn't want to
make this journey. I wanted to stay at home in peace with
Harry.

As we were preparing to mount, Brockley said to me: 'Are
you still carrying your picklocks and dagger in your hidden
pouch, madam?'

In the days when I regularly carried out perilous assignments for the queen, I had adopted the fashion of wearing
an overdress with a skirt open in front to reveal a pretty
kirtle, and inside all my open skirts, I had stitched pouches
in which I could carry useful items. Such as picklocks and
a small dagger, and usually some money as well. But in the
serenity of domestic life, I had ceased to equip myself thus.
I still wore the open skirts, since I liked the fashion, but my
new ones had no pouches for I no longer needed such things
as weapons and picklocks, and could put money into an
ordinary girdle purse.

At least, until now. But on the previous night, I had sat up
late to stitch a pouch into the spare skirt I was taking, and
asked Dale to look out an old one for travelling – one that
had a pouch in it anyway. And I had looked out my dagger
and the key ring on which hung the slim steel hooks which
were my means of getting through locked doors and into other
people's document boxes.

'I'm equipped as I used to be, Brockley,' I said. 'Just in
case.'

'I guessed you might be.' said Brockley. 'We really are
going hunting, are we not?'

It was a long ride. On the first day, we reached London and
crossed the Thames at London Bridge, wanting to get as far
as we could as quickly as we could and bypassing the

well-known and comfortable George Inn south of the Thames.
We finally halted at an inn just beyond London, for we were
all tired, including the horses. The Boar wasn't a good hostelry,
for its customers were scruffy and its food was inferior, and
Brockley, watching a mouse dart across the grimy straw-strewn
cobbles of its main public room, said that even the mice must
be desperate for sustenance; look at the poor thing, risking
itself among the all those clumsy booted feet, in case somebody
dropped a few crumbs. However, it was the only hostelry for
miles. We spent the night there.

Next morning, we rose early but it was more than forty-five
miles to Colchester and we took two days over it. One can't
go all that fast with a pillion rider in the party. Another two
days took us to somewhere called Saxmundham and a further
day brought us to the coast, and a place called Lowestoft. As
we rode in, we were greeted by the salt smell of the sea,
mingled with a strong odour of fish. And there to our right
was the North Sea, grey-blue under a patchwork sky, with a
bristle of fishing boat masts in the harbour.

There were narrow lanes which at first confused us and we
had to turn back from one passageway that only led to the top
of some steep and dangerous looking steps down to the harbour.
Eventually, we found our way to where there were such things
as a church and an inn, and drew rein.

'We must be near the Norfolk border by now,' I said.
'Let's make enquiries.'

'I could do with a tankard of ale,' said Brockley. 'Let's
try the inn first. Landlords always know where every place
of note or important family can be found, within twenty
miles.'

The stableyard of the inn wasn't busy. Brockley gave sharp
orders to the ostler, and then we all went inside, taking our
saddlebags; one can never be quite sure that there are no light
fingers among strange grooms. We found that though the stables
were quiet, the inn was busy, mostly with fishermen who had
been at sea long enough to acquire a hearty thirst. The landlord
was a small, bustling man, out of breath from trying to look
after them all. He waved at a barmaid to attend to our wants,
and we were soon supplied with ale, but it took longer to

persuade him to pause beside us long enough to answer a simple question.

When we finally managed it, what he told us was depressing. We were close to the Norfolk border but we were over thirty miles from Kenninghall and had come in by quite the wrong road. We would have to travel westwards and we'd better keep to the main track that went through places called Bungay and Diss, because there were a tidy lot of marshes and pools and what have you, all about this district. 'But the road, she do run alongside a river but she's a proper road and won't land you in a bog, or not unless we have a heavy rainfall like the one last year . . .'

'After Diss,' said Brockley, firmly interrupting, 'what then?'

'Oh, there's a track, sharp right, after six, seven miles; can't say exactly. Leastways, I think so, but ask in Diss. All that's a way out of my district and if you'll excuse me, I've a dozen things to see to and there's Tom Brothers waving his tankard at me for a refill . . .'

'Can we stay here tonight?' I said swiftly, getting in before the landlord could escape again.

'What? Oh, certainly, certainly; my wife sees to all that, I'll send her to you.'

With that, he was off and we sat sipping our ale and wondering if he really would find time to despatch his wife to look after us.

However, he did, and after a short time, she came to find us. She was a large woman though quick on her feet and with an amiable smile. Oh, yes, we could stay. All these folk, they were local, just brought the catch home and sold it straight away. There was fresh fish on the menu for supper and if we'd finished our ale, she'd show us what rooms there were, though customers' grooms slept over the stables. She was an experienced landlady and had instantly classified Joseph, though she was prepared to grant Brockley the status of manservant.

'If we start out early, we may get there tomorrow,' I said, as we put our tankards aside and rose to follow her.

'I wouldn't make a wager on it,' said Brockley. 'I don't like the sound of all those marshes and pools.'

*   *   *

We didn't get there the next day because Brockley was quite right. The road was a muddy track, which looked as if it had undergone changes over the years, probably because the numerous patches of water had done the same thing. There were frequent forks, and three times, we took the wrong branch and found it petering out at the edge of a bog or the rim of a pool.

Just to make everything even better, during the first afternoon, the warm sun vanished behind clouds and down came the rain. Cloaks were hastily donned, and hoods pulled over heads. All paths became deep in mud, seemingly within minutes. Dale complained that her cloak seemed to be absorbing the rain like a sponge instead of protecting her, and she was afraid she'd take cold.

She had some justification, for all our cloaks were heavy with wet and our horses were muddied to their girths by the time we reached the village called Diss. However, we did find a hostelry there, which provided hot food and mulled wine and rooms where we could change our clothes. Joseph and Brockley spent a long time in the stable, cleaning the mud off our horses' legs and out of their hooves. In the morning, we set off on the last stage of our journey.

By midday we were there. 'At last!' I said, as we jogged through what proved to be a substantial village or small market town, with reed-thatched cottages and a sizeable church, built of grey stone, with a squat medieval tower. The rain had ceased during the night and the road through the village was wide and fairly dry. We halted in the middle.

'Where now?' Brockley said. 'Is this Kenninghall? Where's the Duke of Norfolk's house?'

'I don't know,' I said. 'But we're not going there, of course. We're looking for Wyse's home – well, it will be his mother's home – that's supposed to be close to it. Let's try the vicar of that church.'

We couldn't at first work out which house was likely to be the vicarage, so we dismounted, tied our horses to the church-yard fence, and went into the church itself. We were in luck because we found the vicar inside it. Indeed, we almost fell over him, for he was down on hands and knees just inside the door, apparently searching for something on the floor. He looked up, blinking, as we walked in.

'Good day. I'm sorry to be caught in this undignified manner. I've dropped my eyeglasses. Please don't shift your feet about in case you step on them. They've never fitted my nose so very well,' he explained, coming carefully to his own feet. 'They're too big and they fell off while I was looking to see if the place had been properly dusted. I was stooping, you see, and they just slid off and now I can hardly see anything.'

He was a thin and elderly man whose dark clerical gown looked as though it needed dusting as much as the church. His thin-bridged nose clearly wasn't ideal for keeping eyeglasses in place, and his pale blue eyes didn't look very fit for their purpose either. He gazed round him in a helpless manner.

'Excuse me,' said Brockley. 'I can see them.' He leant down and retrieved the glasses from the floor within a few inches of the vicar's feet. 'Here they are, sir.'

'Thank you!' Their relieved owner seized them, planted them on his nose in a forceful manner, as much as to say *Stay there, confound you!* and then said: 'What can I do for you? I am Dr Herbert Yonge, though I'm not the vicar of St Mary's in the parish of Kenninghall which is where you are now. The vicar's ill and I have been dragged out of my peaceful retired life in Diss to look after St Mary's till he recovers. If you need help of any kind, I'll do my best though I don't know this parish well. Before I retired, I had a living near Norwich.'

I felt discouraged but Brockley said: 'If this is Kenninghall, then somewhere in the village lives a Mistress Wyse who has a son called Roland. Her son may be visiting her and we need to see him. Do you by any chance know of her?'

'Mistress Agnes Wyse? Oh, yes, she helps to dust the church sometimes.' Dr Yonge spoke in slightly disparaging tones. 'Her son has been here lately. He has a post at court, I believe, and she's very proud of him. He's left for London now, I think. I know because of speaking to his mother when she was dusting. I can't claim to know her well and I've never actually met her son. Or anyone here. East Anglians tend to be a race apart, you know,' he added gloomily. 'Descended from Danish Vikings, most of them, I believe. I was born in Bedfordshire myself.'

'We've missed Roland Wyse, then,' I said. 'However, we can still call on Mistress Wyse.' I glanced at the others. 'He may have talked to her – at least we can enquire.' I turned back to Dr Yonge. 'Can you tell us where she lives? And is there an inn in the village?'

'You want lodgings? The White Hart will take you in, I daresay. As for Mistress Wyse, yes, I can point out her house to you. Let me show you.'

He led the way to the door, and pointed to his right.

'There it is – that big house with the beech tree in the front garden. The inn's a little further on. You can't miss it.'

We thanked him and on impulse, because he seemed somehow forlorn, with his bad eyesight and dusty gown, I gave him a few coins for the church. 'To pay for some extra dusting, or to relieve the poor,' I said, and for the first time, he smiled, which made his face unexpectedly youthful. He wasn't truly forlorn, I thought, only unhappy at being summoned from a quiet retirement to resume what had probably been a tiring career spent ministering to a wayward flock whose ancestors had been ruthless invaders, arriving in longships with dragon prows.

We went to the inn first, to arrange rooms for the night and take a quick midday meal. It was quite a big place, with public rooms on the ground floor, and bedchambers upstairs, leading off a gallery with a balustrade and a sheltering roof. Outside stairs led up to either end.

The rooms were spacious and clean, which pleased us. We didn't trouble to ask for a full dinner, but took a quick meal of fresh bread, cheese and ham washed down with small ale. Then, leaving our horses in the stable with their noses in their mangers (after so much journeying, they were no doubt thankful to stay put for a change) we set off on foot to the house with the beech tree in the garden. It was a sizeable house, with steps up to an iron-studded oak front door which had an iron knocker in the shape of a lion's head. There was a first floor above and then three dormer windows, presumably attic windows, poking out of the thatch.

Brockley plied the lion's head briskly and the door was opened by a tall girl with a broom in one hand, although she didn't look like a maidservant. Her brown dress had no farthingale but it was of good material and she wore jewellery too, a necklace and earrings of amber and silver.

'Is Mistress Agnes Wyse at home?' I enquired. 'My name is Ursula Stannard. My companions are my servants, Roger Brockley and his wife, Mistress Brockley. I had hoped to see Mistress Wyse's son but I understand that he's no longer here. A strange situation has arisen at court that he may help to resolve. However, Mistress Wyse may also be able to help. Can we see her?'

'I expect so,' said the girl. 'I am Blanche Lockyer, her cousin. Do come in.'

We stepped inside. From a room on the left, a woman's voice called: 'Who is it, Blanche?'

'Visitors from court. A Mistress Stannard and her servants,' said Blanche, putting her head round a partly open door. The woman inside said: 'Well, bring them in, then,' and Blanche pushed the door wide open. We trooped after her into a pretty parlour, curtained in amber velvet, with matching wool rugs on the floor, embroidered cushions, and honey-coloured panelling. There were two portraits, one on either side of the hearth. I glanced at them with interest, but by then the lady who had been seated by the window with an embroidery frame had risen to welcome us and I transferred my attention to her.

Indeed, I studied her with care. If she were Roland's mother, she must be well into her forties at the least, but although she could not exactly be called beautiful, her complexion was smooth, and her blue eyes were pleasingly set and her nose had a pretty tilt at its tip. She was not expensively dressed but the blue linen gown had been carefully chosen to match her smiling eyes and her ruff, though unfashionably small, was pristine and edged with silver thread. She was slightly built and a big ruff would have overwhelmed her. I wore restrained ruffs myself, considering the big ones to be ungainly.

She had silver earrings and a heavy silver chain as

jewellery, and a cap embroidered in silver to go with the edging
of the ruff. The light red hair that rose in smooth waves in
front of it showed no sign of grey. She had kept her looks
well enough to belie her years, and yet had an air of maturity.
It gave her an aura both of charm and mystery.

I made the introductions again for her benefit, and repeated
what I had told Blanche about the purpose of this visit. Dale
curtsied and Brockley bowed. Mistress Wyse greeted them in
a pleasant voice with scarcely any trace of a Norfolk accent.
She offered us seats and then turned to Blanche, shaking her
head in reproof.

'Whatever are you doing with that broom, Blanche? There's
no need. Lucy will be here tomorrow and she can see to the
sweeping.' She smiled at us. 'My maid, Lucy, is having a
half-day off. I do feel that one should be considerate towards
one's servants, don't you? Do go and put that broom away,
Blanche. Bring some wine for us all. And some of the honey
cakes I made this morning.'

She smiled again as Blanche went out, and I noticed that
her teeth were still in good repair. 'I have a cook but I enjoy
working in the kitchen sometimes. The cakes have raisins in
them as well as honey and a little cinnamon too. I used to
make them with saffron but saffron is too costly for me now.
However, I hope you'll like them. Dear Blanche, she does try
to make up for the lack of servants. I only have one maid
besides the cook; life isn't always kind to widowed women,
and I never wanted to marry again after my dear husband
died.'

'Was that recently?' Dale asked.

'Five years ago. I took Blanche in just after that, for
company, and to give her a home when she was orphaned.
But I want it to be a real home. I do *not* want her to do the
sweeping. I am hoping that she'll marry well, eventually.
Kenninghall House is Crown property now, you know, and
well maintained and there's an assistant bailiff on the estate
there who is interested in Blanche, though I'm not sure that
a bailiff is quite what I want for her. Working on the land,
you know, even as a supervisor – well, it isn't exactly what
I'd choose for my kinswoman, not now that I have a son at

court. Now, you say that you have been brought here because of a strange situation at court. What exactly is this situation?'

Blanche came back with the wine and cakes. Unlike her cousin, Blanche was not only not pretty, but created no impression of charm, either. She was gawky in her movements and her features and mousey hair were unmemorable. She gave the impression of being in Agnes's shadow. I wondered if she was always rebuked if she did the sweeping, or only if there were visitors to be impressed by Agnes's kindness to an orphaned cousin.

While Mistress Wyse distributed the refreshments, I asked after her health. 'We heard that Roland had come to see you because you had been ill. I hope you are quite recovered now.'

Agnes brushed this off. 'It was a passing indisposition, nothing more. I fear I made too much of it, when I mentioned it in a letter to Roland. He came hastening to me but there was little need. I am quite well now.'

I said I was glad of that, and forthwith embarked on the full story of Jane's death. On hearing that she had been found lying stabbed among the flowers in her own garden, Agnes uttered a faint shriek and put down a wine glass in order to clap her hands to her mouth.

I gave her a moment to recover and then went on, explaining that a servant of mine (I didn't name Brockley) had been accused but that I was sure of his innocence, which was why I was making enquiries on my own account instead of leaving them to the authorities. Brockley and Dale remained carefully expressionless throughout all this. Finally, I said: 'I rather hoped to find your son Roland still here. Since he was at Cobbold Hall that morning, it is just possible that he saw something, or someone, that might suggest an answer to the riddle. The only person who was there but has not yet been asked about it is your son. We wondered if he had said something to you about the events of that morning.'

Agnes sipped her wine and slowly shook her head. 'I can't say that he did. No, I'm sorry. He didn't mention visiting this Cobbold Hall at all. He only talked of his work at court, for Francis Walsingham. It's a very good position for him, though

I fear he finds Master Walsingham a hard taskmaster. But there, I told him, you will have to work your way up, and if your employer seems demanding, I'm sure that at least he is teaching you how to do things as they should be done. I want to see Roland do well! And make a good marriage in due course. Ah!' She sighed, reminiscently. 'I was married off by my parents while I was very young – only fifteen. I was happy enough, I suppose, and yet I might have been happier still had they waited and let me have a chance with wealthier, more noble suitors. I could have had them!'

She pointed to one of the portraits by the hearth. Now I saw that the nearest one was of Agnes as a young girl and then, she had certainly been lovely, very bright of eye, with an inviting smile. The tip-tilted nose gave her a look of saucy sweetness.

'I was twenty-three when that was painted,' she said wistfully. 'But I was even better-looking when I was seventeen. That was in 1542, when Henry Howard visited Kenninghall. He was the Earl of Surrey, you know, and the father of the Duke of Norfolk who died so dreadfully on the scaffold last year. Henry Howard never became Duke of Norfolk because his father outlived him. Henry was executed for treason too, poor man. I cried bitterly when I heard of Henry's death. I'm sure he wasn't guilty. He didn't live at Kenninghall but as I said, he visited it in 1542. He was twenty-four and I was seventeen and we met.'

She paused, as though looking back into the past, and there was a silence, until I said: 'How did that come about?'

'Oh, there was a great ball at Kenninghall House and my husband, Robert, was a respected local lawyer, and so we were invited. Henry Howard asked me to dance with him and – well, he fell in love with me. He was a poet and he dedicated one of his poems to me. It's called "Vow to Love Faithfully", and the last line runs *Content myself although my chance be nought.* We were both married, of course, but for men these things don't matter so much. For women . . . well, I would never have betrayed my dear Robert. Master Brockley, do have another cake. I always feel that men need plenty of sustenance. You have a fine-looking husband, Mistress Brockley, and I'm sure he is an excellent servant to you, Mistress Stannard.'

She gave Brockley a sparkling smile and rose to her feet to present him with the plate of cakes. He took one and she patted his arm with approval. 'That's right! It's a joy for a woman to see her cooking appreciated.'

Beside me, I felt Dale stiffen and I saw Blanche give her cousin a surprisingly sharp look. Then she glanced towards the window and said: 'Gilbert is coming along the street! I do believe he's coming here.'

'Gilbert Shore? Your assistant bailiff?' Agnes Wyse turned away from Brockley to look out of the window. As she did so, presenting us with a view of her profile, I experienced a curious jolt in the pit of my stomach. Seeing her side-face in that way meant that I could see the white in the outermost corner of her left eye and the effect was disconcerting. Gone were the charm and the mystery. The outer white of that eye, and presumably the other eye was the same, was a large, fierce, blue-white triangle. I had never before taken conscious note of such a thing, but now, all of a sudden, I recognized it. In the days when I was one of Elizabeth's ladies, I had noticed it in two of the other ladies. Both had doubtful reputations. And once, when Hugh and I were on foot in London and passing through a dubious-looking lane, a woman had stepped out of a dingy doorway and walked past us, close enough for me to see that she also had eyes like that. I had said to Hugh: 'I wonder who that woman was. That gown wasn't showy but it cost something and yet, look at these surroundings! Where are we, by the way? You know London well.'

'Yes, I do. That building's a brothel,' said Hugh. 'Or said to be. I've never put it to the test, I promise. At a guess, I would say that that was the madam.'

I was still staring at this phenomenon when Mistress Wyse said: 'As it happens, I sent a message to Mr Shore a few days ago, asking him to call, at his convenience. I am responsible for you, Blanche, and I felt I really ought to meet him and ask what his intentions are. So far, he's only been someone I once saw you walking with, after which I naturally asked who he was. Yes, he *is* coming here. Well, go and let him in. And bring another glass and more cakes.

I got up. 'We ought to go. You will want to talk to Blanche and her young man in private, I feel sure.'

'Yes, quite so.' Brockley, too, was on his feet.

'No, no, finish your wine first. I would never expect a man to leave his glass while it was still half full. I shan't plunge straight into enquiries about his income and lineage! That would be *most* discourteous!' Agnes's merry laugh invited us to share her amusement, but most of the invitation was directed at Brockley. As we sat down again, I saw Dale flush angrily.

Blanche hurried out of the room. We heard the front door open, and Blanche's voice greeting someone, and then feet went past the parlour door, presumably to the kitchen. Glasses clinked in the distance and there was a giggle from Blanche and what might have been the sound of a kiss. Agnes, hearing it, ceased being amused and sighed instead.

'It's a worry, being in charge of a young girl without a husband to help one. Blanche seems to attract such unsuitable men. First of all, it was a smallholder, one of the tenants of the big house. Samuel Goodbody, his name was. Just a plain man, always with mud on his boots, growing vegetables and fruit for a living and paying rent for his ground. *Not* what I want for my cousin. And now it's this Gilbert Shore and he's not much better. What will become of Blanche, I really don't know. I—'

She broke off as the two of them came in, with Master Shore carrying a dish of cakes and a spare glass. I looked at him with some interest, wondering what kind of man it was who had been drawn to the plain and gawky Blanche. She seemed less plain now, however, for she was becomingly flushed and her eyes were shining. Gilbert Shore put his dish and glass down on the table where the other refreshments were, and politely let himself be presented first to Agnes and then to me and the Brockleys.

'It's a pleasure to meet you all,' he said, accepting an invitation to be seated. His voice was deep and slow, his Norfolk accent marked. 'I've wanted to see where you live, Blanche, and to meet your cousin.'

He wasn't at all what I had expected. I had rather supposed that Blanche's suitor would be himself unremarkable, the sort of young fellow who isn't much to look at and is of modest status and knows it. Gilbert Shore was none of these things. He was squarely built, tow-haired and tanned and had an air of being quietly sure of himself. He wasn't handsome but one day he would be striking. In later life, that bony, arched nose and those prominent cheekbones would make his face craggy. It would be a strong face, but not a harsh one, for when I met his hazel eyes, I saw that they were both intelligent and kind. He had a workmanlike leather jacket on over an open-necked shirt, and stout breeches above well-polished boots. It was a form of dress that didn't go with Agnes's ladylike parlour but he managed to seem completely at ease there.

'Mistress Stannard,' said Agnes, 'and her companions the Brockleys, called thinking they might find my son Roland here.' Like me, she was taking him in, scanning him from head to foot. 'I fear,' she said, 'that my young cousin Blanche was badly named. Blanche means white, but she is a dark horse! I had no idea you were taking walks together until I chanced to see you. Then I asked Blanche who you were, of course. It was wrong of you to be so secretive, Blanche, though I admit you have good taste. You've picked a fine young fellow.' Gilbert Shore remained expressionless and took a draught of wine in a self-possessed manner. 'How did you meet?' Agnes enquired.

'Blanche and my married sister are friends,' said Gilbert. 'My sister is Mistress Susannah Lyon that you've met at the church. Both of you do dusting and cleaning there now and again.'

Badly, if Dr Yonge were anything to go by. Agnes would no doubt like to be known as the pious parishioner who dusted the benches in St Mary's, but I couldn't imagine her enjoying it, or being thorough.

'Susannah invited you and Blanche to supper maybe three months ago,' Gilbert was saying. 'You couldn't come, but you let Blanche accept. We met over my sister's supper table.'

'Ah, yes. I remember. I was expecting a neighbour to sup with me here. So that's when it began. Blanche, refill Master Shore's glass for him. She tells me you work at the Kenninghall Estate as an assistant bailiff, Mr Shore. What does your work involve?'

Gilbert, balancing a plate on his knees, sipping wine and nibbling a cake alternately, began on a description of an assistant bailiff's daily duties. Agnes Wyse commented admiringly on the number of things he needed to know and the masculine skills he possessed and wondered if he could ever spare an hour to deal with a drainage problem in her garden. 'I do have a man to look after the garden, but he has never been able to solve this.'

'I'll help if I can,' said Gilbert neutrally.

'We'll settle a time.' Agnes's attention had veered from Brockley to Shore. 'One evening, perhaps? You could sup with us. I have an excellent cook and I have been teaching Blanche how to cook, as well. If you are truly interested in her, you'll want to know that your future wife can make tasty meals. She shall prove her skill, while we sit and talk of serious matters, worldly or godly, as the fit takes us.'

Her smile had become unmistakeably conspiratorial. They might have been alone together. The atmosphere in the room had become suddenly tense and when I looked at Blanche, I saw that she was now eyeing her cousin not just sharply, but with something remarkably like hatred. My glance flickered to Dale and Brockley and I knew that they too felt uncomfortable.

Gilbert said, 'Thank you,' very quietly. A silence fell.

It was time to leave. I got to my feet for the second time and the Brockleys did the same. We made our farewells. Outside, the air was chill with the approach of more rain.

'That *woman*!' said Dale. 'She must be nearly fifty and she makes eyes at everything that wears breeches!'

'If young Gilbert isn't careful,' said Brockley, 'he'll find himself in bed with her, wondering how he got there. She's the kind of woman that has to show that she's more attractive than other women are.'

'I wonder,' I said. 'That young man didn't strike me as easy prey. But you're right about her. I saw it in her eyes. I wonder if she was really quite the virtuous wife she claims.'

'Probably not,' said Brockley with a snort.

'Did you think she was attractive?' Dale asked suddenly.

'In a way,' Brockley told her. 'Only a man would recognize

it, but there is a . . . pull. As though one were a compass needle that has to point to the north.'

'Dale,' I said solemnly, 'if you wish to hit Roger, I sympathize, but there are people about and you'd do best to wait until he's alone with you.'

We laughed as we made our way towards the inn.

TEN

The Last Hope

N ot that the laughter endured for long. Our anxieties were too serious for that. 'We leave for London tomorrow,' I said, as we entered the White Hart. 'We *must* track Wyse down. He's the last hope. If only he hasn't been sent off on an errand to the Scottish border! But probably not – they'll want him to tackle that cipher. He can do it if anyone can.'

'I'll talk to the landlord about routes,' Brockley said. 'There ought to be a quicker way home than the one through Lowestoft.'

The landlord, as we found later on when we were enquiring about supper, answered to the name of Ezra Spinner, which to my mind didn't suit him. For me, it conjured up a picture of a thin man with spidery arms and legs, while Ezra was in fact a fat, jolly soul with slightly short ones. He was well into his fifties judging by the silver colour of his wild and curly hair. His laugh was a resounding guffaw, which he demonstrated to us in most hearty fashion when we told him that we'd come from London by way of Lowestoft. There was laughter, too, from some of the others present, for several local men had called in for a pint of ale to round off a day's work.

'Round by Lowestoft? From Lunnon Town! It's a wonder your horses' legs ain't been worn down by six inches!' said a man who was surely a farmer, judging by the earth on his practical leather boots and under the nails of his strong, broad hands.

A man who had been sitting unobtrusively in a quiet corner remarked: 'It must have taken you a week, for sure.' His voice sounded familiar and we realized that it was Dr Yonge. 'There's a far better route than that,' he said. 'Ezra, haven't you got a map?'

'That I have,' said the landlord. 'Cat! Where are you? Where's that map I keep for confused travellers! Bring it here!'

His wife appeared from a back room almost at once, carrying a scroll which she spread out on a table. She was a striking woman, though not young, for her face had mature lines even though her wavy hair was dark and she was probably proud of it for she let two long tresses escape from her cap and snake down on either side of her face, to brush against her little ruff. She was quite well-dressed, as was her husband, and the room was well maintained, its cobbled floor swept clean and its settles polished. Drinks were served in good pewter goblets and tankards. The White Hart was prosperous.

'Turned off the road from Diss, did you?' Cat Spinner said, pointing to Diss on the map. Her accent was strong but agreeably so, as Gilbert Shore's had been, with the musical up and down cadences of East Anglia. We agreed that we had come from Diss. 'Then you goes back to that turn, and goo on west a way, to Thetford. Then you turns south and goo through Newmarket and this place here, Bishops Stortford, so it's called, not that I've ever been so far. That's your road. Just straight on south from Thetford and then bearing a bit west, but all on the one road, and there you are, Lunnon Town.'

'Many thanks,' I said. And then asked civilly: 'You were born here in Kenninghall?'

'That she was,' said her husband with one of his hearty laughs. 'Blacksmith's daughter, then got a place as maid to Mistress Wyse, as lives just along the road, till I took a fancy to her and wed her – and her plump stocking full of her savings!'

'Mistress Wyse was generous enough in her way, for all her faults,' said Cat.

'We've met the lady,' I said. 'We called on her today, as it happens. We thought her son, Roland, was there. We had a . . . a business matter to discuss with him – and we hoped to catch him up. It seems now we'll have to chase him back to London.'

'Met our queen bee, have you?' said the farmer, breaking in unexpectedly. We looked at him in surprise. 'Oh, we all know her. Pretty well, some of us.' He sounded sour.

'Now then, Samuel Goodbody.' Ezra shook a disapproving

head. 'I don't like that kind of talk in my inn, and well you know it.'

I caught Dale's eye and knew that she had recognized the name. So had Brockley, who muttered, very softly, so that only Dale and I could hear: 'I suppose she nipped his romance with Blanche in the bud.'

Dr Yonge, however, said very seriously: 'Quite right. It's a sin to destroy a woman's character.' Whereupon another man, who had put a wicker basket containing dead marsh birds down by his feet and was probably a wildfowler, remarked: 'There ought to be a few laws against destroying marriages. She's had a hand in spoiling one or two. A tiresome woman, that one. I cast no stones at her virtue; there are folk who never put a foot wrong and still cause trouble. I'm sorry for that niece of hers that lives with her.'

'Cousin,' said Ezra. 'Blanche is her cousin.'

'Cousin, then. She'll eat all Blanche's young men afore Blanche ever gets to taste them. She's done that afore.' His gaze rested candidly on Samuel Goodbody, who buried his nose in his tankard. 'And Gilbert Shore'll be next, mark my words,' the wildfowler added.

'I fancy,' whispered Brockley, 'that after spoiling Blanche's love affair by ogling Master Goodbody herself, she dropped him once the mischief was done. He hasn't forgotten, I fancy.'

'Hush,' I said.

'I repeat, I don't like this sort of talk,' said Ezra, addressing the wildfowler. 'Mistress Wyse has had her troubles. Robert Wyse was a stern man. The daughters had to marry where they were told and one of them's very miserable with the man her father picked. She didn't want to wed him but her father thrust her into the marriage. Whole village knew about it.'

'Could be that Robert got to be stern after provocation,' hazarded the wildfowler, swigging ale.

'Now, thass enough,' said Ezra. 'And she's good to her servants, like Cat says. Cat knows. Don't you, Cat?'

'Well, I was her maid till I married,' Cat said. 'She don't have a personal maid these days. Yes, I'd say she was a generous mistress and still is, I daresay.'

'Ezra's right. We shouldn't tattle,' said Dr Yonge, and Ezra nodding agreement, turned to us and said: 'Is that map of any help to you?'

'Yes, it is,' Brockley said. 'I think we should write down the places we're going to pass through. Thetford, Newmarket, Bishops Stortford . . . Madam, did you bring any writing things with you?'

'Indeed I did,' I said. 'I'll fetch them.'

We had a good supper at the inn. The White Hart charged quite reasonable rates and it was plain that unlike Agnes Wyse, they could afford saffron, which had certainly been used in the spicy bread and butter pudding. Joseph ate with us and I told him to enjoy his fill.

In the morning, we set off early. It took only four days to reach London by the new route. I longed to get back to Hawkswood and to little Harry, but first of all, I must go to court and Walsingham's office, and try to speak to Roland Wyse.

Walsingham's offices at Whitehall were much like the ones he used in the other palaces. He usually travelled with the court although not always. Since Lord Burghley (though I still thought of Burghley as Cecil) had now ceased to be the Secretary of State and become Lord Treasurer instead, Walsingham had been promoted to share the duties of Secretary of State with another court official, a man called Sir Thomas Smith. I had never met Sir Thomas but had been told that he was older than Walsingham and very learned and from observing the offices they both used, I assumed that they had much in common.

All the suites consisted of three or four well-proportioned rooms with elegant panelling, patterned leading for the windows, and red and white Tudor roses in the ceiling beams. All the rooms were also furnished with plain tables and stools, and fitted with shelving so laden with document boxes and bulging folders and weighty reference books that most of the panelling was hidden. Some rooms also had maps pinned up on the walls. Little that was decorative had been left on view.

After some delay while my credentials were investigated, I was admitted and found Walsingham at his desk, dark-clad as ever, with his black hair as usual cut short. His personal secretary, a quiet, greying individual called Humphrey Johnson, was reading letters at a second desk, and on the way in, I passed through an outer office where three clerks were seated at a table and busy with whatever mysterious tasks were given to clerks in this department. But Wyse was not there.

'Yes, he came back, but I've sent him into Hampshire,' said Walsingham, 'with a squad to ask awkward questions in a house there.'

Walsingham's idea of humour was always grim and apt to appear at unexpected moments. His smile invariably made me think of Death in a jovial mood. 'These foreign priests,' he explained. 'They are constantly creeping into the country, like a plague of mice, trying to convert decent Protestants to their Papist faith. There are seminaries devoted to preparing them. There is one particular order – the Jesuits – that is said to be planning a virtual crusade. None of them just want to spread their faith; they also want to convince our people that our good queen ought to abdicate in favour of that pestiferous woman Mary of Scotland. The house that Wyse has gone to has almost certainly been harbouring them.'

'When do you expect him back?' I asked.

'Soon,' said Walsingham, 'though I'm not exactly certain when. If you want to talk to him, I'll send him down to Hawkswood. I don't mind sending him off on errands. The truth is, he's hardworking and fairly competent, but I find it wearisome to have him at close quarters. I don't think he's ever liked me much, but some time ago, I began to have the feeling that he really hated me. I don't know why. I've never done him any harm, though I am beginning to feel that I would like to! However, I assure you that I have questioned him myself, about Jane Cobbold's death, and he remembers nothing to the point. He says he caught up with Sir Edward Heron at Cobbold Hall, took dinner and then got on his horse and started for London. He passed Jack Jarvis's cottage and stopped to pass the time of day with him, but nothing more. He went into the cottage but only for a few minutes. He saw no strangers, observed nothing out of the way.'

'And I've been chasing him round the countryside just to

find that out,' I said wearily. 'I've just been to Norfolk, hoping to catch up with him there. I managed to have a few words with his mother, but she didn't know anything useful.'

'My poor Ursula. You've wasted your time. You might have known that we would question him. After all, he does belong to my department. If any of my men are close to a serious crime, I'm bound to make enquiries.'

'Did he have a chance to look at the cipher letter?' I enquired.

'Oh, yes. He decoded it in a few hours. He's extremely gifted that way, you know. But it told us nothing helpful – either about Jarvis's death, or Mistress Cobbold's.'

'What did it say?'

Walsingham frowned. 'It's so unlikely that I've lain awake puzzling over it. Unlikely, I mean, because I just can't see how Jack Jarvis, cottager at Cobbold Hall, rearing chickens and growing vegetables, came to be making for Dover with a letter for an illicit worsted mill – not named – giving details of likely customers and markets, including fairs in France and the Netherlands.'

'*That's* what the letter was about?' I said, astonished.

'Yes, it was! Now, who would pick a scruffy, elderly cottager as a messenger for such a purpose? Anyone running such an enterprise and wanting to find custom would send his own agent to collect information and if an agent wanted to send a confidential interim report while he was still out in the field, as it were, he'd hire an ordinary courier and send the letter to his employer's private house.'

'*Is* there an illicit loom in Dover?' I asked.

'Oh, yes. We've known about it for quite a long time. So far, it hasn't concerned my department. Worsted looms are small ale as far as we're concerned; we leave it to the weavers' guilds to bring prosecutions if they think fit. The fact is, people want this new worsted and where there's demand, someone usually comes forward to supply. The worsted looms will all be made legal one of these days. Though this one *may* attract my attention before too long. I've heard a whisper that this is another place that's being used as a safe house for Catholic priests coming in through Dover, in disguise. But the letter doesn't refer to that in any way.'

'Could the decoded letter itself be in a form of code? A second line of defence?' I hazarded.

'I thought of that,' said Walsingham, sounding slightly offended at the idea that he might have failed so to do. 'All I can say is that I and my staff tested the notion as thoroughly as possible and either the clear version of that letter is *not* any form of code, or it's an impenetrable one. Frankly, the cipher is complex enough to make a second line of defence pointless.'

From the desk in the corner, Johnson remarked: 'Sir, would Mistress Stannard care to see the key to the code and see for herself how difficult it is? She has some experience of such things, I believe. It might interest her.'

'Oh, yes. Would you like to see it, Ursula?'

'Very much,' I said.

Walsingham gave Johnson a nod, and he delved into a drawer beneath his work table, from which he took a piece of folded paper. 'I have another copy; Mistress Stannard can have this one. I believe that even Wyse had to sit up all night to break it.'

I examined the key with interest, taking the opportunity to learn, even though I hoped I would never have to use my knowledge for another dangerous assignment. Dangerous assignments had to be over for me now that I had Harry.

'I've never dealt with an alphabetic code before,' I said, studying it. 'Yes, I can see that it might well have kept Roland awake all night!'

It seemed that the letters of the alphabet had been shifted, so that, for instance, the letter A was represented by Z, B by A, C by B and so on. But throughout the letter, the method of shifting changed at every tenth word. For the second ten, the shift was in the opposite direction, so that A was represented by B, B by C and so forth. For the third and fourth tens, there were other variations. Then the sequence began again. I wondered if Wyse had had a headache after unravelling it. I also wondered aloud how on earth he managed to do it at all.

Johnson laughed and Walsingham said: 'I make him work. He's well paid.'

I thanked them for the code and folded it away in my secret pouch. I also thanked Walsingham for asking Wyse the questions I had wanted answered, useless though the answers had been. Then I said farewell and rejoined Dale and Brockley, who were waiting in an anteroom. They looked at me with questions in their eyes. Regretfully, I shook my head.

Home. The last familiar mile, through heath and farmland and an oak wood; and then the sight of Hawkswood's chimneys ahead. Hawkswood's chimneys were of grey stone like the walls, but their stones had been set in ornamental patterns and they had beauty, above all when the kitchen chimney was sending soft grey smoke into the air, an announcement to all the world that the hearth was alight and food was cooking. Then came the sight of the gate arch, and a joyful welcome from Sandy and Hero as we rode in. Sandy bayed with excitement; Hero, as usual, greeted us with her short *wuff*, which was much the same as the *wuff* with which she commented on the scent of a prowling fox. But when we dismounted, she bounded up to us, to ask for caresses.

Simon and Arthur came out to help Joseph lead the horses away to their reward of trough and manger and an enjoyable rub down. I went in through the door to the great hall, taking the Brockleys with me. And there was Tessie, smiling, and Sybil, and with them was little Harry, toddling forward and tumbling into my arms. I was so glad to be with him again that I was almost tearful.

'Darling, I *hate* going away from you! Have you been good? Has he kept well, Tessie?'

'He's a sweetheart and full of life,' Tessie said. 'He's trying out his legs, these days, learning what they're for!'

'We've watched him carefully,' said Sybil, 'to see he doesn't totter into any danger, but he's got good sense for his age. He's been no trouble, Mistress Stannard. I think Phoebe has put jugs of hot water in your rooms already; I saw her going upstairs with a pitcher a moment ago, anyway.'

'Wilder was upstairs just now,' Sybil explained. 'From a window, he saw you coming and warned us.' She laughed.

'And there Phoebe was, rousing up the kitchen fire for all she was worth and getting in Joan Flood's way!'

Then came all the agreeable business of washing away the travel stains and changing into fresh clothes. Later, we sat down to an excellent supper – even though it didn't include spicy bread and butter pudding. John Hawthorn was interested, though, by my description of the one served at the White Hart and said he would try to match it. 'You guess at cinnamon, nutmeg and ginger, madam? And saffron?'

'Yes, certainly saffron.'

'I don't usually use that,' said Hawthorn thoughtfully. 'I think we might lay in a supply, if you agree.'

'Why not?' I said. We had had good harvests in the last few years, and done well with rearing and selling young stock, too. We could allow ourselves a little luxury.

But my bright tone did not reflect my feelings. It was a joy to be home like this, hugging Harry and discussing recipes, surrounded by people I cared about. But it wasn't so long since Hugh had died, leaving a wound in the fabric of my household, a wound that had not yet healed. And now I was afraid that further wounds, further losses lay ahead.

I was so afraid for Brockley and I knew that both he and Dale shared my feelings, all too thoroughly. But we all tried to be cheerful. We passed the evening talking of our journey, describing the travails of our rain-swept ride from Lowestoft to Diss, and our encounter with Agnes Wyse, and the byplay between her and Blanche and Gilbert.

It was Gladys who remarked that by the sound of it, Agnes had come down in the world and probably felt it. 'And, look here, you, it's hard for a woman who's been beautiful, when her mirror tells her she's past her prime. Don't I know? I didn't always have brown teeth and there was a time I could keep my bowels in better order.'

'Oh, *Gladys*!' said Dale. 'Must you?'

'Facts are facts,' said Gladys. 'But I had a good wash afore supper. And I *was* a beauty, once.'

I believed it. Her dark eyes were still pleasing and beneath her wrinkled brown skin, the bones of her face were still shapely. I gave her a smile, before gently steering the conversation elsewhere.

Facts are facts. Before long, we would have to face them.

I gathered the Brockleys and Sybil into the Little Parlour after breakfast and set about this uncomfortable duty.

'We went to Norfolk and to London,' I said. 'And we do now know that Roland Wyse saw and heard nothing that day that can help us. He was our last hope, and it's failed. Who else can we talk to?'

'There's nowhere to go,' said Brockley frankly. 'I've known that ever since you came out of Walsingham's office. Your face told us all we needed to know, madam. But if we can't find another lead, another scent to follow, then Heron will have me back in Lewes and up before a judge at the Assizes.'

'Roger, don't!' Poor Dale looked terrified.

'It's no good pretending,' said Brockley. 'That is what will happen. If no other believable suspect can be found, then Heron will summon me again, and I will probably be found guilty. Madam, I hope you believe me when I say I am not, but I wouldn't altogether blame you if by now you were wondering.'

'*Roger!*' wailed Dale.

'I'm not wondering,' I said. 'I *know* you, Brockley. We've worked together, been in peril together. You learn about people that way. I have Gladys in my household because when we met her in Wales, she was in danger of being arrested for witchcraft, and you went chivalrously to her rescue. That's the kind of man you are.'

'She wasn't a threat to any of us, madam.'

'You wouldn't have harmed her even if she had been. And you have sense. Murdering Jane Cobbold because she'd set some nasty gossip going, concerning me – good God, Brockley, we knew from the start that Jane Cobbold's tongue would be a nuisance – *and* we knew that hers wouldn't be the only one. We'd just have to ignore them all until people found something else to gossip about. Killing Jane wouldn't help. It would have been *silly*. You're not silly.'

'If you're sure, madam.'

'Of course I'm sure! Now then. If we can't find any further scent to follow, as you put it, then there's only one thing to do. You and Dale must get out of the country while you can. To one of the Protestant lands – Sweden, Norway.'

'But the bail money!' cried Dale.

'Selling Withysham will cover it.'

'We couldn't let you do that, madam!' Brockley protested. I gave him a fierce look.

'Brockley, I won't let you hang! If I order you to leave the country, then just for once, you'll do as you're bid! You'll go – and I'll dispose of my own property as I please!'

'But we don't *want* to leave you and live in a foreign country!' Dale protested.

'You don't want Brockley to lose his life either,' I said. 'Sweden or Norway would be Paradise by comparison with that. And you have passports. There won't be any difficulty about travelling.'

Many years ago, I had journeyed to France as a secret queen's messenger. Since then, it had been tacitly understood that I might one day journey abroad again on the queen's business, and would take my personal servants with me. Our passports were withdrawn for a time when Elizabeth feared that I might return to France because of Matthew, but she restored them when I married Hugh. The Brockleys and I had never since then been without them.

'But Roger didn't do it,' Dale protested. 'He *didn't do it*! There *must* be *something*! If he didn't do it, then someone else did. Whoever it was must have left *some* trace, *somewhere*!'

'I know,' I said desperately. 'But what? We've found no sign of such a thing! It's a dead end. I even took my picklocks and dagger to Norfolk with me in case they came in useful, which they didn't. *Nothing* has led anywhere. *Nothing* has been useful. I – we – have tried everything we can think of and all in vain. I'll go anywhere, do anything, if only I knew where to go, what to do!'

Brockley's eyes met mine. His were without hope.

'You don't have to leave at once,' I said. 'I must try to think. Perhaps I *will* think of something. But we mustn't wait too long. I don't want Heron's men turning up here to be the next thing that happens.'

But the next thing to happen was entirely different. Three days later, Roland Wyse came to see me.

ELEVEN
Unwanted Opportunity

Wyse arrived unexpectedly just after dinner. Sybil and I had settled down in the East Room to do some embroidery. Both of us enjoyed the art. I was more skilled with the needle, but Sybil could draw and had a real gift for inventing designs. This time, we were making covers for settle cushions. We talked as we worked and as so often at that time, we talked of Brockley's predicament.

There was always the chance that by continually mulling the matter over, and tossing ideas to and fro, we might chance upon some new way of seeking the truth. With our hands and eyes occupied by the embroidery, while our brains and tongues were immersed in our conversation, we had little attention to spare for anything else and though we did hear Sandy barking, the East Room windows overlooked the gardens, not the courtyard, and we paid no heed until Wilder appeared at the parlour door to say that Master Roland Wyse had arrived and wished to speak with Mistress Stannard.

'All right, Wilder, bring him in.' Wilder withdrew and I said to Sybil: 'Perhaps Walsingham has sent him. Perhaps he *has* remembered something he heard or saw that day! Perhaps this is the new hope we've been longing for!'

A moment later, Wyse was in the doorway, bowing and wishing us good day. I noticed that he was carefully dressed, in a deep-blue doublet and puffed hose, slashed with pale green, pale green stockings and highly polished boots. 'Mrs Jester,' he said, 'may I ask you to let me have a few words alone with Mrs Stannard? I have something to say to her of a most private nature.'

Sybil at once folded her work into its box and left the room with it. I waved a hand to invite the hovering Wyse to be seated.

'This is a surprise, Master Wyse. I can't imagine what kind of errand it is that's so secret that even my close friend Sybil mustn't know what it is. Does it concern Roger Brockley? Because if so, believe me, everyone within these walls knows all about his troubles.'

'Roger Brockley?' Wyse seemed taken aback. 'Why, no, Mistress Stannard! Mr Walsingham questioned me about the day of Mistress Cobbold's death, of course – I understand that you know that – but I was little help to him. Naturally, I'm sorry about Roger Brockley's unhappy position. I imagine you are all very anxious, especially his wife. But no, I'm not here to talk about him.'

'Oh. Well . . .' I broke off as Wilder reappeared with the usual refreshments and then said: 'Master Wyse, did you come alone? What about your companions, if any?'

'I'm alone, Mistress Stannard. You can leave the tray, Wilder, We'll serve ourselves.'

Wilder compressed his lips and looked at me. I nodded. He took himself off obediently, but achieved the feat of expressing indignation with his back view. Visitors were not supposed to give him orders.

I poured wine and offered Wyse a choice of nuts and raisins in one dish and little mincemeat pasties in another. He commented that the nuts had evidently come from abroad. 'It would seem that your affairs are prosperous.'

'We are able to enjoy a few modest luxuries at Hawkswood,' I said, thinking of the saffron I intended soon to buy.

He put a pasty on a dish but then set the dish down on a small table. He seemed ill at ease and as a good hostess should try to make guests feel comfortable, I said politely: 'Please tell me why you've come.'

'It's difficult,' said Wyse. The boyishness of his face was more marked than usual, and the stone-coloured eyes, that I had always found off-putting, seemed oddly vulnerable. He looked diffident.

'What's difficult?' I asked encouragingly.

'All the way here, I've been trying out words in my head but now that I've arrived, I've forgotten them all and I just feel shy. However, I must get it out somehow. Mrs Stannard, your late husband, Hugh Stannard, died over two years ago. But you are still quite a young woman and you have the heavy responsibility of looking after two houses and the lands that go with them. You have Withysham as well as Hawkswood, have you not?'

He hesitated and I prepared to explain that for the time being, Withysham was, as it were, mortgaged to the state. But he drew breath and spoke before I did, in a rush.

'You must surely have considered remarrying. I've come to offer you marriage. To me.'

I sat absolutely still. It was that or topple off my settle and fall to the floor in shock. There had been Hugh's death. And then had come that brief, passionate, painful reunion with Matthew de la Roche, and our final parting. Since then, something within me seemed to have died, as completely as Hugh, as completely as my one-time feeling for Matthew. I had not considered re-marriage for a single moment, and if I had, I certainly wouldn't have regarded Roland Wyse as eligible. I knew nothing that was really to his disadvantage but I had never been able to like him, and I was well aware that others felt the same. It was the kind of reaction he seemed to inspire.

Finally, I managed to say: 'You are, I think, a good many years younger than I am, Master Wyse. It wouldn't be . . . suitable.'

'I am thirty. I am no youth.'

'I shall be forty next year. There are nine years between us.'

'Mistress Stannard, there are many happy marriages where the man is younger than the woman! It makes little difference, if there is true fondness. I have admired you from the first moment I saw you. I have several times called here when I chanced to be in the district; surely you have wondered why? I had no errands to you – I only wanted to see you. I believe I could make you a good husband. I have good health and a good position at court and hopes of further advancement and I promise I would be good to you. As I said, you bear a heavy burden with two homes and their farmlands to care for. You are a woman, and women aren't fitted for such responsibilities.'

'Queen Elizabeth,' I said, 'is responsible for an entire realm.'

'But she has advisers, her councillors and her statesmen, to tell her what to do,' said Wyse, smiling slightly. His diffidence was fading. He was sure of himself again. I studied him carefully, thinking that if he believed that England was ruled by the Royal Council, and that Elizabeth meekly did what the councillors told her, he knew very little about her.

He was continuing to talk. 'Women cannot take complicated decisions. Your minds are not adapted to them. God gave that gift to men. I could take your burden over for you. You have clearly done as well as you can' – his eyes flickered to the dish of imported nuts – 'but it must be hard for you. I could see that your estates do better still. If we acquired one or two farms for renting out, that would do wonders for our income. Also . . .'

He glanced past me to the window. 'Your little boy – Harry, that's his name, is it not? – is out there, being given a ride on a horse. He's a fine-looking child.'

I turned, and saw that Arthur Watts had indeed put Harry astride placid Rusty, and was holding him in place while Joseph led the horse slowly round the paths of the knot garden, which had wide walks. Harry was still so small that his legs stuck out absurdly on either side of the horse's back. Seeing him, I smiled.

'He likes horses,' I said. 'I hope he'll be a good rider one day.'

'You have a charming smile, Mrs Stannard. I'm sure your boy will prove a good horseman, but boys need fathers, you know. They need to grow up with a man in charge of the household, who can set an example, show them what a man's duties are in this world and answer the questions growing boys might not want to ask their mothers. I'll gladly do those things for your lad. He needs companions, too. If we have one or two children of our own, his half-brothers or sisters, he can grow up as part of a real family.'

I sat still, wondering how best to word my answer. This was an honourable proposal, and I must try not to cause him pain when I refused it, but refuse, I must.

I knew from bitter experience that the curious jerk in the

stomach which a woman feels when confronted by a man who attracts her physically isn't always the best guide towards happiness, though there may for a time be ecstasy. My union with Matthew de la Roche had been like that. I did not regret those heights of passion. They had been a glorious experience. But never, with Matthew, had I known real happiness. With Hugh I had not known those giddy heights, but instead, Hugh had given me reassurance, security and kindness and I had found contentment in settling for those.

Roland Wyse did not inspire me with either reaction. He did not attract me, nor did I think I would find peace and safety with him. I couldn't immediately work out why not, but the instinctive knowledge was there.

My silence clearly disconcerted him. After a pause, he said: 'I know you're not in love with me. But love would come, I'm sure of it. My dear . . .' I bristled, but tried not to show it. 'I am offering you a worthwhile opportunity. Please consider it carefully. Men and women need each other, Mrs Stannard, or perhaps I may call you Ursula . . .'

I bit back a desire to retort, *No you may not*, and wondered why I felt so fierce about it. I was being offered a perfectly reasonable opportunity to remarry, to acquire a male partner to share my responsibilities, perhaps give me more children. I had once feared childbirth very much, and for good reasons, but Harry's birth had been surprisingly easy. I was not so nervous of the prospect now. Women in my position did remarry, more often than not, and were glad of the chance.

But I was not glad of it and I didn't want Wyse's children. I didn't want Roland Wyse. He was not my kind of man. I struggled to make sense of my aversion to the idea of marrying him, and then understood.

He had said it himself. *You bear a heavy burden with two homes and their farmlands to care for. I could lift that weight from your shoulders.*

Oh, yes, he would. Undoubtedly. If I let him into my life, he would take charge of Hawkswood and – if I retained it – Withysham. They wouldn't be mine any longer; they would be his. I knew it, with a certainty that would brook no denial. He would decide how they were to be run; I would have no say. He would decide how Harry was to be brought up; I would have no say. He would probably take it upon himself to hire or dismiss the servants. He might decide to get rid of Brockley!

If Brockley were still there to be got rid of in the first place.

Wyse picked up his discarded pasty and took a thoughtful bite from it. He swallowed and then, as if he had heard me thinking, he said: 'I imagine you have Roger Brockley much on your mind. Am I right?'

Damn the man. Of course he was right. 'Naturally,' I said.

'You may be mistaken about him, you know. I daresay you believe that you know him through and through, since he has been in your service for so long, but do we ever know another person so thoroughly? It might be best to let a judge and jury decide whether he is innocent or guilty. As a woman, you naturally think with your heart rather than your head. As I said, women's minds are different from men's. It is wisest for ladies to let the menfolk take the hard decisions. You are a lady, and therefore not fitted to judge.'

'I know what I know. Brockley is innocent,' I said, and I heard the ice in my voice.

'Well, let us not dispute over that,' said Wyse. 'I understand that in your concern for him, you may find it hard to put your mind to other matters. I do realize that you may need time to consider my proposal.'

I needed no time at all. This must come to an end at once. I finally took refuge in formality.

'Master Wyse, you have offered me marriage, which is a compliment and I recognize that. I thank you for it. But I have no wish to marry again. It is a firm decision and I shall never change it. Please accept that.'

TWELVE
Terror by Night

Wyse did not linger after that. I accompanied him into the courtyard to see him off and before he mounted his horse, he bowed over my hand and urged me to think over his proposal. He hoped with all his heart that I would change my mind. Might he visit me again before too long?

I said, as politely as I could, that there would be no point; that my decision would not alter. 'Either about remarriage, or about Brockley,' I said. 'He is innocent, and I do believe that I shall soon be able to prove it. Please don't go about smearing his name.'

'I wouldn't dream of such a thing. It would offend you – and I still have hopes.' said Wyse. He then gave a gratuity to Simon, who had saddled the horse – a good-sized gratuity, judging by Simon's widened eyes and appreciative thanks – and took his leave with dignity.

I, however, was trembling as I went back indoors. In the East Room, I found Sybil, Gladys and the Brockleys all waiting for me. Sybil had presumably collected the others. They looked at me with anxiously questioning eyes – except for Gladys, who said candidly: 'What did that man want? I don't like him. He *smells* wrong. I'd curse him if you'd let me.'

'Don't talk like that, Gladys. Sit down, everyone.' I sat down myself, thankful to do so because I felt so shaken. 'He came to propose marriage to me.'

There was a silence. Until, once more, Gladys took it upon herself to comment. '*That* one? Asked you to wed with him, did he? There's impertinence for you!'

'No impertinence,' I said. 'It was an honourable offer, made in a perfectly respectable way. He told me he had good health, a good position, hope of advancement, and was willing to lift all burdens off my shoulders, be a father to Harry and provide him with brothers and sisters.'

'But what did you *say*?' cried Dale, while Sybil's compressed features seemed to buckle further still, as if she were about to weep.

'I said no, of course,' I told them. 'What else? If I were to marry Roland Wyse, he'd take us all in charge, as if he'd arrested the entire household. I know he would. He's pushy among his colleagues at court and I expect he's the same in private life. He would decide everything. He would call Withysham and Hawkswood his. He would buy land – or sell it – without reference to me. After Hugh, how could you possibly think I would marry Roland Wyse?'

'It would be pleasant, ma'am, if you did marry again, a good man, and have more children,' said Dale. 'But somehow . . . not Mr Wyse.'

I smiled at her. I knew, because Dale had told me, that when she and Brockley were first married, they had wondered if they would have any children. It was still a reasonable hope at that time. I also knew that when they realized that it was no longer even remotely possible, they had decided that they were content without. But there had no doubt been disappointment at first. It was kind of Dale not to envy me my own children, and even to hope that I might one day have more. It was also perceptive of her to sense that Wyse was not the right man to provide them.

'There's nothing obviously wrong with him,' said Brockley. 'But I don't care for him, myself. I don't altogether know why. It just is so.'

'I've made it clear that I've rejected him,' I said. I saw the relief in their faces and a little strength returned to me. Here, surrounded by my dearest friends – I included Gladys in that list – I felt protected. Though, I reminded myself, Brockley needed protection more than I did.

'Wyse asked if he could visit me again and see if I'd changed my mind, but I said no to that as well,' I told them. 'Let's forget him. We need to talk. We've got nowhere by asking people who were at Cobbold Hall on that day if they noticed anything significant. Nobody did. But we *have* to go on, to find another approach. Has anyone got any ideas?'

'What sort of man *might* have done it?' said Dale. 'Either a passing madman, or someone who'd gain if Mistress Cobbold died – isn't that right? If she gossiped nastily about you, ma'am, maybe she did the same to others.'

Brockley's eyes narrowed in thought. 'Or does anyone gain from something left in her Will? Did she have wealth of her own? Or . . .'

'Maybe she had a lover and her husband found out. What about that, then?' Gladys demanded. 'Maybe the lover killed her because she wanted to finish with him. Or maybe Anthony Cobbold hired someone to kill her because she was unfaithful.'

It was hard to imagine the conventional and virtuous – and overweight – Jane Cobbold taking a lover, or even getting the chance, and equally hard to imagine the not very effectual Anthony Cobbold hiring an assassin. Even if he had wanted to, I couldn't believe he would know how to go about it.

All the same, there were lines here that might be worth following.

'I can enquire about her Will through Cecil,' I said. 'I don't want to ask Christina if her mother and father have been quarrelling . . . she might take exception to that and no wonder. But Hawthorn's cousin is still the butler at Cobbold Hall. I shall speak to Hawthorn. As for finding out about rumours; has anyone heard of gossip about other scandals than mine?'

They all frowned, thinking. There was silence, until we were interrupted by the sound of running feet and there was an agitated tap on the door. I called: 'Come in!' and Tessie rushed into the room.

'Ma'am, it's Harry!'

I was on my feet at once. 'Harry? What's amiss with him? He was having a ride on Rusty just now!' I swung round to look through the window but the garden was empty. 'Has there been an accident? He was all right just a little while ago . . .'

'There's been no accident, ma'am, but I think he's ill. He didn't eat much of his dinner but he wanted to have a ride – the grooms had promised him – and I thought maybe fresh air would make him hungry. So I let him. But when he came in, he was flushed and fretful and he started to cry when I picked him up, and he felt so hot! I think he has a fever! I've put him to bed but . . .'

'Go on thinking,' I said to the others. 'Brockley, speak to Hawthorn for me, about his cousin. I will write to Cecil later. Gladys, Sybil, come with me to the nursery.'

Gladys always kept a supply of ingredients for her various potions and after a brief look at Harry, I sent her to make a fever-reducing drink for him. I coaxed him to take it, though he didn't like the taste and spluttered and made faces. As Tessie had said, he was fretful and feverish. When I took his hand, it felt alarmingly hot.

'I'll stay with him,' I said. 'I'll have my supper here. Sybil, perhaps you would take over from me for two or three hours after that. I'll get some rest then, and after that I'll spend the night here. Tessie, you can have a good night's sleep in my bed; then you can be with him for most of tomorrow. If we can get him to eat, he'd better have something soft for supper; bread in hot milk with a little honey, perhaps.'

It was a long, worrying night. I sat by Harry all through the hours of darkness, watching by the light of an oil lamp. It wasn't a good enough light to let me keep awake by doing embroidery but I had a book of verse, printed in a strong black ink, and read some of that from time to time. Every now and then, I got up to give Harry a drink of milk. He was restless, but he had been able to swallow a little supper and he did sleep intermittently. In the morning, however, he was still feverish and as soon as there was enough daylight to let me see properly, I realized that he had a rash.

It was all over his face, small pink spots. He kept rubbing them and whimpering.

'I think they itch,' I said to Tessie and Sybil when they came to relieve me and bring Harry some more bread and milk with honey. 'Ask Gladys for something to soothe that. What is it, do you think? Is it measles?' Children had to have these things, I thought, and remembered hearing that children sometimes recovered faster than adults, and that one couldn't catch measles twice.

I also knew that children didn't always recover. Measles didn't often kill, but it could happen.

Sybil had sat down by the bed and was spooning the bread mixture into Harry's mouth. 'I don't know what it is, but I don't think he's dangerously feverish. I had an illness like this when I was about ten. My mother called it the Little Measles. It's a mild kind, too mild to stop you from getting the other sort of measles, but my mother said it wasn't serious. If this is the same, then he'll be better in a few days.'

The day passed. Harry continued to take small quantities of food and Gladys duly made an ointment that seemed to soothe the discomfort of the rash which had started to spread over his body. But he was miserable and we kept watch over him constantly. I stayed with him again that night, but this time got some sleep on Tessie's small bed.

It was a broken sleep, but not because of Harry, who this time was peacefully in dreamland, breathing evenly. The nursery rooms were on the top floor, and were above the courtyard. What roused me was the sound of Sandy barking. He stopped after a few moments, however, and I dropped back into unconsciousness, only to be woken up again a little later, because he was now whining, as though in pain and I could hear Simon's voice, talking to him. Evidently Simon had been awakened as well, and had got up to see what was amiss. Well, he would deal with whatever it was. Once more, I settled down.

In the morning, Harry was definitely less feverish and the rash on his face seemed to be drying up, which was encouraging. But when Sybil came with Harry's breakfast, her face was grave.

'Simon came to the kitchen while I was there and told me some sorry news. Sandy's dead. He fell ill during the night. He started crying and Simon went to him, and found him lying down, whining and dribbling from his mouth. He died a few minutes later.

'Oh, poor Sandy! He was still hardly more than a puppy!' I was truly saddened. I had liked the young animal very much. He had all the makings of a reliable but not vicious guard dog. 'What about Hero?'

'Hero's all right but she's had years to learn sense. Simon says that Sandy was a young dog and greedy and would gobble up anything even vaguely edible. Arthur Watts took the dogs out into the woods yesterday and let them run; very likely, Sandy ate something he shouldn't. Christina did say that he'd eat anything.'

'Tell Simon to bury him, somewhere in the grounds. *Poor Sandy!*' He had been calling for help when he woke me the first time, by barking. The second time, he had just been crying in distress, as dogs will.

'It seems,' I said to Sybil, 'that troubles never come on their own; they always arrive in a downpour. What next, I wonder?'

We didn't have to wait long to find out. It came the very next night. Harry was much better, and although I had meant once more to spend the night in the nursery, Tessie said that I was surely tired and that she would be happy to stay with him instead, sleeping on her usual bed while I returned to mine. So at the last minute, I went down to my own room, which was on the floor below the nursery, next to the bedchamber used by Dale and Brockley, who were already abed by the time I reached my room. Sybil slept in the one on the other side of me. Gladys, Wilder and the other servants were on the same floor, though some distance away, above the kitchen regions, and on the far side of the main staircase.

It was a beautiful night; clear and lit by a full moon, bright enough to drown the stars close to it. It silvered the garden and shone into the bedchambers. Some people believe that to sleep in the moonlight can cause madness but Hugh and I liked it and on moonlit nights we often had the bed curtains open and the windows unshuttered. Brockley and Dale, over the years, had adopted the same habit. Dale was a little nervous of it at first, I knew, but Hugh's continued sanity and mine finally convinced her that there was no danger.

That night was warm, and I pushed my window open, to let in air, and the sweet scents of the rose garden outside. Then I lay down and Tessie had been right to say that I was tired for I fell asleep immediately. But some time in the small hours, I was summoned back to wakefulness, by bumps and bangs in the Brockleys' room, accompanied by terrified screams from Dale, and Brockley's voice, cursing.

I hurled myself out of bed. In the past, I had heard Dale and Brockley quarrel, but screams and crashes had never occurred before. I rushed barefoot from the room, slinging a dressing robe round me as I went and shouting to know what the matter was.

The Brockleys' door was shut, but I thrust it open without ceremony and then froze on the threshold. The moonlight, streaming through the open window, showed me the room clearly, without colour, but with ample detail. The bed had been thrust askew and one of its curtains hung at a haphazard angle, partly torn from its rings. Dale was sitting up in the bed, clutching the sheet to her and still screaming in fright while Brockley, in his nightshirt, was up, flourishing a sword and in the act of flinging himself towards the window, where, for one fleeting second, I glimpsed something moving, as though something or someone had scrambled out through the casement and was just letting go of the sill as they made their escape.

'Brockley!' I shouted. Ignoring me, he reached the window and leant out of it, bellowing imprecations. '*Brockley!*' I shouted again.

This time he turned and at once made towards me. 'Where did you spring from, madam? I thought you were still upstairs! Fran, be quiet!' Dale's screams sank down and melted into sobs. 'Madam, let me by! The window was open and a man got through and he had a knife. He's fled the same way but I'm going after him!'

'No, don't! He might kill you!' Dale shrieked. Brockley, unheeding, thrust me out of his way, but pulled up short as a crowd of people surged towards the door. Sybil had rushed from her room, while Wilder, John Hawthorn, the maid Phoebe and the two Floods, in various states of undress, had all come pelting from their quarters, clutching candles and wide-eyed with alarm.

'Our window was open. We heard shouts and screams . . .' The Floods were not young, and Joan's candle was wobbling wildly because her hand was shaking. At her side, her husband Ben was not much better.

'I looked out – there's a ladder up to your room, Brockley!'
That was Hawthorn.

'There's been an intruder!' Brockley shouted. 'Get out of
my way!'

'An intruder?' Wilder said. 'He'll be well away by now if
he got out by the window and down that ladder.'

'He had a knife!' said Brockley furiously, 'and we've got
to get after him! Wilder, Hawthorn, come on!'

'Barefoot and in nightshirts?' protested Sybil.

'There's no point,' I said. 'Wilder's right, he'll have made
good his escape by now. He'll be a mile off before you get
out there – had a horse nearby, as like as not. Let's just be
thankful no one's hurt.'

Brockley muttered something under his breath, but there
were too many people blocking his path and he abandoned
the chase, though unwillingly. I looked at the sword, which
he was still holding. 'Do you always sleep with a blade to
hand?'

'Life in your service has sometimes been perilous, madam,'
said Brockley dryly. He went towards the bed, picked up the
scabbard which was lying on the floor, sheathed the sword
and laid it on a chair.

We had all now crowded into the room. Sybil had gone to
Dale and was comforting her and my massively built chief
cook was looking curiously at Brockley's weapon. 'You need
a meat cleaver rather than that,' John Hawthorn remarked.
'Something you wouldn't have to waste time unsheathing in
an emergency. And could use easily at close quarters. I've got
a spare; you can have it if you like.'

'I prefer the sword. It kept him at arm's length tonight,'
said Brockley.

'A cleaver's heavy and if it's crude, well, it don't need much
skill to kill with it. Believe me . . .'

'Will you two stop arguing about weaponry!' shrieked Dale.
'Have men no sense?'

'Brockley, just what happened?' I said.

The answer told us little. A sound had awoken both Brockley
and Dale, and they had opened their eyes to see a man climbing
through the window, which they had left open for coolness,

just as I had done. 'He had a knife in his teeth,' Dale said, her voice shaking. 'The moon shone on the blade. He had something dark over his face.'

'So I sprang out of bed and the sword was on the chair where I always leave it. I snatched it up,' said Brockley, 'and drew it and went for him. He dodged and the sword caught in a bed curtain and when I wrenched it free, I dragged half the curtain off its rings. He threw the knife at me . . . where is it?'

'I've just kicked something,' said Phoebe. She peered at the floor, holding her candle low. 'Yes! It's here!'

Hawthorn picked it up and handed it to Brockley. 'Yes,' Brockley said. 'He threw it at me, I flung myself aside – I crashed against the bed and knocked it sideways, and the knife fell on the floor. And then the fellow, whoever he was, lost his nerve and bolted for it. He was up on the window seat and slithering over the sill and out of the window in a trice and then you came in . . .'

'Did you recognize him?' I said. 'The moon's bright enough.'

'He was masked. That's the something dark that Fran saw.'

Hawthorn said, 'We all need something to steady our nerves. Where's Gladys?'

'Slept through it, I fancy,' I said. 'But a serving of wine will do. Wilder?'

'At once, madam.' Wilder disappeared, taking Phoebe with him. I, seized suddenly by a new fear, called to Sybil to let Brockley look after Dale, and we went in haste, up to the nursery to make sure that Harry was safe. But the nursery was peaceful. If any sounds had carried there, they hadn't woken Harry or Tessie, who were both sleeping quietly. Once assured that they were unharmed, we crept away and went back to the others.

Reaction had set in. People had sat wearily down wherever they could; on the wide window seat, on the bed, on the stool in front of Dale's mirror. Wilder and Phoebe had brought the wine. We all had some and then I sent most of my household back to their rooms. But Brockley and Hawthorn and I stayed up for the rest of the night, while Dale, reassured by our company, once more fell asleep.

In the morning, we were all tired and jaded, but after breakfast, Brockley asked for a private, serious word with me.

'I was going to say the same to you,' I told him. 'Come outside. We will walk round the garden and hope the fresh air will wake us up properly.'

'I want to say,' said Brockley as we walked among Hugh's roses, 'that I don't think now that Sandy died because he ate something unhealthy in the woods. I think someone poisoned him. So that he wouldn't bark and warn us of an intruder. Hero wasn't poisoned. What do you make of that?'

I was slow-witted with tiredness. 'What is there to make of it? I don't understand what you're trying to say, Brockley. Perhaps she wouldn't eat the meat because she smelt that something was wrong with it. If there ever was any poisoned meat.'

'Perhaps. But it's my opinion,' said Brockley, 'that Sandy was poisoned because whoever did it, meant to return to attack someone here and knew that Sandy would give the alarm, but Hero wouldn't. Which means that whoever came through my window last night was someone Hero knew. You know she only gives a little *wuff* if the person smells familiar.'

'But . . .' Inside myself, I had begun to shake. 'Who . . .? And who was meant to be murdered? Suppose whoever it was came in through the wrong window? Suppose he was really looking for me? Could this be anything to do with Jane Cobbold?'

'I'm inclined to think so. It would be a wild coincidence if it were otherwise, don't you think, madam?'

'But . . .'

'The intended victim could have been me, of course,' Brockley said. 'If someone wanted me to be blamed for murdering Mistress Cobbold and was afraid, when I was released, that after all, the finger was going to be pointed elsewhere – at him, perhaps! Maybe I was to be found, dead by my own hand because I was truly guilty and had despaired of escaping the gallows or else was riddled with remorse. Perhaps I would be discovered with my fingers clasped round the hilt of the knife that had been driven into my heart while I slept.'

'But what about Fran?'

'Maybe he hoped to make a clean kill without waking her.'

'Unlikely!'

'Or perhaps he meant to kill us both and make it look as though I'd slain her first and then myself. It's been known, madam. Men in despair have killed their wives and children before destroying themselves; they do it thinking to save their families from scandal, or poverty after the death of their bread-winner. Or just so as to take company with them into the hereafter.'

'Dear God,' I said. 'But *who* was your midnight visitor? Who?'

'I have a name in mind, but . . .'

I had a name in mind too and, like Brockley, I felt hesitant about uttering it. I needed to think it out, to see if it made any sense. I was about to say so, when Wilder came hurrying out to us.

'Madam, Mistress Stannard, you have a visitor. Master Anthony Cobbold is here, with a Master Peter Poole.'

THIRTEEN
The Missing Piece

Anthony Cobbold had lost weight and his face was hollowed, the bones of his skull painfully obvious, his eyes blurred, as if by recent crying. Whatever other people had thought of Jane, he at least was grieving.

His companion, Peter Poole, was a stranger to me and I had no idea who he could be until Anthony introduced him. Then I remembered that when Anthony called on me just after Brockley's arrest, he had mentioned the man. Yes, of course, Poole was a Cobbold tenant, and was the smallholder that Jarvis, just before he disappeared, had asked to take charge of his poultry. He was a large man in middle life, fleshy and weather-beaten, very much a farmer in his sleeveless leather jerkin and gaiters. He was ill at ease in the Little Parlour, hesitant about taking a seat, as though he feared that he might make it dirty. Brockley, who had accompanied me, finally got him to sit down on a stool. He did so with an air that said that cushioned settles were only for the gentry, not for common folk like him.

'Master Poole has something to tell you,' Anthony said to me. 'He told me first, and I persuaded him to repeat it to Sir Edward Heron, but Heron didn't seem very interested. Only, I think you might be. Will you hear what Master Poole has to say?'

Master Poole twisted his big, calloused hands together and stared at them as if wondering whether he had washed them properly before coming to Hawkswood. 'I dunno how important it be. Sir Edward, he thought not.'

'Just tell me what it is,' I said. 'Please.'

'It were the day Mistress Cobbold, she got killed. Not a day I'd be likely to forget, or anyone would! I'd been to Woking, come back by that path that goes past the hall on the west and winds about, but in the end there's a track leads off to my place . . .' He seemed to become entangled in his own words and stopped. I nodded encouragingly. I was familiar enough with the Cobbold lands to follow what he meant. Brockley also nodded agreement. 'We understand,' he said.

I said, 'Please go on.'

'It was hot. I was tired. Sat down on a fallen tree to take a breather. Thing is, that there track I mentioned does wind. Like a snake. There's a point, just afore it gets to where the turn-off for my place is, where it bends quite near that straight path between the hall and Jack Jarvis's cottage, the path that was only made not that long back.'

'Two years ago,' said Anthony. 'It's a good deal shorter than the old track to the house was. Meant felling a lot of trees, but the timber fetched good money.'

'That's right,' Poole said. 'Well, it's mostly woods round there, but there's an open patch where I sat down. Looks as if some cottager in the past cleared it for a crop, though Master Jarvis, he didn't use it . . .'

'Quite right,' Anthony said. 'The previous tenant grew a patch of corn there, though it never did too well, with woods all round it keeping the sun off.'

'Well, from where I were sitting,' said Poole, 'I could see straight across to the new path and the cottage. It sits at a kind of funny angle from the path so I could see some of the front as well as the back and there were a horse tethered at the front gate. And then Mistress Cobbold comes along on foot, on the path, and she goes in at the gate and then I saw her stop a moment, like she was listening to something – might have been voices inside the cottage. On a fine day like that, there were windows open and all.'

'Yes, it was warm that day,' I said. 'What happened next?'

'The lady knocks on the door and she's let in. After a few minutes, out comes Master Wyse. He unties the horse, gets astride and turns right, as if he was heading towards the hall, only he didn't go far. He turns off into the trees, far side of the track from me. Just disappeared. And just after that, two fellows arrive with a ladder and start setting it up against a tree by the track – seems they had some trouble positioning it right.'

Brockley broke in. 'You say that Master Wyse turned back towards the hall, that he'd just come from? That makes no sense. He'd said he was in a hurry to get on the road to London!'

'Yes, he did,' Anthony agreed. 'And that's just it. That's precisely why I think that this could matter, only Sir Edward didn't agree. Go on, Poole.'

'There's not much more. Out comes Mistress Cobbold, taking her leave, and she sets off back towards the hall, and then, well, I can't be that certain who it was, but I thought I saw someone moving, on foot, among the trees where Master Wyse had gone, almost as if . . . as if whoever it was were following her, only out of her sight. By then, those two fellows with the ladder had it settled and they're climbing up it. They start work with a saw and then Master Jarvis, he comes out and starts doing summat in his garden. I didn't think anything about anything then,' said Poole. 'No one ever asked me questions except about what Master Jarvis said to me when he came to ask me to look after his chickens. Only I've heard things since, like you've just said, about this man Wyse being in a hurry to get on the road to London, and so what was he doing, turning the wrong way and then riding into the woods and then – if it was him – sneaking through them on foot as if he was following Mistress Cobbold?'

I said, 'You are saying you think Master Wyse left his horse tethered in the woods and set off to follow Mistress Cobbold, on foot and keeping among the trees?'

'Summat like that.' Poole twisted his hands together more unhappily than ever. 'Didn't think much about it *then*,' he burst out. 'Only now, with hearing things, like . . .'

Anthony said, 'You say that Master Wyse turned into the trees before the gardeners came with their ladder. So they never saw him. That explains why they never mentioned him when they were questioned. The woods are dense. Well, you know them. Big oaks, spreading branches, thick in leaf in July. The gardeners who were up the ladder could see the cottage and the garden and a good length of the path, but not down among the trees. They didn't see him leave the cottage and they couldn't have seen him once he was in the wood.

They wouldn't be able to see a horse if one was tethered there, or anyone slipping off on foot and keeping under the trees.'

'I got up and went on home just after the gardener fellows started with their saw,' said Poole. 'Didn't see no more.'

'Did none of them see *you*?' I asked.

'Don't think so. I were sittin' in the shade, very quiet, like. None on 'em looked my way, even.'

'Why didn't Sir Edward think any of this was important?' I wanted to know.

'He said Wyse had already told his tale and explained that he stopped for a short talk with Jarvis, and went into the cottage, and yes, Mistress Cobbold did arrive not long after that,' said Anthony. 'But he said she only greeted the two of them and then he left her to talk with Jarvis. That's Wyse's version. He didn't mention riding off into the woods but Heron said it was a warm day, and he might have wanted to ride in the shade. Or he had some other errand taking him out of the way – Priors Ford village lies in that direction. And Sir Edward said how could anyone be sure where the rider went after he'd gone into the wood? And if a man were glimpsed there, walking, why should it be Wyse? Could have been a farmhand taking a shortcut to somewhere. *No, no. All this is making too much of too little.*' Anthony was by now doing what amounted to a mimicry of Sir Edward's somewhat portentous voice.

'Sir Edward still thinks the guilty man is myself,' said Brockley.

He and I looked at each other. I was sure that we both now harboured the same suspicion but neither of us had yet spoken the name. It was time to do so. I said, 'For various reasons, I am beginning to think that the guilty man is Wyse. That occurred to me before you arrived, Master Cobbold. I believe Brockley here would agree.'

'Yes,' said Brockley. 'I would. I always have said that he looked like an assassin.'

'Though why he should want to harm Jane Cobbold, I can't think,' I said, 'but all the same – Brockley, could last night's intruder have been Wyse?'

'Intruder? What's this?' demanded Anthony.

We explained. Anthony was horrified. 'Has this been reported to Sir Edward, or one of the local magistrates or constables? To anyone?'

'Not yet,' I said. 'We were all very shaken after our disturbed night and Brockley had some points he wished to mention to me before we reported what had happened. But reported it must be, of course, and quickly. I think I'll go to Sir Edward direct.'

'The man could have been Wyse,' Brockley said. 'Hero knows him well. She wouldn't have given tongue if she scented him. Though admittedly, the man's face was masked and by moonlight . . . well . . .'

I had sat down on a settle and now found myself sagging tiredly into the corner. 'All the same, it makes precious little sense. Wyse decoded that cipher letter and it was about business for an illicit loom in Dover. What on earth has that to do with anything? With Wyse himself, or Jane Cobbold? Or Jarvis, come to that, and yet the letter was on him when he was found. It's all *absurd*.'

'If Wyse did the decoding, is it certain that the letter really said what he claimed?' Anthony asked suddenly.

'All this talk of ciphers – you mean letters that look like jumble and nonsense and aren't?' Poole asked, bewildered.

'Yes, precisely,' Anthony told him.

'And you think this Master Wyse made up what the letter said and it really said summat else?' Poole, for all his rustic demeanour, was no fool.

'Yes, just that,' Anthony said.

'I wonder,' I said. 'Wyse handed the key to the cipher over to Walsingham once he'd found it, and I would expect Walsingham to have it checked against the letter by someone else, just to make sure it was accurate. He's thorough.'

Brockley was running his fingers through his hair and I would have liked to do the same, except that when I was getting up, Dale had as usual crimped my hair and fixed my headdress securely and I couldn't.

'*Nothing* makes sense,' I said. '*Why* should Wyse want to attack Mistress Cobbold? Did she overhear something when she first arrived – when she was still outside in the garden? I suppose that's possible. But where does the unlicensed worsted loom come in? It's like a pattern that isn't complete – there's a missing piece in the middle!'

Anthony and Poole left shortly after that. When they had gone, Brockley said: 'I was going to tell you, out in the garden, but before I got to it, our visitors arrived all of a sudden and distracted us. I have had a word with Hawthorn. He says his cousin at Cobbold Hall has never hinted at any kind of dispute between Master Cobbold and his wife, and certainly, if either of them had been having a love affair, you can place a wager on the servants knowing. They always do. If there'd been any trouble between the Cobbolds, of any kind, Hawthorn's cousin would have told him. Seems that Hawthorn's cousin isn't the most discreet man in the world.'

'So that theory looks unlikely,' I said. 'We won't find the missing piece there. Brockley, we have to tell Sir Edward what happened last night and we should do it at once.' My disturbed night had left me very tired but I knew I must not give way to it. 'Now,' I said.

It was an hour's ride from Hawkswood to Edward Heron's house. I went in formal fashion with an escort. Sybil, the Brockleys and Joseph all accompanied me. The sky had clouded over by dawn but the day was dry and pleasantly cool for August. We made good time and found Sir Edward at home. Joseph took care of the horses, while a butler ushered the rest of us into a lofty if not very welcoming parlour.

The house dated from the last century and had tall but narrow windows like glorified arrow slits, very unlike the generous mullions of Hawkswood. As a result, the rooms were shadowy, and made darker still by the oak panelling and furniture, and the heavy tapestries, which were all in sombre colours and depicted gloomy scenes, such as the Last Judgement (that one included a lurid view of damned souls in hell), the assassination of Julius Caesar, and the like.

Within a few minutes the household chaplain, Parkes, came to us. I had met him before, and had good reason to dislike him. He had dark, rounded eyebrows the same shape as Norman arches, and an unsmiling face, with long, vertical lines between his eyes and from nostrils to chin. He was, as usual, gowned

in black and had ink-stained fingers. He asked our business
and then said that we could entrust it to him. He would take
careful notes and make a report to Sir Edward.

'We need to see him ourselves,' I said. 'The matter could
be of grave importance.'

There was a chilly pause, during which Parkes tried, with
a steely silence, to intimidate us into doing as we were bid,
and we stood our ground in mute determination. I had been
right to bring companions. Four to one is a good arrangement
when you need to overcome resistance.

Finally, we were admitted to Sir Edward Heron's study.

To meet with disappointment.

I had found myself in front of Sir Edward – and Parkes – to
face questioning when I was suspected of witchcraft. That was
when I learned that Sir Edward, though he was a man of
integrity, was also capable of getting fixed ideas into his head.
I had had the horrible experience of hearing evidence that
should have been in my favour, twisted to point a finger at
me instead, while Sir Edward remained blind to what was
happening.

'But,' he said when Brockley and I, talking by turns, had
given our account of the night's events, 'you say you couldn't
identify the intruder? Who is to say who it might have been,
and why assume that it has anything to do with the matter of
Mistress Cobbold? It is more likely to have been a common
housebreaker, entering the wrong window by mistake. That
is, of course, if there ever was a housebreaker at all.'

We stared at him, astounded. Dale, in a voice high with
indignation, said: 'But I *saw* him! I saw him coming in at the
window! I've never been so frightened!'

Sir Edward smiled at her. 'A loyal wife is a precious gem,
and I don't doubt that you are such a gem, Mrs Brockley.' He
turned the smile towards me. 'And you are an honest woman,
Mrs Stannard; of that I have no doubt. But what did you see?
You were wakened by alarming noises in the next room, and
you ran to discover what was wrong. You saw your tirewoman,
Mrs Brockley, sitting up in bed. She was screaming. Mr
Brockley was lunging towards the window with a sword in
his hand. But did you see the intruder?'

'I think I glimpsed the tips of his fingers, just as he started back down his ladder. We found the ladder still there in the morning. It was one of ours. It's usually kept in an outhouse shed. Anyone could get at it and plenty of people know it's there. People who visit the house from time to time would mostly know. Work is forever being done in the grounds.'

'Never mind the ladder. You *think* you glimpsed fingertips. That's all. And only by moonlight, and there was Mr Brockley here, waving a sword and rushing towards the window; all in a poor light and flying shadows. I put it to you, Mrs Stannard, that you may not have seen fingertips at all, only shadows, and after all,' said Sir Edward, shaking his head over my gullible female nature, 'Mr Brockley is under heavy suspicion of being the killer of Mrs Cobbold. What if he and his no-doubt devoted wife arranged this pretty scene for your benefit? She screamed. He banged about. Then, when you came to the door, he made his leap across the room, sword in hand. All to help you feel quite sure that Mr Brockley is being hounded, perhaps to suggest that someone unknown wanted to make it seem that he had slain himself in fear or remorse. What about that?'

'It's nonsense!' Sybil was as outraged as Dale. 'Mistress Stannard is not so easily gulled!'

'Also,' I said, 'Brockley did not know I was sleeping in the next room. My little son has been ill and I have been spending my nights in the nursery with him. He's better now, and I came back to my own room late last night. Brockley didn't know that. He was surprised to see me when I ran in, hearing the disturbance.'

'I expect he did know,' said Sir Edward, smiling indulgently. 'There are few secrets among household servants.'

Groaning inwardly, I began to talk about Jarvis and the cipher letter. Surely, I said, Jarvis's death and the discovery of the letter suggested that something was amiss somewhere that might have something to do with Jane Cobbold but not with her gossiping habits or Brockley's attitude to them. Sir Edward only smiled indulgently once more.

'I cannot believe for a moment that there is any connection between Mrs Cobbold and whatever it was that Jack Jarvis was mixed up in. That, I feel sure, was quite separate. He was up to something, evidently, but unfortunately fell victim to footpads as many others have done when travelling alone. No, I must dismiss that. I also fear that I have serious doubts about this story of an intruder, though I am sure that you ladies are here in good faith – except perhaps for Mrs Brockley, and she can be excused on grounds of wifely devotion. I will, of course, think the matter over, and I thank you for bringing it to my attention. Now, I am busy this morning and have no more spare time. Parkes, however, will call my wife and she will see that you have refreshments before you leave. Good day to you. How fortunate that you have cool weather for travelling.'

We declined the refreshments and took our leave, politely, although we were inwardly seething. Dale burst out in fury on the way home. 'He's determined to make it be Roger! He twists things! I don't think he's even *tried* to consider anyone else. It's not right. It's not right!'

'No, it isn't,' I agreed. 'But what we can do about it, heaven alone knows.' I thought hard, though, as we rode on. Wyse was in the forefront of my mind. Nothing that I had learned so far seemed to make the slightest sense, but Wyse was there, always there. He had been at Jarvis's cottage when Jane Cobbold arrived, and she had very likely overheard some of their conversation before they knew she was within earshot. It brought the three of them close together just before Jane's death.

I puzzled and wondered. Wyse had deciphered the mysterious letter found on Jarvis's body, and the result didn't fit in anywhere. He *could* have been the intruder who threatened Brockley, though there was no certainty. Wyse had offered marriage to me. Was that as straightforward as it seemed or was it a ploy to gain command of my household – and of me – so as to control anything we might say? Wyse! Wyse!

I said aloud: 'I think I want to know a great deal more about Roland Wyse. I must decide how best to go about it.'

Brockley said, 'Wouldn't Lord Burghley or Mr Walsingham be able to tell us something? They must know his background.'

'I do intend to write to Lord Burghley,' I said. 'I had better do that today. I must think what questions to ask. Well.' I patted Jewel, and encouraged her into a trot. 'Let's get home in good time for dinner. Hawthorn wants to go marketing in Woking this afternoon and I daresay he'll keep to his plans, in spite of last night's disturbance.'

Hawthorn often did his own marketing, vying with Brockley for the chance to visit Woking or Guildford. He would hitch Rusty or Bronze to a small cart and set off, returning with bags of flour or rice or salt, or foreign goods that never reached the shops in Hawkswood village, such as oranges or grapes or certain spices.

He did indeed intend to go to Woking that afternoon. 'I'm low on a good many things,' he said, coming into the hall to present me with a list to inspect, along with an estimate of the cost. 'Life has to go on, even if we have been invaded in the night. It would still have to, even if we had a foreign army quartered on us.'

'I hope we'll never have *that*,' I said with feeling. 'That woman Mary Stuart would like to snatch the crown from Queen Elizabeth and she'd bring a Spanish army here to help her do it, without a second thought, but I hope her scheming has been stopped now.'

The last conspiracy I had helped to uncover would undoubtedly have led to a Spanish invasion, had it been allowed to ripen. I shuddered at the thought.

Ben and Joan Flood adhered to the Old Religion, and occasionally slipped away to somewhere – I never asked where – to hear an illegal Mass. Quite probably, they believed that Mary Stuart ought to be queen of England. I had never asked them about that, either. Just now, they were out in the kitchen and therefore out of hearing. But if they had heard me, I knew they would have ignored my comments. They and others like them seemed unable to imagine what a Spanish invasion would mean. In any case, I had other things on my mind just now. I added an item or two to Hawthorn's list, amended the quantity of flour he wanted to buy, and sent him off. I wanted to rest, and sit with Harry, and *think*.

My efforts to think bore little fruit that afternoon. I was too tired after my broken night and the wearisome and useless ride to call on Heron. I took a short rest and visited Harry, who was mending fast, and then sat in the hall, trying to draft a letter to Cecil. Somehow I couldn't get it right. I was still there, frowning over a second unsatisfactory draft, when Hawthorn came back at frantic speed, clattering into the courtyard at a canter, the wheels of the cart bouncing on the cobbles.

Drawn by the sound of headlong hooves, I went to the window that overlooked the courtyard and stared in astonishment as Hawthorn's cart came through the gate arch at full pelt. Hawthorn was standing up at the front like a Roman charioteer, brandishing his whip, while Bronze, his bay coat streaked with sweat, had foam round his mouth, ears laid flat back and eyes ringed with white. I rushed outside.

'Madam! Mistress Stannard!' Hawthorn almost fell off the cart in front of me. Simon and Arthur had run to see to the sweating Bronze, and were soothing him and giving Hawthorn indignant looks, which he ignored.

'I got everything!' Hawthorn gasped. I had never seen my big and occasionally aggressive chief cook look so panic-stricken. 'Then I tipped a groom to watch the cart while I went to the inn for a drink and my cousin from Cobbold Hall was there so we drank together and my cousin said . . . he said . . .'

'Said what? Hawthorn, tell me!'

'Master Cobbold went today to dine with Sir Edward Heron! He came back and . . . He talks to my cousin a lot, now his wife's gone. A man has to talk to someone . . .'

'I daresay!'

'He – Master Cobbold – must have got to Sir Edward's house just after you left. Sir Edward told him of your visit and said in his opinion, the story about the man who got in last night and attacked Brockley here was a tarradiddle and meant to lift suspicion off Brockley – and he's made up his mind, he's going to have Brockley arrested again and he'll see to it within the next two days!'

'What?' My stomach began to turn somersaults.

Brockley had appeared from somewhere and was at my side. 'What's happening? Hawthorn?'

'Master Cobbold argued with Sir Edward, it seems,' said

Hawthorn. 'But Sir Edward was determined, and Master Cobbold's that upset, that's why he talked so free to his butler. He's a law-abiding man; he doesn't feel he ought to interfere with the law and send to warn you, but he can hardly bear to think of what's going to happen! Well, my cousin doesn't like Sir Edward and his conscience isn't so tender but he wasn't sure he ought to come and warn you directly, either. But he had the chance of telling me so he did, and left it to me to decide. And I've got no doubt! I got back here as fast as Bronze could go and I've half-killed him, poor animal, but . . .'

I looked at Brockley. He was a man of courage but his eyes now were full of fear and his skin had turned almost grey with it. I shared that fear, which was for him, for Dale, for all I held dear at Hawkswood. Nothing would ever be the same if Brockley were taken and condemned.

'Hawthorn,' I said, trying to keep my voice calm, 'bless you for this warning. I think we have time to get away. We shall leave at dawn.'

'Where are we going, madam?' Brockley enquired. His voice, too, was carefully calm.

'London,' I said. 'The best thing to do, anyway, if we want to find out more about Wyse. If he's our man, then somewhere in his life, in his past, there is something that is the key to all this mystery. I shan't write to Cecil now. I want to see him and Walsingham face to face and you're coming with me.'

'So I'll be a fugitive from the law,' said Brockley bitterly. 'I never thought to see the day.'

'No fugitive,' I said. 'We're not supposed to know Sir Edward's plans. I am going to London and, as part of your duties, you will escort me. But you'll be out of his reach for a while. I doubt if he'll chase you to Whitehall. He won't charge into Whitehall Palace or Cecil's house to lay hold of you. He'll most likely wait for us to return. And meanwhile, it's just possible we may find out something out that will *help*!'

FOURTEEN
The Nature of Cats

The south of England in August can be so beautiful. The trees are heavy in leaf, the tracks bordered with long grass and white cow parsley, and the pinky-red of foxglove and valerian. Wheat is ripening into expanses of gold, starred with red poppies and blue cornflowers, and in the meadows, sleek cattle enjoy the rich grass and the sunshine on their backs. In our own pastures, my dappled mare Roundel was grazing contentedly with her second foal, now two months old, at her side. I have always loved such summer days.

But when we fled from Hawkswood before Heron's officers could get there, we raced through the August paradise without noticing it. When I say *we*, I mean myself, Brockley and Dale. Because we needed speed, I insisted that Dale should ride on her own and for her we took Rusty. I was on Jewel and Brockley rode his sturdy cob, Mealy. We went as fast as possible, galloping and walking alternately, to get the best out of the horses.

Before reaching London, we halted at a small inn, to refresh both the horses and ourselves. While we were hurriedly swallowing our ale and cold chicken, Brockley said quietly: 'Madam, do you know exactly where we're going? The queen may still be away on her summer progress. If she is, Lord Burghley will be with her, and possibly Walsingham. Even if they're not away, they could be at their homes or at any of the Thames-side palaces.'

'We're not going to London,' I said.

'Not . . . Ma'am, what do you mean?' Dale asked.

'Back at Hawkswood, I said we were, so when Sir Edward's officers arrive, everyone there will say London's where we've gone. They think it's true, so they won't have to lie and they'll sound convincing when the officers question them, as they assuredly will. In fact, Brockley, I wouldn't dream of taking you into London. I was talking nonsense when I said that Heron wouldn't send men to London after you. He'd only have to send one man – a messenger to the London authorities, stating that he had issued a new warrant for Brockley's arrest, and London would become a trap. Even Cecil and Walsingham might feel obliged to apprehend you. They have to uphold the law, and the authority of County Sheriffs. Oh, they can – as they did – give private advice, but if Heron insists on taking you in, they can't gainsay him. We're going to Norfolk instead. I think the questions we want to ask might be better asked in London, but as we dare not go there, let's see what we can learn at Wyse's home.'

'How do you mean?' said Brockley, puzzled.

'When we went to Kenninghall before, I simply wanted to find Wyse to ask him about the day Mistress Cobbold died. We talked to Agnes Wyse only because Roland wasn't there. Now, it's different. This time we'll make a point of talking to Agnes Wyse – and anyone else who may have known her son well. I think we should find out . . . well . . .'

At this point I had to pause to collect my thoughts. As yet, I had hardly clarified them myself. At length, I said: 'I think we should ask who his closest friends are – old friends from his childhood in Kenninghall, new friends he made while he was away studying law; perhaps friends he's met in London. And enquire about his interests, business interests especially. Has he ever, for instance, invested in the wool industry – in a worsted loom in Dover, for example? Things like that. Anything – *anything* that might shed light on him. And just hope and pray that when we return from Norfolk, we'll be armed with the kind of information that will keep Heron at bay.'

'I can't see it,' said Dale plaintively. 'How would that sort of information help? What might Agnes Wyse know that has to do with either Mistress Cobbold or Jarvis?'

'God knows,' I said frankly. 'But there has to be something somewhere! Nothing in this business seems to make any sense whatsoever but the sense must be there even though we can't see it. Every day, I feel more and more certain that Roland

Wyse is at the heart of all this. Heron has dismissed Poole's story and so we *must* find out more.'

'Poole's story makes a link between Wyse, Jarvis and Mistress Cobbold. Heron's dismissed it but it seems like something to me. But what if we *don't* learn anything else that could be useful?' said Brockley.

'If the mission fails,' I said, 'then you won't come back. You will run away and escape to Sweden or Norway, as I advised once before. I shall be shocked and grieved by your flight and I'll set about selling Withysham.'

'Madam!'

'I mean it, Brockley.' I did mean it too, though at that moment I was seeing Withysham clearly in my memory and to talk of selling it hurt. It was smaller than Hawkswood and I had not spent much time there since I married Hugh, but it was still dear to me. It was a quiet, grey stone house in Sussex, and because it had been an abbey until King Henry dissolved the monastic world, it had the narrow ecclesiastical windows common to most abbeys, and all its rooms were shadowy. But it was not like Sir Edward Heron's gloomy house. Its tapestries depicted pleasant scenes and its atmosphere was serene. I had happy memories of being there with Meg; of the two of us studying Greek together, seated by an open window on sunny days, looking out towards the green Sussex downs. But compared to Brockley's safety, I said sternly to myself, it meant nothing.

I'd be taking another risk, as well, naturally. Heron might well suspect me of helping Brockley to escape. I would have to invent a very convincing tale of how he and Dale slipped away one night, unknown to me. But once again, I said to myself, Brockley's safety came first.

Within the next two days, John Hawthorn had said. His messenger would not yet be on the way to London. We had time in hand. Our straightest route did brush the edge of London, so we pressed on hard, all day, so as to be across London Bridge before evening. Once more, we made our first stop at The Boar. It hadn't improved since our last visit. Its clientele was as scruffy as ever and its floors even dirtier, but this time we did at least think of asking for a private parlour, though we were slightly surprised to find that there actually was one. It wasn't all that comfortable, for it needed dusting and its settles had no cushions, but it was at least quiet.

The landlord was a thin, harried-looking man with broken veins in his nose, suggesting a liking for his own wares. His wife was a grey-haired wisp of a woman with an air of being anxious to please and never quite succeeding. I would have hesitated to bully them but Brockley, though he looked and sounded tired, was still strong-minded enough to insist in a loud voice that we should be provided not only with a parlour but also reasonably sized portions of food for our dinner. They did as he told them, though I can't say the cooking was any better. The most that can be said for The Boar was that the beds were clean (if lumpy) and the stableyard was quite well run, though Brockley as usual insisted on overseeing the care of our horses himself. At breakfast, however, the bread rolls were yesterday's and the omelettes leathery. Leaving promptly was no hardship.

We knew the best route this time, and reached Kenninghall late in the afternoon of only the third day. We at once made for the White Hart.

We found few customers there, for it was well past the time for dinner. We took a private parlour and asked for ale to be brought to us there, and as we hadn't taken dinner anywhere, enquired if hot food was still available.

Ezra sighed and muttered but finally said that they could provide something. 'We've plenty of bread and there's a mutton ham, only just cut into, and some bean stew we can heat up. And Cat'll make some almond fritters if you like. Will that do?'

It seemed to me that Ezra wasn't his usual hospitable self. His voice was flat and his jolly smile was missing. We accepted what was offered and when Cat came in to put spoons and bowls and wooden platters on the table, I saw that she wasn't her usual self, either. Her mouth was turned down at the corners, giving her a sullen air and she did her table-setting with an ill-tempered rattle.

Brockley noticed it, too. 'Is anything wrong, Mistress Spinner?' he asked.

'Nothing that need trouble you, sir. A bit of lost business that's taken the shine off the world for a while. That needn't spoil your food. What brings you back here?'

'We've come to visit Mistress Agnes Wyse,' I said. 'It's possible she can cast a light on something strange that may concern her son. You knew her well at one time. Do you know Roland Wyse, too?'

'Not really. He was still just a little boy when I married Ezra and left off being maid to his mother. Can't say I've ever exchanged more than good day with him since then.'

'Were you happy when you worked for Mistress Wyse? I remember you said, last time we were here, that she was a generous mistress.'

'So she was and I can't say different.' Cat rearranged a couple of spoons in a pensive way. 'All the same,' she said, 'I didn't like the post that much, truth to tell, but there isn't much choice hereabouts for a wench that needs to earn a living. I tried to get work at Kenninghall, the Duke of Norfolk's place as it was then – said to belong to the queen now the duke's dead – but there weren't any vacancies, and yes, Mistress Wyse paid a good wage, I have to say that. But I was that glad to wed Ezra and come here, where we can work for ourselves, not other folk. I've got your stew heating. I'd better go and look at it.'

She disappeared.

'What are you after?' Brockley asked me in a low voice. 'Is she likely to know anything useful?'

'I'm after anything I can get. Gossip! Master Stannard told me once about the way miners pan for gold or tin. They dig out shovels full of earth and stones and put it all in water and shake it about and if the metal's there, it'll separate out – sink to the bottom, being heavier. I want to make everyone who knows Wyse at all talk about him, and maybe somewhere in it will be a few flecks of gold.'

Cat and Ezra came back together, Ezra bringing a tray of pewter goblets and a jug of ale, and Cat a serving dish laden with ham slices. A kitchen wench came behind them with a tureen of stew. The wench went straight back to the kitchen after putting the tureen on the table, but Cat and Ezra stayed, Ezra to fill the goblets and Cat to serve the food.

I said, 'What was it about working for Mistress Wyse that you didn't like, Mistress Spinner?'

Cat's mouth curled. She had an expressive mouth, and her eyes, which were a greenish hazel, had a glint in them. 'She weren't so prim and proper as she made out, that's what I didn't like. Well, you heard some of the talk, last time you was here, didn't you?'

'Now, Cat,' said Ezra warningly.

Cat, however, tossed her head and I ventured further. 'Didn't the Earl of Surrey write a poem for her?' I asked innocently. 'She mentioned that to us. Were you working for her at that time? Was it true?'

'Yes, I was and yes, it is!' said Cat, almost belligerently. 'A love poem, too!'

'Well, that were a compliment,' said Ezra reasonably. 'No harm in that. That's court folk for you. Young gallants writing verses to pretty ladies. It's what gentlemen like Henry Howard do, and no evil in it. I remember that visit the earl made to his brother of Norfolk. A fine young man was Henry Howard of Surrey, and no one here ever believed he was guilty of treason, for all King Henry had his head off.'

Brockley said, 'Our three goblets have taken nearly all that jug of ale. Could we have another jugful, master landlord?'

Ezra was obliged to leave us, jug in hand, and I seized my chance. 'I expect having a poem written for her turned her head a little. It would turn mine!'

I had judged her aright. Cat Spinner disliked Agnes Wyse and wanted to talk about her.

'Did more than turn her head, I'd say. Truth to tell . . .' She lowered her voice. 'I rather think that Roland Wyse is Henry Howard's son.'

Into the startled pause that followed this, Dale eventually asked: 'Why do you say that?'

'Like I said, I were her maid then. Robert Wyse was away – had been away two months – when the earl came visiting. Only . . .' Cat, having filled my bowl, clattered the serving spoon angrily into the tureen. 'Only,' she said, 'to start with, it wasn't her he was after. No, indeed it wasn't!'

'Who was it, then?' I asked quietly.

'To start with, it was me!'

I looked at her, startled anew, but held my tongue, not knowing what to make of this.

'Oh, I daresay I was well out of it!' Cat's voice was harsh. 'I'd have ended up left with a baby, likely as not, and lucky if its dad were honest enough to help us. Great lords with noble wives don't take much account of servant girls in trouble, even if they've caused the trouble in the first place. But I never had the choice. See, he'd talked to me at Kenninghall when I'd gone there with Mistress Wyse – she'd been asked to a Christmas ball. I was to attend on her if she wanted aught, and look after her cloak. There was a feast too and a to-do over it all; I offered to help the Kenninghall servants. Better than sitting by, doing nothing. I didn't think my lady was likely to want much service. Henry Howard, he met me when I was carrying a tray down some stairs. I tried to step out of his way and the tray began to slip. He put out a hand to steady it . . .'

Her voice had become softer and her mouth was no longer turned down at the corners. They had lifted into a little reminiscent smile. 'I thanked him and tried to curtsey and nearly dropped the tray again, and he laughed and said be careful, no need to be so formal and you're a pretty thing, who are you? I hardly knew what to say. I knew who he was; one of the maids of the house had pointed him out to me. *That's the Earl of Surrey, Henry Howard. Isn't he handsome?* That's what she said. And another maid said he was a bit of a rogue, though maybe it weren't surprising – she'd seen his wife once, and she was nice-looking enough but there was no sparkle and all she ever talked of was their children. They had a fair-sized family. *No marvel if he likes an adventure now and then.* That's what she said.'

Cat paused, apparently lost in reminiscence. Her eyes weren't seeing us; they were seeing back into the past, and looking into the face of a young man who had long since died on the block. At length, she said: 'Well, it's true he was handsome, and he weren't a bit haughty, like you'd think an earl would be. Just a fine young fellow with such a smile! I told him who I was. He asked when I'd be out and about on my own, and I said I'd have shopping to do on the morrow, while my lady rested in bed after her late night. He promised to meet me. And so he did! And we walked and talked as I went here and there – buying this and that; can't remember what. He asked when next I'd be free and I said the evening after next. Madam would be supping with neighbours and wouldn't need me. Late September, it was, but still light for a fair time in the evenings. He said to meet him under a certain oak tree on the edge of the duke's land. We would walk and talk again, he said, and get to know each other.'

Cat's voice sounded as though she were speaking from a long way off, as though she were far away in time. 'I was only sixteen,' she said. 'An innocent. I didn't see then where it would lead, or if I half saw, I wouldn't look. But earls don't take blacksmith's daughters or lady's maids up to their four-posters and feather mattresses. I knew well enough that there was a hay barn not far from that oak tree. That's where we'd have ended up, sure as can be. But I didn't let myself think about that. I was bemused. I thought he was wonderful! He saw me home.

'Yes, he saw me home.' Now her voice was bitter. 'He took me to the door and *she* saw us coming and stepped out to meet us. She was so welcoming! Invited him in – I think they'd danced at the ball – as if he were an old friend and then, if you please, sent me off on another errand! While I was gone, she entertained him in her parlour and by the time I come back, she'd got him dazzled. Oh, she was young, no more than seventeen, just one year older than me, but she knew all the tricks. Born knowing, if you ask me. He was just about to leave and he said goodbye to me as if I was nothing, but he kissed *her*. I kept the tryst under the oak tree but he didn't come and when I got back home, he was there. With her. She hadn't gone out to the neighbour after all. They were in the parlour. She told me to bring them wine. He did smile at me, kind of apologetic like, but . . .

'He came back two or three times to see her. Always, I was sent out. But once I got back early and they weren't in the parlour; they came down the stairs in a bit of a hurry just after I came in. Must have heard me saying, *Where's madam?* to one of the maids. Robert Wyse came back home not long after that and Henry Howard left Kenninghall and went back to *his* home, wherever that was. But by then, she'd missed a course. I was her personal maid. I'd know, wouldn't I?'

'God's teeth!' said Brockley softly.

'Well, I've been happy with Ezra but I hear things about her; she hasn't mended her ways, don't you think it, and no wonder her husband grew so stark and hard with his family. Keeping her on a tight rein, he was, I don't doubt it, and not always succeeding, either! Not that all of it's her doing, I grant you. Why men have to behave like wasps falling into a jam pot, I'll never know. Well, I'll leave you to your meal.'

She whisked out of the room, leaving us to finish the serving ourselves. We stared at each other.

'What caused all that?' Brockley said. 'What made her burst out like that, all of a sudden, and to strangers?'

'She may feel it's safer to talk to strangers,' I said. 'She's still bitter, that's plain enough. Ezra probably tries to make her be discreet. But strangers wouldn't be so likely to spread talk round the district.'

'There's been talk already,' said Brockley. 'Remember the gossip we heard last time we were here? There's something odd about this. Something's changed. It's as if the very name of Mistress Wyse makes our landlord's wife angry, in a way she wasn't last time. What's happened?'

'Maybe Agnes has been making eyes at Ezra?' I suggested.

'After all these years?' said Dale reasonably. 'She must have known him most of her life.'

'Getting desperate now she's getting older, perhaps?' Brockley offered. 'Or maybe Ezra's changed – started to stray.'

'Let's eat,' I said.

We finished our meal. Brockley went to arrange rooms for us, and came back saying that Ezra seemed irritable and almost brusque, but a couple of rooms were to be had, the same ones that we had had before.

'And now,' I said, 'let us talk to Agnes, if she's home.'

'But even if Roland Wyse wasn't fathered by Master Wyse, what difference can that make to anything?' Dale grumbled as we set off on foot to Agnes's house. 'Mistress Cobbold can't have been murdered because of *that*! Even if she'd found out and he thought she might spread the news around, why should Roland care? He's a man with a position at court and don't tell me he's the only one there who isn't quite sure who his father was!'

'Maybe he's in love with some lass whose parents think the son should be burdened with the sins of the father,' hazarded Brockley as we reached Agnes's house and I applied the knocker. 'We haven't gone into Wyse's romantic life.'

'Since he proposed marriage to me,' I said with asperity, 'I hope he hasn't got a romantic life at present! Still – yes, we could ask Agnes about his love affairs, if any.'

He and Dale nodded. The door was opening to reveal a youthful maidservant, probably the Lucy who hadn't been in evidence during our previous visit. She showed us into the parlour, where we found Agnes rearranging ornaments on a shelf next to a tapestry wall hanging that hadn't been there before. 'I think I shall have to have this shelf moved,' she remarked, by way of a greeting. 'It distracts the eye from the tapestry. The theme of that is the death of Cleopatra. Very dramatic – don't you agree? It should have the wall to itself.'

I looked at the tapestry and thought it not merely dramatic but repellent. Cleopatra, inadequately clothed, lay on a couch in a limp, dying attitude. With one hand she held a snake to an exposed breast, while the other caressed the reptile in a loving manner. Two other women, also minimally clad, knelt weeping beside her. Weakly, I said something about the excellence of the workmanship. Beside me, Brockley exuded disapproval and Dale was embarrassed by Cleopatra's nakedness. I didn't even have to look at them to know that; I knew them both far too well.

'It's very pleasant to have visitors I can show my fine new things to,' said Mistress Wyse, probably taking their silence for admiration. I noticed that she was wearing what, from its pristine appearance, was surely a new gown, and a silk one at that. It was black with silver and green embroidery on the sleeves and her ruff was edged with the still fashionable Spanish blackwork. The ensemble suited her.

The maidservant was hovering. 'Cakes and wine, Lucy,' said Agnes, waving her out of the room, and us into seats. 'It is kind of you to call,' she said. 'Is there any special reason for it, or were you just in the district? Have you news of my son?'

'We did just happen to be in Kenninghall,' I said, feeling my way. 'We have seen nothing of Master Wyse lately but thought we might take news of you back to *him*.' Asking my questions, I realized, was something to approach with caution. Polite social exchanges had better come first. 'How are you faring? How is your cousin Blanche?'

The effect of this harmless enquiry was remarkable. Agnes's face went pale with anger, and in her lap, her fingers curved like claws. I noticed for the first time that she kept her nails unattractively long. *'Blanche!'* She fairly spat the name. 'That saucy, ungrateful, impertinent fool! I've no idea how she is and I don't want to know, either.'

'But . . . whatever is the matter?' I infused my voice with sympathy. 'What has Blanche done? I see that she isn't here just now.'

'I gave her a good home here, every kindness. All I wanted from her was a little gratitude and to know her place and not push in and put herself forward when I had company! She's run off, that's what she's done. She's run off with that Gilbert Shore! They set it all up without my knowledge. The deceit of it! Oh, it was all legal! Banns called and everything, the way the church likes, but called where I couldn't hear them! Sly! Deception!'

She broke off as Lucy appeared with a tray. Lucy took one look at her mistress's furious face, put the tray down in haste, bobbed and fled. The rest of us sat still. As soon as Lucy had vanished, Agnes resumed as though there had been no interruption.

'Do you know what that pair did? No, of course you don't. Gilbert went to stay for a while with his parents in the next parish and had the banns called there. He rode over to his work every day. Must have got up at dawn to get there on time. Then one market day, out goes Blanche to buy needles and silk thread, *so she said*. But she didn't come back, just left me to worry and panic and ask the neighbours if they'd seen her!'

Her sense of grievance, her bitter indignation, were pouring out in a torrent. 'And then a messenger boy arrives!' she said furiously. 'With a note to say she and Gilbert are married – over in his home parish – and she'll be living from now on in a cottage somewhere in this village. Well, I hope she won't regret it, that's all, but I've no doubt she will. Blanche hasn't got what's needed to hold a man, mark my words, and Gilbert's no catch. Just works on the land! My husband was a lawyer, a professional man! I suppose she snatched at one of the few men who looked at her twice. Well, more fool her!'

I could think of nothing to say and from her silence, nor could Dale. As for Brockley, his distaste could almost be smelt but his voice was as smooth as cream as he said: 'I can understand why you wanted someone better for your cousin. After all, yours is a well-connected family, is it not? Isn't Roland the son of an earl? Earl of Surrey, I believe. Did you have Roland in mind for Blanche? These days, you wouldn't need a dispensation for the marriage of cousins. I believe some vicars still object, but not all.'

Agnes's mouth opened. Or rather, her jaw dropped, while her eyes widened. 'So she's talked! That woman Cat Spinner! Cat by name and cat by nature, that one. She said she would but I told her, won't people wonder why you never told what you know before? But she's not one to think clear, oh no, not her. She's just angry because I won't let her bleed me any more. That's what's wrong with her!'

'Bleed you?' I asked.

'Yes, *bleed* me. Of money! Ever since Robert died. Not till he was gone – she was frightened of him; everyone was, me as well. I never wanted to marry him but he had money and a profession and when he came courting, my parents said I had to take him; I'd never catch a better bridegroom. I was terrified of him. I was only fifteen when I was married. He was a hard man. Henry Howard was kind, smiling, affectionate. I was still only seventeen when he fell in love with me and I needed some kindness. And then . . .'

Agnes's mouth twisted sourly. 'Robert knew who Roland's

father was. There was servants' talk and he could add up the months, could Robert, and he knew when he saw Roland that here was no baby born early. He didn't do me any harm over it; oh, I'll grant him that. He was hard but he was decent and he wouldn't beat a woman who was suckling a child. But from then on, he never melted. Always cold, he was. Polite and a million miles away. Used me when he wanted to, got two daughters from me and then lost interest. He wouldn't let me tell Roland the truth and I thought it best not to myself, but that was the first thing that woman Cat Spinner threatened to do; tell Roland. So then I did let him know the truth. After all, why shouldn't Roland know that his father was an earl, and the Duke of Norfolk his half-brother?'

I opened my mouth to ask how Cat had managed to go on bleeding Agnes, once Roland knew of his paternity, but Agnes had merely paused to gulp in a breath, and now overrode me, surging on.

'At least Roland gained from knowing. The duke came to his house here in Kenninghall now and then. Roland got to know him somehow and let him know of their relationship. I'd told Roland this and that about his real father; things Henry Howard said to me, about his family, details most people couldn't know, and that's how Roland got the duke to realize they really were brothers. They became friends. They never made anything public, but Roland had studied law and the duke helped him to his first post at court. Not a big one; just a junior in Walsingham's office, but that was his start. The Duke of Norfolk, God rest his soul, was a better friend to my Roland than Robert ever was, for all he pretended that Roland was his. He was always harsh to the boy. Always!'

Not all that surprising, I thought. Most men would find it hard to be kind to the cuckoo in the nest, though admittedly, I pitied the cuckoo.

'Roland was fond of the duke,' said Agnes. 'He was near falling ill with sorrow when Norfolk was executed. He works for that man Walsingham because it's a position with prospects but he hates Walsingham for hounding his brother to death. And now that Spinner woman . . .'

I got my question in at last. 'But if your husband was dead

and Roland knew of his parentage, then how could Cat Spinner have gone on bleeding you, as you put it?'

'No one *here* in Kenninghall knew! The duke and Roland kept even their friendship quiet, let alone their being brothers. I said they never made anything public. That Cat said she'd tell the world if I didn't pay her, every month, on the first. There'd been gossip about me already, just because I make an effort to look well. Cat said she'd have all Norfolk knowing for sure I was an adulteress and knowing about Roland, too. It was all right for him to know, but do you think I wanted the whole world to hear about it? So I paid her, and paid her high, as well! Her husband knows all about it, I fancy. That inn's a mighty prosperous place!'

'Does your son know anything about this?' Brockley asked. 'Surely, you've told him? Can he do nothing to help you?'

'I didn't dare tell Roland.' There were tears now in Agnes's eyes. 'I was afraid of what he'd do. He can be violent. While he was still just a lad, my husband beat him often, but when Roland was fifteen, he put on some muscle and then, when Robert tried one day to take a whip to him, Roland turned on him and knocked him down. Knocked him *out*, as a matter of fact. And since he's grown up and gone out into the world, he's grown harder. He'd be so angry about the Spinners that he might do anything! I hardly know him these days. He doesn't tell me things any more; he's not open the way he used to be. I know nothing of his friends, nothing of his interests. I'm just glad of the money he sends me. It keeps Cat quiet. *Kept* her quiet. Not now!'

'What has happened to change things?' Brockley asked.

'I've kept up appearances as best I could,' said Agnes angrily. 'For five years I've only had one maidservant and no new dresses. I got tired of it, just tired of it, and two weeks ago, I told Cat to tell the world if she liked; I'd pay her no longer. She didn't like that! Just then, money came from Roland – he's generous enough that way – and for once it didn't go to put silk on Cat Spinner's back or buy pewter goblets for them as drink at the White Hart. This time, it went on a tapestry and this new gown for me! If you do tell the world, I said to Cat, *I'll* tell people why you've kept silent all this time. So as to extort money from me! I'll hold my tongue as long as you hold yours but no longer. She tried to defy me. *You won't do that*, she said to me. *If you do, then the world'll know you really were unfaithful; that I've not made it up. You wouldn't have paid me a penny else.* Well, she was wrong. If she's started pointing her finger at me, then I'll point a finger at *her*! Yes, I will! I will!'

Abruptly, Agnes's tears overflowed. She turned her head away to sob into a cushion. We all looked at each other, embarrassed.

'I've remembered something,' I whispered, careful to make sure she couldn't hear. 'Roland Wyse witnessed the execution of his half-brother Norfolk, as I did. I saw him there. It's true he was very upset. He cried.'

FIFTEEN

Encounter in a Second-rate Inn

'Well,' I said as we walked back to the inn, 'our questions have been answered before we even asked them. Agnes knows little or nothing of her son's friends or interests, and most of those, these days, are surely in London. I should have gone there first and sent you off to Norfolk without me, Brockley. My mistake!'

'We do now know what's made Agnes and Cat so talkative,' said Brockley. 'Only two weeks ago, Cat lost what by the sound of it was a healthy slice of income, because Agnes ran out of patience and told her so. They're both sore and spitting.'

'I don't like either of them,' said Dale primly.

'Nor me,' Brockley agreed. 'No wonder Ezra never wanted people to gossip about Agnes! Once some really juicy gossip was circulating, there'd be little point in Agnes paying the Spinners to keep quiet! And now he's probably afraid that Agnes will tell the world about the extortion, so he's still trying to get Cat to hold her tongue. My God, what a pair! Well, we'll deal with them.'

We had spoken further to Agnes before leaving her, explaining that it was quite possible that Cat had not talked to anyone but us and if so, we thought we could make sure it stopped there. We parted from her on quite friendly terms. When we reached the inn, Brockley, in the kind of voice that isn't easily gainsaid, declared that we must speak to Cat and Ezra in private. Accordingly, they showed us into a very small room which, to judge by its ledgers and the ink stains on the scarred little table, the chipped earthenware writing set, the pot of spare quills and the small abacus with the cracked beads, was where they did their accounts and made lists of things to be done and stores to be purchased. It was quite difficult to squeeze us all in. Clearly, Agnes's contributions to their income hadn't been spent here. Brockley closed the door. Then he spoke.

'We have a warning for you,' he said to the Spinners. 'A warning that you should take very seriously.' His voice held authority, although looking at him, I noticed once more that he looked very tired. His eyes were slightly bloodshot, as though he hadn't slept. 'We know that you have been wringing money out of Agnes Wyse, by threatening to spread scandal about her, and about the parentage of her son. She has now refused to pay you any more, and quite right, too. Extortion is a very serious crime indeed and carries some terrifying penalties. Agnes told us that she has had to pay high for your silence. No, she didn't tell us the amount but we had already noticed how prosperous your inn seems to be. There must be no more of this.'

They stared at him without speaking, their faces half defiant and half frightened. Ezra's chins were wobbling and there was sweat on his forehead but his eyes were angry. Cat's were sly, and the locks of dark hair flowing down the sides of her face suddenly gave me the creeps. They reminded me of Agnes Wyse's nasty tapestry, with Cleopatra caressing a snake. The hair lay in sinuous curves that made me think of snakes.

'*Never* attempt to take money from anyone again, by threats,' said Brockley. 'Agnes will not report you as long as you are silent from now on. We have her word on that. I hope that we were the first you tried to feed with scandal. If you've talked to anyone else, I advise you to find a way to retract, to say you were mistaken.'

'I warned you, Cat. I said, don't talk about her; she'll find a way to get back at you.' Ezra glowered at his wife.

Cat glowered back and said: 'She took the earl's fancy away from me. Maybe it was best in the end but no wench would like it. She brushed me aside as if I were nothing.'

'Over thirty years ago,' I said. 'Time to let it go, surely. Don't dare to rob or harm Agnes again. Leave her alone.'

'There's talk about her without us!' Ezra snapped.

'Then you'd best contradict it,' said Brockley. 'You've always forbidden it in your inn, haven't you? Go on forbidding it. That was a way of guarding your private pot of gold, I suppose. No use threatening to tell what's already being said! You'd be wise to go on defending Mistress Wyse's good name. We'll leave in the morning. No doubt you would like us to leave now but it's too late in the day to get far. I recommend you to see us as good business. We'll pay our bill as we should. You can hardly complain about *that*. That's all.'

He turned on his heel and both Dale and I followed him out of the congested little office. We made our way to the stair that led up to the gallery at the nearest point to our rooms. As we were about to separate, Dale suddenly said: 'What *is* the penalty for extortion, Roger?'

'I don't know,' said Brockley frankly. 'But then, neither do the Spinners. I expect it's unpleasant. We've done them a favour, warning them.' He paused, with a hand on the latch of their bedchamber door. 'After Lewes, I wouldn't throw anyone into the jaws of the law for anything short of rape or murder – or maybe arson. But the Spinners don't know that, either.'

That night, I found it hard to sleep. I didn't like the feeling that we were under the roof of two people who hated us. I didn't really suppose that they would murder their own guests in the night, but I felt their hatred as though it were a loathsome smell, oozing under the door of my room.

The night was too warm for comfort. I left my bed curtains open and opened a window as well, but still sleep eluded me. Restlessly, I turned and turned again, seeking a cool place on my pillow and then losing the pleasant chill because my own hot skin warmed the linen. At last, cross and weary, I got up, put on a robe and slippers and went out on to the gallery to lean on the balustrade and gaze into the courtyard. A misshapen moon, two or three days past the full, cast a pallid light into the courtyard. By it, I saw a dark figure emerge from the shadows below, and begin to prowl back and forth.

I leant further over the balustrade, trying to see more clearly. Then I recognized the figure. Its shape, its proportions, the set of the shoulders, the manner of the stride, were all familiar to me. For some reason, Brockley, too, was sleepless and was now pacing about in the open air as though in desperate unease.

I made for the stairs and hastened down to the courtyard. When Brockley's ramblings brought him within earshot, I said his name in a low voice. He stopped short and spun round. 'Who's there? Who is it?'

'Ursula Stannard,' I said. 'Brockley, why are you out here in the middle of the night? Did the heat keep you awake?'

I saw his shoulders slump. 'Did it do the same for you? I hope it's only been this once, at least. I've not had a good night's sleep since we heard that Heron was out to re-arrest me.'

'I've thought once or twice that you seemed tired.'

'Tired! It's like a continual ache. Madam, what progress have we made? Didn't we come to Kenninghall hoping to learn something, anything, new about Roland Wyse, something that might point to a new solution, a new answer to these deaths, Mistress Cobbold's and John Jarvis's? Something that would make sense of all that and this business of worsted looms? But have we? It's plain that even if we'd asked the questions we had in mind, Mistress Wyse didn't know the answers. I can't suppose that anyone else in Kenninghall does either. Most of Wyse's life is at court, nowadays.'

'But we did learn a few things we didn't expect,' I said. 'Maybe coming here wasn't a mistake after all. Perhaps the answers we need are hidden in the things we did learn. We know now that Wyse can be violent – enough to worry his mother. We know that he has become harder as the years go by. And we know that he has a grudge against Walsingham. Admittedly, I can't quite see how that connects up, but it looks like the beginning of some sort of track. Brockley, I think I *must* go to London.'

'I can't see what you mean by the beginning of a track, madam. Yes, we now know for sure that Wyse has a violent temper and we've found out that he was half-brother to the Duke of Norfolk and grieved by Norfolk's execution and detests Walsingham on that account, but does that really help? Will any of that send Heron off on another scent?'

'Not on its own,' I said. 'And that's why I must go to London. I think I ought to look at that cipher letter for myself. I know I said to Master Cobbold that Walsingham was sure to have had it checked, but how do I know? If he didn't, then there may have been some deception by Wyse. That was a clever idea that Cobbold and Poole came up with. I have the key – what's supposed to be the key – and I want to decode it and make sure that the letter really is about that loom. I should have thought of that before.'

'Perhaps,' said Brockley carefully, 'no useful piece of evidence exists.' He paused and then said: 'Have you ever *really* considered, madam, that perhaps I might be guilty?'

'*Brockley!*' I was taken completely aback. 'Of course not!'

'It would make sense.' His voice was cool, without inflection. 'Perhaps I did slink into the Cobbold Hall garden, catch Mistress Cobbold there alone, tax her with the way she had slandered you, receive a dismissive answer, lose my temper with her and kill her?'

Moonlight shows outlines more than detail. I could see Brockley clearly enough but I could not see his eyes. He was a shape and a voice, a voice so devoid of feeling that it was almost sinister. Which was nonsense. This was *Brockley*, whom I had known for years, who had shared danger with me. We had protected each other, been loyal to each other. That Brockley could not possibly have done what he had just said.

'Well, did you?' I asked, keeping my own voice as brisk and normal as possible.

'No, I didn't,' said Brockley. 'But will I ever be able to prove it?'

'You were in Woking, within two miles of Cobbold Hall at the time of her death, and on previous occasions you were rough with men who repeated the slanders. That is all the evidence against you that there is. No, Brockley. I don't believe you did it and unless you are prepared to go into a church and put your hand on the Bible there and swear that you are guilty and are making a true confession, I never will.'

'I'm sorry to be causing you so much anxiety, madam.'

'There's no need to be sorry, Brockley. It isn't your fault.'

'Thank you.' He turned his head away from me as though he didn't want me to look at his face, even by the inadequate light of a waning moon. Then, painfully, he said: 'The truth is, I'm afraid. I'm more than afraid. Lewes was . . . Dear

God, I've been a soldier. I've fought. I've killed – in battle, not in cold blood; but yes, I have killed. I have also been in danger, many times. But I've never been afraid like this before. The thought of that place . . . the thought of hanging . . . I can't . . .'

I made a quick decision. 'I shall go to London, as I said, but I'll go alone. You and Dale must make for . . . Lowestoft would do, I should think. You know how to get there. I'll give you some extra money.'

'The ports could have been warned, madam. If Heron has sent word that he's issued a warrant to take me, a port could be a trap.'

'I doubt it,' I said. 'He'll have been told by now that I've gone to London, taking you, and he doesn't know we were aware of the new warrant. I think the ports are probably safe for the moment. It shouldn't be too hard to get a passage across to Norway, Denmark, Sweden – any of them. One day you'll be able to come back; I'm sure of it. But no, you must never return to Lewes.'

Brockley was shaking his head before I was halfway through this speech. 'No! You can't travel all the way from here to London unescorted, madam. I can't allow it.'

'Of course I can! I've travelled alone before and stayed in an inn alone – don't you remember? You had been captured and I came to your aid. I'm perfectly able to—'

'I daresay, but it wasn't right or safe. Lone travellers – lone women above all – are always at risk. Footpads exist. I repeat, I can't allow you to make such a journey with no escort.'

'And I can't allow you to risk yourself for me, Brockley!'

'I know my duty,' said Brockley. I could hear the tremor in his voice and it tore my heart. 'And Dale would agree. We can't run off and leave you alone. We're your servants; we take wages from you. We have duties.'

'Your duties include doing as I tell you!'

'Not always,' said Brockley.

'I'm trying to protect you!'

'And we, you,' Brockley pointed out. He added: 'Dale is afraid for me, just as you are. I think that now that things seem to have come to a head, she finds even the idea of exile in a strange country bearable. But she knows it would be wrong to desert you so far from home. That is final.'

'*Oh, really!*' I didn't know whether or not to be furious with him. I also knew that if I lost my temper, it would have no effect on him. I searched for a compromise. 'Very well, but neither of you are to enter London. On that I do insist. You know the danger. God's teeth, I can surely ride unescorted for just a short distance through London, in broad daylight to wherever Walsingham is – assuming he's *in* London! Through thronged streets and on a good horse I'm not likely to come to harm. I need not spend a night away from you, or if I do, it will be at court or perhaps with Lady Mildred in Cecil's house. But you and Dale must stay outside the city. If, when I get to Walsingham, I can't lift the threat from you, I'll get word to you. Either in person, or by hiring a courier privately. *Then* you and Dale must pack up and make for the coast – Lowestoft, Dover, as you choose – and do it immediately. If Cecil isn't there, Lady Burghley will see I have an escort when I go home. On this matter I *won't* be argued with. Do you hear me, Brockley? I can't bear to think of you being taken again and nor can Dale. Will you at least obey *this* order?'

There was a silence. I could feel him hesitating, struggling to decide, his sense of duty battling against his fear. I waited. At last he answered me.

'Very well, madam. Fran and I won't enter the city. We'll come with you to its outskirts and wait there. If I am taken,' Brockley said grimly, 'well, I didn't kill Jane Cobbold but I think I might kill myself.'

'Brockley, for the love of heaven! Well, that settles it. If I learn nothing to help you when I reach Walsingham – which I fear very much may be the case – then you must leave England at once.'

'You'll find yourself selling Withysham,' said Brockley painfully.

'It doesn't matter!'

'And I know it does. But I can only thank you – and pray it won't be necessary.'

There was a stillness between us as we stood there in the midnight courtyard. It was a long time now since we had realized that our friendship was hurtful to Dale and that we must step away from each other, back into the persons of mistress and servant. Now I knew that the old bond had never broken; only been stretched. Here, in the mingled shadows and white moonlight, it had drawn us together again. *I love this man.*

But I must not. And at that moment, to my alarm, I felt within me a treacherous jab of desire, something I had long since sworn I must *never* feel for Brockley, never again. I was within an inch of walking into his arms and at the same moment, he took half a step towards me.

We must not.

I stepped back. 'Go back to bed,' I said. 'That's an order, Brockley. Did you leave Dale asleep?'

'Yes.'

'If she wakes, she'll wonder where you are. Go back to her. Let her comfort you. I noticed an apothecary's shop here in Kenninghall when we arrived. Tomorrow, if he has the makings, I'll get him to make up a brew to help you sleep. I can give him one of Gladys's recipes. I know it by heart. Brockley, somehow, some way, I will one day have us all peacefully living at Hawkswood together. Even if you do have to spend some time in exile first. Go upstairs, Brockley. Now.'

We set off early the next morning, although we didn't leave Kenninghall quite as soon as we would have liked because first we had to stop at the apothecary's and then, just as we were passing a little shop where bronze and brassware were on view on tables set out in front, a young couple stepped out of it, arm in arm. The girl, who was carrying in her spare hand a basket with bronze dishes in it, glanced up at us and exclaimed: 'Mistress Stannard!'

We pulled up. 'Blanche!' I said, and then looked at the young man and recognized the tow-head, beaky nose, jutting cheekbones and intelligent hazel eyes. It was Gilbert Shore. They beamed at us and I gazed at Blanche in astonishment. Here before me was a girl who was happy and in love and the difference between her and the mousey, gawky Blanche I had met in Agnes Wyse's house was staggering. This girl was graceful and assured and even the hair in front of her linen hood now gleamed golden brown. 'Blanche . . . Shore?' I said.

'Blanche Shore,' said Gilbert proudly. 'And we are buying things for our new home. I have begged a morning off by promising to make up the time by working late for a few days. I've rented a cottage in this street – that one.' He pointed. 'I couldn't take Blanche to the cottage on the estate; I was sharing that with three other young men. Can you spare a little time to take some ale with us, at home? There's a stable at the back, for my cob, but there are empty stalls as well.'

They were longing to entertain, longing to show off their very first home. We could only say yes.

'We heard from Mistress Wyse that you had married,' I said, when we were sipping ale in their tiny but cosy parlour.

'I don't suppose she was happy about it,' said Blanche, without concern. 'I never did understand what she really wanted for me, whether she hoped for a wealthier marriage than this, or no marriage at all so that I could go on being her companion. But either way, I prefer Gilbert!' She gave him a sparkling look and he grinned back.

'I can tell you exactly what she wanted for you,' he said. 'To be the unworldly, admiring little cousin, walking in the shadow of an oh-so elegant and fascinating older woman. You escaped and I hear she's furious. I find it a pleasant thought!'

'You really did dislike her!' I said.

'Dislike her?' Gilbert's Norfolk accent deepened under the influence of emotion. 'I nearly never got born because of her!'

'Er . . .' I said, not understanding.

'I'm twenty-two,' said Gilbert. 'Twenty-four years ago, my father was betrothed to my mother, but still living with his own parents and they were neighbours of Agnes Wyse, on visiting terms. She never took much heed of my future dad then. *Until* he was betrothed, and then sometimes my mother, just a young girl, would join him and her future in-laws when they went visiting. Agnes didn't like that! That woman can't bear to see a man more attracted to another woman than to her. Oh, she couldn't have shown it so openly if her husband had been there, but Robert Wyse was often away and then my lady was free to ogle.'

'You mean she . . .?' said Brockley, looking as though he had just bitten into an unripe lemon.

'Dunno whether it would ever have gone beyond ogling,' said Gilbert. 'But she flattered my dad, who was no more then than a lad of nineteen, and offered him the best of the pasties she made with her own pretty hands – *so important that a young woman should cook well; can you cook, my dear?* That's what she said to my mother. As well as advising her on beauty, the kind of advice that makes it clear to a wench that she ain't beautiful enough as she is, and asking my dad if he was clever about repairing things – a chair of hers needed a new leg and there was a leak in her cottage roof; maybe he could come round some time and see to them.'

'Good grief!' said Dale.

'Oh, I know all about it,' Gilbert said. 'My granddad – my father's father – told me. It was him put a stop to it. Seems my father was fair bemused by it all, and started going to see Agnes on his own and my mother's parents heard about it and came near to breaking the betrothal off. But they had the good sense to tell Granddad, and he said enough was enough and forbade any of his family to go near Mistress Fascinating Wyse. He hurried the marriage on – *and* saw to it that my parents went to live in another village, away from here. But it was a near thing. I came very close to never existing! Think of that, Blanche!'

'I do, and it's a dreadful thought,' said Blanche. 'All the same, she was kind to me in her way. She did take me in when I was orphaned.'

'Just as well,' said Gilbert. 'The likes of Mistress Wyse need *something* on the credit side of the Recording Angel's ledger! You're too soft-hearted, my love. That one's the sort as has to be queen of the hive, and women like that are dangerous.'

But as he looked at her, he was smiling, and she smiled back. They would be all right, I thought. Blanche had got away and Agnes had never had a hope of snaring Gilbert. She'd nearly kept his parents from marrying, and he clearly didn't mean to forgive that.

Blanche said, with laughter in her voice: 'Her son, Roland,

he made her cross once by speaking up for us. During the last visit he made, just after she'd found out that Gilbert was courting me. He met us out walking and talked to us and got on well with you, didn't he, Gilbert? Then, when he came back to the house he said to Cousin Agnes, how nice it was that I had a suitor, and that he approved of Gilbert. Oh, she didn't like that. Said she had other plans for me and would he please mind his own business. I wasn't in the room, but I overheard.'

'He seemed a curious character,' Gilbert remarked. 'I can't quite say why, but he did. But generous. Before he left, he quietly slipped Blanche and me a couple of gifts. He gave Blanche a pretty necklace of freshwater pearls, and he gave me a very handsome dagger. I'd never owned one before. That's it, up on the wall above the hearth.'

We all turned to look, and my stomach jolted, for I immediately recognized the silver hilt with its pattern of curving, interlinked lines. I had seen it last in unforgettable circumstances.

Jutting out of Jane Cobbold's heart.

'It isn't that valuable, I understand,' Gilbert said. 'The hilt's not solid silver or anything like that. But it's a handsome bit of work and daggers like that are popular among young men in London and at court, so Roland said. He said he'd bought several of them because they made such acceptable gifts – for Christmas and so forth.'

'It doesn't prove anything,' I said to Brockley and Dale, as we made our way out of Kenninghall village. 'Those daggers are common in London. Roland Wyse owned several, and such a dagger was used to kill Jane Cobbold, but that isn't evidence that it belonged to him.'

'No,' Brockley said thoughtfully. 'No, it proves nothing. But it's another pointer. Not a strong one, but . . .'

'It's a straw in the wind,' Dale said emphatically. 'It was him. I know it was! And somehow or other it's got to be proved.' Her protuberant blue gaze was turned towards me. 'You'll find a way, won't you? You'll show the world the crime was done by Wyse, and set my Roger free?'

'I'll try,' I said. 'I'll try.'
I wished I knew how.

'I really think,' I said fastidiously, as we stood holding our
saddlebags and letting our shoulder satchels slide to the floor,
'that it would be doing this place a great favour if the Spinners
took it over! Whatever one can say about their honesty, they
do know how to run an inn. They have *some* standards.'

I stared across the floor of the taproom in The Boar. As
ever, there were mouse droppings in the straw and if the
cobbles had ever been swept, let alone washed, it probably
wasn't since the previous century. 'I'm sorry to be leaving
you in such a place, but I can get to Whitehall from here quite
quickly. Brockley, will you see if there are rooms free? And
what sort of supper we can have?'

Brockley went to find the landlord. Dale and I waited. The
taproom was gloomy, with no lights as yet though the day
was dull and evening was near. The room was crowded with
its usual rough and ready clientele. The smell of unwashed
humanity mingled with the reek of ale and old straw. I noticed,
though, that the inn did have some customers of a better type,
for when a serving boy with a tray of wine opened the door
to the parlour that we had once used, I glimpsed a card table,
lit by two branched candlesticks, and card-playing gentlemen
with smart ruffs and slashed doublets, striped hose and polished
riding boots.

Brockley came back, bringing tankards of ale and the news
that yes, there were rooms for us. 'And there's pigs' trotters
or beef sausages for supper along with pottage, and some sort
of fruit pudding to follow. It'll do. I said don't skimp the
portions; we've been travelling and we're hungry.'

We drank our ale, went to look at our rooms and deposit
our bags in them, and then went down again to find a table.
The parlour now occupied by the card players was the only
private room there was and clearly we couldn't use it this time.
Our food arrived and with it, a flagon of wine. I poured for
us all and sipped my own, which turned out to be horrible.

At the same moment, I noticed that another tray of wine
had been taken into the parlour, and as I once more caught a

glimpse of the fashionably clad occupants, I wondered – and doubted – if they were being fobbed off with the same sour vintage. Opposite me, Brockley had sipped at his own glass and was making a face. 'Madam, this liquid is . . . is . . .'

'Cat's piss,' said Dale inelegantly, having tried it in her turn and setting down her glass with a bang.

'Brockley,' I said, 'can you ask for a flagon of the same wine that has just gone into the parlour? If the gentlemen in there are meekly drinking this, I am Philip of Spain.'

Brockley obliged. After a short altercation with the landlord, he came back with a fresh flagon and glasses, and a sulky potboy who removed the first consignment. 'That's better,' I said to the Brockleys, after trying out the fresh offering, which was a considerable improvement. 'Now, we have things to talk about.'

Shortly before reaching The Boar we had stopped at the vicarage attached to a big church and asked the incumbent if he knew where the court was. He did. The queen was back from her summer progress and the court was at Whitehall. 'Tomorrow I make straight for Whitehall,' I said, 'and I must see Walsingham and ask to examine that cipher letter for myself. I shall want you to stay here and be as unobtrusive as you can.'

Privately, I had little hope that examining the cipher would bear any fruit; I was certain at heart that Walsingham had had it checked. But I must know for sure whether Wyse had been falsifying the evidence. It didn't seem probable that he could have done so undetected but no path, however faint, must be ignored. Not with Brockley's life at stake.

I would also tell Poole's story to Walsingham. It *did* link Jane, Jarvis and Wyse, however tenuously. I must plead Brockley's case somehow. I must also try to learn from Walsingham what friends, what interests, Wyse had. My fear for Brockley was steadily growing, and more swiftly than ever since he had talked of killing himself if he were taken back to Lewes. Nor could I hope that he and Dale would be happy in exile. Somehow or other, his name had to be cleared.

We had finished eating and were sipping the last of the wine, when the door of the parlour opened and one of the card players

came out. He looked round, and then made straight for us. In
the dull light, he was beside our table before we recognized
him. Then Dale said: 'Master Ryder!' and Brockley stood up,
and so did I, reaching out a hand to the newcomer.

'Whatever brings you here? But I'm very glad to see you,'
I said.

'And I,' said Brockley with sincerity. 'How are you, old
friend?'

It was John Ryder, solid, reliable, fatherly Ryder whose stiff
hair and beard seemed to have gone a little greyer than they
were when I had last seen him, but who nevertheless looked
as fit as he always did. He was smiling broadly.

'I thought twice that I'd caught sight of you when the door
was opened by serving men. The second time, I was certain.
Well, the others are playing a game that doesn't need all of
us to play, so I stepped out to find you. What brings me here,
you say. What brings *you*?'

Brockley had looked round, found a spare stool and was
bringing it over. 'Sit down, do,' I said. 'We'll all exchange
our news.'

SIXTEEN
Wild and Impossible

Ryder was a reassuring sight. There was something about him that seemed to make even the most perilous situations feel less alarming. 'You first,' I said to him. 'It's a surprise to find you playing cards in this tiresome hostelry. Where have you come from, today?'

'Hertfordshire. We meant to go on to The George at Southwark and be comfortable, but the horses were tired,' Ryder said. 'We're a squad sent out by Francis Walsingham . . .'

'You're working for Walsingham, now?' I enquired, surprised.

'I get seconded from time to time, as you know,' said Ryder with a grin. 'I am leading the present expedition – Captain John Ryder, in charge of ten men, including a second-in-command that I think you know – Roland Wyse.'

'Wyse is here?' I asked.

'Oh, yes, indeed. Dealing the cards when I left the parlour. He's a good card player,' said Ryder carefully. 'Good at his work altogether.'

I sensed that Ryder, too, had reservations about Roland Wyse. 'I interrupted you,' I said to him. 'What took you to Hertfordshire?'

'Master Walsingham's favourite quarry. Catholic priests bent on leading English Protestants astray,' Ryder said. 'One of our number is a former strolling player. He was imprisoned for debt, but – did you know this? – Walsingham visits prisons now and then, looking for useful men. Ones who will gladly take risks, just to get out of gaol. Walsingham does get them out, on condition that they work for him. He has found himself some valuable agents, believe me. This man is an example. He can act any part. We had suspicions of goings-on in this big house in Hertfordshire – some of the servants seemed to have stopped attending their parish church regularly – so we sent our actor ahead to present himself as a man searching for a smallholding to buy, and also as an unhappy Catholic, anxious to choose somewhere where he might hear Mass regularly. He wormed his way into that house and he found that it was a regular hiding place for the priests who are being slipped into the country – and yes, three of the servants have apparently been converted. At least, they're attending the secret Masses held there. The owner provides the priests with a list of other houses where they'll be welcome and where they may be able to raise money for the cause of Mary Stuart.'

I sighed. The tale was all too familiar. It was the sort of thing Matthew was involved in, all too often. There never had been any hope of lasting peace and happiness with Matthew.

A serving boy came over to ask if we needed more wine. Ryder ordered it, saying that he would pay, though Brockley interposed with: 'Make sure it's the same as what's in here,' and handed the lad the flagon we had almost, but not quite, emptied between us.

'Our expedition was a success,' Ryder said as the boy hurried away. 'But it was unpleasant. We crept into the house after dark and caught the household at Mass, behind a closed door, and before we burst in on them, we listened outside. We heard the priest praying, loudly and ardently, for the accession of Queen Mary and for the return of the true faith for England. Then we flung the door open and caught them, with candles and incense and all, two French priests and all the servants. There were hysterics from the women, and children screaming. We sent the priests, the master of the house and his steward off to London as prisoners with five men to guard them – I have ten men now but I set out with fifteen. We let the wife and the other servants off with a caution and left them to cope with the children and each other. The wife was distraught, throwing herself about, weeping herself nearly into an apoplexy . . . No, it *wasn't* pleasant.'

'I'm sure it wasn't,' I said, visualizing it. The boy came back with the wine and Ryder paid him.

'I did some questioning,' said Ryder, 'and I had the

impression that despite the enthusiastic prayers we overheard that priest declaiming, the family actually had little idea of what he was really after. I think the household just consists of devout Catholics – which isn't a crime unless they refuse to put in their obligatory appearances at the local Anglican church – and I think they imagine that the priests they harbour are simply in England to provide Catholic rites for those in England who want them. I'm fairly sure they don't fully understand that the conversion of their servants is now a crime, nor do they seem to realize that the houses they direct their secret guests to are places where money may be raised for Mary Stuart. They know about the money but they think it's just for food and clothing for the priests.'

'In spite of the prayers?' said Brockley, surprised.

'Yes,' said Ryder regretfully. 'In spite of the prayers. Those are just words, you see. Wishes. Not . . . practical deeds.'

'You mean that quite harmless people are being caught up in something they don't understand?' said Brockley.

'Yes. Just that. One of the children upset me quite a lot,' Ryder confessed. 'The eldest boy – he's about ten, I think. You see, our spy in the enemy stronghold, so to speak, had told us that yes, there were priests in the house, and that they would be there for some days, and were saying Mass every night, after dark. He also told us there were three dogs, two big lurchers and a small mongrel. They were let loose at night. To get into the house unheard, we had to deal with the dogs. We provided our strolling player with poisoned meat and on the chosen evening, he fed it to the dogs.'

'That's horrid!' said Dale.

'Yes, I know.' Ryder shook a regretful head. 'Roland Wyse supplied the venom. He offered to bring it in case we had to deal with guard dogs. He knew where to get some, he told us, and he said he'd mixed it with something that would make the animals drowsy so that they'd die without making much noise. There would be noise, otherwise. I had the feeling he was speaking from experience but I decided not to ask *what* experience.'

I thought grimly that I could probably enlighten him, but held my peace.

'None of us liked doing it to the poor brutes,' Ryder said, 'and that young boy apparently was very fond of the mongrel; it was his special pet. To us, of course, it was as much of a menace as the lurchers. It had a fine set of teeth and a very loud yap. But it broke the boy's heart. I think he minded the dog's death more than he minded his father's arrest!'

'That's so sad,' said Dale.

'The boy's grief for the dog, or his lack of it for his father?' Ryder asked dryly.

'Both,' said Dale.

I changed the subject. 'You're bound for Whitehall tomorrow, are you?' I enquired. If so, Brockley would be pleased, for I could travel with an escort after all.

'No.' Ryder shook his head. 'No, we're going straight on to Dover.'

'Dover?' Brockley asked sharply.

'That illegal loom,' said Ryder. You know – the one the cipher letter mentioned. Oh, yes, I know about it; Walsingham told me. He wouldn't normally trouble himself over anything so trivial as an unlicensed worsted loom but there have been vague rumours about that workshop for some time and then, recently, some anonymous information was laid that was a lot more specific. It was already known that it's run by a man called Julius Ballanger, who's a lifelong resident of Dover and has a reputation as being willing to turn a dishonest penny. He has been suspected of smuggling dutiable goods into the country. He is also known to have Catholic leanings. Our nameless informant suggested that the Ballanger weaving shed is another safe house for proselytizing foreign priests. We start for Dover in the morning, to find out. And now, Mistress Stannard, what of your story?'

Brockley looked at me uncertainly, wondering what I would say. I was wondering, too. It didn't seem right to undermine Ryder's relationship with Wyse when the two of them were working together; nor did I want Ryder to know of Heron's new warrant. I decided on discretion.

'Forgive me,' I said, 'but the errand we've been on is very confidential. Without permission from Cecil or Walsingham, even discussing it with you might not . . . well . . .'

'Is it something to do with Brockley here?' Ryder asked. 'Oh. yes, I know about the accusation against him, and that he's out on bail. That's so, is it not, Brockley? I'm glad. I find it difficult to believe in your guilt, my friend. I take it that you are innocent.'

'Entirely,' said Brockley. 'And we have other suspicions – but as Mistress Stannard says, we ought to be discreet.'

'I won't ask awkward questions. I wish you a happy outcome,' Ryder said formally.

'Thank you,' I said. And was glad that I hadn't begun to talk about our suspicions of Roland Wyse, because the parlour door had opened again and Wyse himself had come through it, and was making straight towards us.

He arrived at our table, smiling broadly. 'May I join you? What a surprise to see you here, Mrs Stannard. How does that come about?' He sat down without waiting for my permission. Ryder looked at him expressionlessly and said: 'I understand that Mistress Stannard is engaged on a private errand and we should not, therefore, ask her to discuss it.'

'Really? Then we won't. What are you all drinking?' He surveyed the table, picked up the flagon and sniffed at it, and nodded approval. 'An agreeable wine. Shall we have some more? And what about some hazelnut comfits and dried fruits? Where is that boy?' He craned his neck to see behind him, caught the serving lad's eye and beckoned imperiously.

The daylight was fading fast now and the wispy landlady was at last lighting the candles in the wall sconces. However, the uncertain light was still good enough to show me that Wyse's lordly summons had made the boy's face turn sullen. Wyse really did have a knack of annoying people, though he would probably retrieve himself by giving the lad a good tip. He was an odd mixture of a man, I thought, and I looked at his stone-hued eyes and thought about his knowledge of how to poison dogs. My suspicions were hardening with each passing moment.

The boy arrived at our table and that was when the wild idea came to me. It came all in a moment, complete except for one thing, which was the sheer difficulty of putting it into practice. I couldn't see how to manage it.

Ryder, meanwhile, was quietly taking the initiative away from Wyse by saying: 'Let me be the hospitable one, Roland. I'm your superior officer, after all,' and then turning to the boy to command another flagon and the fruit and comfits that Wyse had suggested.

As the boy turned away I put a hand on his sleeve, and heard myself say: 'Oh, and one more thing. I wish a flagon of this most excellent wine to be put in my room, with a glass, of course, in case I fancy a drink in the night. It's the first room on the left, upstairs – the room allocated to Mistress Stannard. That's who I am. Please see to it straightaway; I can see that the inn is busy and it could easily be forgotten. I'll pay you now.'

I pulled out my purse and shot warning glances at Brockley and Dale, who were staring at me in astonishment. I wasn't in the habit of wanting wine by my bedside. They met my eyes and wiped the amazement from their faces. Whatever I was up to, I could trust them not to interfere.

I had taken the first step towards setting my trap, though how on earth I would achieve the subsequent steps remained beyond me. They seemed impossible. If only I could imagine a way . . .

SEVENTEEN
A Trap for a Dangerous Mouse

J ust once in a while, providence is kind. Perverse luck afflicts us much more often, but every now and then, fate relents, and the one thing that is needed, is granted at precisely the right moment. Or to put it another way, very occasionally the enemy makes a mistake and, as it were, bows politely and hands one a sharp and shining sword.

'Captain Ryder,' said Wyse, 'I am well acquainted with Mrs Stannard, and there is a private matter which we should talk about – nothing to do with any errand she is carrying out at this moment; something between ourselves. This chance meeting has given us an opportunity. Have I your permission to ask our companions to take their card game upstairs? They can go on gambling in the big bedchamber we're all sharing. Then, if the landlord allows and the lady is agreeable, she and I can have the parlour for a quiet talk.'

Ryder looked at me. 'I'm agreeable,' I said.

He got to his feet. 'Very well. I'll arrange it.'

Dale said softly: 'Ma'am, shall I come with you? For propriety?'

'Thank you, Dale, but no. There won't be any need for that.'

There certainly wouldn't. Here was my chance. My plan had begun to clarify and I would not need or want either Dale or Brockley to be present.

The card players grumblingly abandoned the parlour and went upstairs while the wispy landlady went in to clear up their leftovers. Then Wyse nodded to me and the two of us, carrying our wine glasses and, in his case, some raisins and comfits that he had tossed into a spare dish, betook ourselves into the vacated parlour. He shut the door after us. The table and its benches had been left tidy but Wyse motioned me towards two cushioned settles that stood against the walls and met at a corner, so that they were at right angles to each other. I took one and Wyse the other, and we faced each other across the corner. I sipped my wine and left it to Wyse to speak first. I had already guessed what he was likely to say and he duly said it.

'Tell me, Mrs Stannard, have you given any more thought to the proposal I made to you back at Hawkswood, not so long ago?'

I looked down at my feet, as if shy or embarrassed, and let the silence grow, until at length, he tried again. 'You don't reply. But surely you have thought about the matter, at least sometimes.'

'Yes, of course. But it's all very difficult.'

'Difficult?'

'There is so much to consider; the feelings of my household to think of as well as myself; my own reluctance to enter into another marriage in any case . . . and . . . well . . .'

I let him think that I was stammering and tiptoeing round things I didn't want to say outright. In the course of this second silence, a mouse ran across the floor and paused under the table, nosing at a crack between the cobbles. Wyse threw a couple of raisins to it. It started back in alarm as they pattered down, and then, scenting food, darted forward to investigate the offering. We watched as it sat up, like a squirrel, with a raisin between its front paws and nibbled at the fruit.

'Poor little things. They have to live, just like us,' Wyse said.

'And perhaps,' I said, 'they do less harm than some human beings do. Maybe they've a better right to their lives!' I helped myself to some raisins and ate them and then took a deep breath. This was the moment for the next step in my wild scheme. 'But you were very sad, were you not,' I said, 'when, whatever he had done, your brother Thomas Howard of Norfolk was executed? I saw that for myself, though at the time I didn't know that you were brothers.'

Wyse stared at me, with astonishment and something so near to outrage that my courage faltered and I retreated into asking a harmless question. 'Who was the friend who witnessed the execution with you?'

'What is all this?' Wyse demanded. 'We were talking of marriage.'

I must go on. I was launched now, like a small ship on a perilous sea. If it really was perilous. If Wyse had indeed been the man who climbed into the Brockleys' bedroom, then he was certainly dangerous, but if he wasn't then I was wasting my time.

'We were also talking about mice,' I said, 'and whether they had more right to live than some human beings. That made me think of executions, and then the Duke of Norfolk came to my mind. Who *was* your friend, though?' Having asked the question, it seemed natural to seek an answer. 'I wondered at the time. He didn't belong to the court, I think.'

'Why are you interested? He was just a friend, from France. Gilles Lebrun. He's an agent for a French merchant who sells wine to England. I've known him for years, on and off, because he's often in France, of course. How did you find out that Norfolk was my brother?'

'I've visited your mother in Kenninghall and talked to her. She told me.'

'Whatever did you do that for?'

'I wanted to know more about you. It came as a surprise to find that Thomas Howard was your brother – well, half-brother.'

'I daresay! He was a dear fellow and yes, I grieved for him most bitterly. He was good to me, a true brother, however unwise he was in other respects. But *why* did you want to know more about me? Oh!' His eyes widened, as an answer occurred to him. 'So that you could better judge what kind of husband I would make?'

'Partly,' I said, and once more stared at my feet, wondering how to phrase my next words and remembering that Ryder thought Wyse had previous experience in the matter of poisoning watchdogs. That was a new piece of evidence, another pointer. I did not think I was wasting my time. In which case, I was inviting danger.

Presently, he said with a touch of impatience: 'You seem unwilling to give me a plain answer – to any question. But surely there are answers. My dear, I wouldn't, of course, do such a thing without an invitation, but if I were to come to your room tonight, you would learn how capable and how loving a husband I would make you. Would you consider inviting me?'

I raised my eyes to study his face. Candlelight is kind to the human countenance. It had softened Wyse's eyes, blurred the pugnacity of his jaw, and he had dropped his voice to a gentle, almost purring note. The fingers round the stem of his wine glass were shapely and masculine.

How nature can betray us. For a long time, in fact since I first knew that I was carrying the child who had been christened Harry and was at Hawkswood, being cared for by Sybil and Tessie, desire had not troubled me. But I was not yet forty and I had for years been used to the comfort of regular love-making. Of late, I had felt uneasy stirrings. That moment with Brockley in the courtyard had been one such. Now, as I looked at Wyse's fingers, I experienced another.

My face felt hot. To cover my confusion, I seized a hazelnut comfit. I was horrified by my own treacherous body, appalled to find myself so vulnerable. How could I possibly feel the slightest desire for this man? I didn't like him, wouldn't like him or want him for a husband even if I were not so suspicious of him. And I was here in this room with him only because of those suspicions which I must either confirm or dissipate, for I owed that to Brockley and Dale. If this man were innocent then I must seek further, to discover who was guilty. If he was not, then I must see that justice was done. And I had no other business with him.

'Tell me, Master Wyse,' I said at last, 'was it you who came *uninvited* into the Brockleys' bedchamber at Hawkswood one midnight, with a knife?'

Wyse stared at me and then burst out laughing.

'You think that?' he said, with scorn, and took the last of the comfits. 'Mrs Stannard, how could you? How foolish women can be! Why should I do such a thing?'

The scorn dispelled my carnal urges most effectively. It also drove me forward, a wind in the sail of my fragile ship. It reminded me so strongly of something that Wyse had said when he came to Hawkswood to propose.

As a woman, you naturally think with your heart rather than your head. As I said, women's minds are different from men's. It is wisest for ladies to let the menfolk take the hard decisions.

Only a foolish person would say to his face the things I now intended to say, but he clearly considered all women foolish. He even imagined that Elizabeth was ruled by her council instead of the other way round.

'I have been probing into the deaths of Mistress Cobbold and John Jarvis,' I said. 'Did you know that on the day that Jane Cobbold died, she may have overheard you talking with Jarvis when you visited him in his cottage? She was seen there, pausing outside, near a window. It links the three of you. Sir Edward Heron wasn't impressed when he was told but I do intend to tell Francis Walsingham. He may think differently. I am on my way there now. Tell me, how can I possibly even think about your proposal, while you are under such a cloud?'

He was staring at me again. And no longer laughing.

'I told you when you visited me at Hawkswood that I did not intend to remarry,' I said. 'I don't think I will ever change my mind, but as things are, I can't even consider such a thing. I have not confided my misgivings to anyone else, by the way, not even to my closest associates. That would be quite improper.' *Will he really swallow such blatant bait? Well, I can but try.* 'That,' I said virtuously, 'would be to slander you and that I will not do. For the misgivings themselves, I pray you will forgive me. But I must clear my mind.'

'There's nothing to forgive,' Wyse said. 'I am armoured in my innocence. But I am sorry that you think so ill of me, when I admire you so much. You have hurt my feelings, Mrs Stannard.' He stood up, looking affronted, and abandoning his wine glass. 'I think I must bid you goodnight. Be thankful you are but a woman. A man, I would call out for the kind of things you have . . . hinted. Goodnight. I shall go upstairs now, and salve my wounds in private.'

He went out, shutting the door after him almost with a slam. I let him have a minute or so, during which I hoped he would indeed go upstairs. We had finished the comfits and raisins and he had left their little dish lying on the settle. Thoughtfully, I picked it up and slid it into the hidden pouch inside my divided skirt. Then I went out of the parlour in my turn. There was no sign of Wyse but Dale, Brockley and Ryder were waiting for me, still seated round their table. I joined them.

'Did Wyse go upstairs?' I asked. 'He said he intended to.'

'Yes, a minute or two ago.' Dale eyed me with open interest, obviously longing to know what had passed between us in the parlour.

'I think it's too early to retire,' I said. 'Master Ryder, tell us more about this errand you have in Dover.'

When finally we went upstairs, Dale came into my room with me as usual, to help me undress. The wine I had ordered was there, on the table by the curtained bed: flagon and glass. She gazed at it in puzzlement and a degree of disapproval, but I paid no attention. Instead, I said: 'Dale, it may be inconvenient, but I wish to sleep in your room tonight. None of us should sleep in here. Is there a truckle bed I can use?'

'There is but Roger will insist on sleeping there, for sure, if you have to be with us. He'd say you and I must share the bed,' Dale said. 'But ma'am, what is this all about? What did that man say to you?'

'He renewed his proposal, of course,' I said. 'Without success, naturally. But I took the chance of making myself into the cheese in a mousetrap.'

I was running an eye over the room. At the foot of one wall, there was a hole – a mousehole, surely. I took the comfit bowl out of my pouch, placed it carefully beside the hole, and then unstoppered the wine flask. While Dale watched me in amazement, I poured a little into the bowl. 'Now,' I said, 'we'll join Brockley next door and I'll explain.'

Brockley, after hearing what I had to say, shook a disbelieving head. In fact, he was near to laughing at me. 'Madam, it can't work! Even if he did think of . . . of doctoring your wine – or creeping into your room in the night to harm you – he won't do it. He'll see the trap for what it is. He can't be that simple-minded.'

'He thinks that I am. He believes that all females are simple-minded! He virtually said so, the time he came to offer me marriage. He offered to take over all my burdens. He said the female mind isn't suited to running estates or taking decisions, or words to that effect. I told him tonight that I hadn't confided my misgivings to anyone, even those closest to me.'

Brockley actually clawed at his hair, in a mixture of horror and something like admiration. 'You used the enemy's weakness against him! Very good soldierly tactics. But if he *is* guilty . . . madam, how could you put yourself in such danger?'

'If this dangerous mouse takes the cheese,' I said, 'I really will have some evidence to put before Walsingham. There's what Ryder said about Wyse knowing how best to poison the dogs, as well. It will all add up to something stronger than just the fact that Wyse owned several daggers like the one that killed Jane Cobbold, stronger than the little fact that on the day she died, Jane Cobbold *may* have overheard him and Jarvis talking, though for all anyone knows, they were discussing the weather.'

'I'll sleep in your room tonight,' said Brockley. 'And if he comes creeping in . . .'

'You'll sleep in here. No one occupies my room tonight,' I said.

Brockley frowned but met my eyes and gave in. 'All right,' he said. 'But before we settle down, I'll slip in there and leave a marker to tell us tomorrow if anyone did intrude. I'll put a couple of my hairs in the crack of the door as I close it. If anyone opens the door in the night, the hairs will fall. Then we'll know. I'll use the truckle bed tonight.'

'Wake up! Wake up, Fran; madam.' We came awake, to find Brockley, already dressed, leaning over us and gently agitating the bed. We sat up. It was after dawn, though still early, by the sound of the birdsong outside and the quality of the light. 'What is it?' I asked.

'I've been up since cockcrow,' said Brockley. 'I slept well, thanks to Gladys' recipe, but I made sure not to sleep for too long. Ryder and Wyse and the rest of them have risen and gone. That poor downtrodden landlady was up as well, making breakfast for them. I crept down the back stairs and heard her grumbling to herself. She and her husband sleep in a room at the foot of those stairs and he was still snoring; I heard him. Selfish lout,' said Brockley censoriously. 'It's time we had a look at your room, madam. I'll wait in the passage until you're dressed.'

Dale and I lost no time in getting some clothes on. In a very few minutes, we joined Brockley and approached the door of my unused bedroom. It was dark in the passage, which had no window except a small and dirty one at the far end but Brockley had sensibly brought a candle. He held it close to my bedroom door, just under the latch.

'The hairs I left are still here,' he said, beckoning me to look. 'No one went in here after you came upstairs last night. Well. Let's go inside.'

We did so. I had left the windows unshuttered and the room was full of the early sunlight. It was also full of a disagreeable smell, though not an unfamiliar one. Most householders are bothered by mice and most set traps or else keep cats to hunt them. Trapped mice lie where they have died and injured mice sometimes escape from cats' claws and die inside their holes. One knows about it soon enough for the decaying body will start to stink within hours. My room reeked of dead mouse. I went to the hole where I had left the little bowl of wine.

It was empty, and there were two dead mice beside it. They had died unpleasantly, in puddles of their own faeces.

'Oh, ma'am!' said Dale, holding her nose.

'So it worked!' Brockley was awed. 'No one entered this room after I placed those hairs but he had time before you ever came upstairs, and he put something in your wine, just as you hoped he would. He'd assume it would be put down to food poisoning, I fancy. In a place like this, who'd be surprised!'

'Yes. He did what I thought most likely,' I said. 'As I said last night, I purposely annoyed him in the hope that he'd walk out, leaving me in the parlour and then I kept us downstairs until he'd had his chance to get at my wine – which I'd ordered in his hearing. When I gave that order, Dale, I was afraid you were going to exclaim in surprise!'

'I couldn't understand it,' Dale said. 'You'd never done such a thing before. But madam, what made you think of it? What gave you the idea?'

'It was when Ryder said that Wyse provided poison for use on guard dogs,' I said. 'Apparently, he told Ryder that he'd mixed it with something to make the dogs sleepy as well, to keep them from making much noise. It was obvious that Ryder thought that Wyse had poisoned guard dogs in the past and perhaps they did make a noise, so this time he added something that would prevent that. Well, poor Sandy cried. Maybe *that* was Wyse's piece of past experience. I kept thinking about it. Then I remembered that Sandy once had his nose in Simon's ale tankard. If dogs liked strong drink, I thought perhaps mice might. And if so, maybe it would be a way of finding out if anything had been done to my wine. It was chancy. The mice might have crept off and died out of sight under the floorboards but they didn't. We have our evidence for Walsingham.'

Brockley had unstoppered the wine flask and was sniffing at it. 'There's a queer smell,' he said. 'Faint, but it's there.'

'We've got to get rid of it,' I said. 'What's below the window?'

Brockley, flask in hand, went to look. 'A dusty-looking bush,' he said. He wrestled for a moment with a stiff latch, got the casement open and emptied the flask out of it. 'I don't know whether it can harm the bush but the poor thing looks half-dead already.' He turned back into the room. 'The flask will need a good wash.'

'Better break it,' I said. 'I'll apologize for the accident and pay for it. Lucky it's glass and not metal or leather; it'll be easier to destroy. And then, Brockley, I must leave you and Dale here, while I make haste to Whitehall. And Walsingham.'

EIGHTEEN
Beyond Reason

I was recognized this time and admitted to Walsingham's presence with little delay. As usual, he was busy at a cluttered desk while his clerks were also busy, three of them in an outer office and Humphrey Johnson, their senior, in the same room as his master. Walsingham wasn't in a good temper, and his face looked drawn. I suspected a return of the mysterious stomach trouble from which he so often suffered. I wondered if perhaps his ailment was the reason why he so often seemed so stark and joyless and wished I could ask Gladys to advise him.

Still, he was gracious enough to grant me an interview though his response to what I had to say was disappointing.

'Granted, it sounds as if there are some bits and pieces of evidence that point at Roland Wyse, but what do they really amount to? You say you have learned from his mother that she once had an affair with the Earl of Surrey, the father of the late Duke of Norfolk, and that Wyse and the duke were brothers. And Wyse wept when at his brother's execution. I urged that on, which explains why he probably detests me, but where does that get us? Then there is what you say about Jane Cobbold . . .'

'On the day of her death, she may have overheard him talking to Jarvis. It brings the three of them together,' I said, interrupting him and repeating what I had already told him. And others. *Ad nauseam*, I thought irritably.

'He has always said that when he left Cobbold Hall, he paused to speak to Jarvis,' Walsingham said ruthlessly. 'Then someone broke into your house at Hawkswood just after one of your dogs was poisoned. *If* it was deliberately poisoned and its death wasn't an accident. You say the other dog wasn't poisoned but didn't bark at the intruder and that this proves it was someone it knew. Well, possibly, but that someone wasn't necessarily Roland Wyse! There must be a fair number of people that the dog would recognize. That doesn't prove that it was he who fed venom to *your* dog! Or that anyone did. Yes, dogs were poisoned in Hertfordshire, when a squad including Wyse went there in search of priests, and it seems that he supplied the poison. But quite a few of my staff know how to obtain venom for dealing with guard dogs. Some of them have actually had to do it and therefore could be said to have experience in that unpleasant task. It's evidence of nothing at all.'

'Something killed those mice!' I protested.

Walsingham uttered a dismissive snort and Humphrey Johnson remarked: 'Mice aren't very big. Was the wine strong?'

'Yes, fairly. It was a good wine. But . . .'

'Perhaps the mice just died of poisoning by alcohol.'

'I think Humphrey feels as I do,' said Walsingham. 'Wyse isn't popular but that doesn't make him a murder suspect.' The secretary cleared his throat. 'Yes, Humphrey?' said Walsingham.

'I can't see him as a criminal,' Humphrey said. 'Just an ambitious fellow who hasn't got quite what's needed to achieve his ambitions. He tries to buy favour, you know. Presents for all at Christmas and he tips too well in taverns. But it doesn't really work. *He* works, I grant you – wants to get on. But he panics if things go wrong. Remember, sir, when he mislaid the report on that Hertfordshire house? He ran about like a beheaded hen until he found it. He was *sweating* in case he lost his job, but all he'd done was put the thing in the wrong file.' I remembered that according to Christina Ferris, her father had said that Wyse was panicky because he had had difficulty in tracking Edward Heron down. 'I don't like him,' said Johnson. 'But as a cunning criminal – no, I don't think so.'

Brockley had said he looked like an assassin. Maybe he hadn't quite got what was needed to be an efficient assassin, I thought. I did not however repeat Brockley's comment. It wasn't evidence.

'I take your point, Humphrey,' Walsingham was saying.

'Look, Mistress Stannard, nothing you have told me adds up to anything definite. I have great respect for you but I do find this attempt to point a finger at one of my staff a little annoying, even when the man concerned is not my favourite personality. Well, I am no favourite myself with quite a number of people. Wyse does in fact have much ability and time may mature him out of his faults. Now, if you'll excuse me, I have much work on hand. There have been a number of reports of Catholic sedition, in widely scattered places. If I had my way, I would simply declare Catholicism itself illegal. I and my family were in Paris during the Massacre of St Bartholomew's Eve and we feared for our lives. But the queen will not have it. I am forced to use the new legislation against proselytizing as my best weapon. I need to have these reports followed up and . . .'

'Please,' I said, 'would you tell me just one thing. When that cipher letter, the one found on Jarvis, was decoded by Wyse, did anyone check his work afterwards? He gave you the key.'

'Of course it was checked, and by me! Once in a while I like to carry out such tasks in person, and decoding that cipher was good mental exercise. The decoding that Wyse did was correct in every respect.'

'Do you still have the original?'

'Yes, I took charge of it when he brought it back to me along with the clear version.' He pulled out a drawer from his desk and took a folded document from it. 'Here it is.' He handed it to me. 'Do I read you aright?' he asked. 'You want to check the decoding yourself?'

'Yes, if I may. I can sit in the other room with the clerks so as not to disturb you. It may be a slow business – it's a complex key.'

'Yes, that's what foxed my other clerks. I tried to speed matters up by telling them to make copies so that all three of them could work on it at once. They did so but none of them broke the code. Very well, you may sit in the outer office and test Wyse's work and mine, but you'll be wasting your time. You'll find— Yes, all right, come in, what is it?'

A knock on the door to the clerks' room had interrupted us. The clerk who now entered in response to Walsingham's irritable summons was a gangling young man with intelligent dark eyes and longish dark hair that flopped into them. I liked the look of him, but Walsingham glared at him.

'I didn't wish to be disturbed and when, Master Wentworth, are you going to the barber to get your hair cut? Or do you propose to start curling it with tongs? Now, what is it you want?'

'A report from France has just come in, sir; we can expect a new wave of priests from the Continent at any moment, it seems. I felt you should see it at once.' Young Master Wentworth, apparently unperturbed by Walsingham's tone, came up to the desk and placed some papers in front of his master. His glance lighted on the letter in my hand.

'Is that another enciphered message that will need decoding, sir? Master Wyse isn't here but I'll gladly tackle it, and so will the others, and perhaps we'll have more success this time. We couldn't break the Jarvis code but I think we learned a good deal, trying.'

'That *is* the Jarvis code,' said Walsingham. 'It's the original. Mistress Stannard wishes to examine it for herself.'

Master Wentworth, interested, gave the letter a closer glance and then stiffened. 'But, sir, it isn't.'

Walsingham and I both stared at him and at his desk, Humphrey, who had resumed his work, paused, quill in hand. 'What do you mean?' Walsingham demanded.

'I made the copies of the original for us clerks to work with, sir. I did all three of them. I worked from the original, of course, but then gave it back to you, and you kept it, if you remember, and passed it to Roland Wyse to tackle, when he returned. But I recall it very clearly. I know what the first few letters were and these are different. May I?'

He held out a hand and I gave him the letter. He felt it with his fingertips and studied the text minutely. 'The paper is the same texture, and the hand that wrote this is the same, or so I think, but the letters aren't. The first ones are certainly different, and there's this paragraph halfway down, where I know there was an amusing sequence of letters in the first line . . . a trifle rude, in fact . . . just a minute. I still have the copy that I used when I tried to decode it. May I fetch it?'

Walsingham's expression was alert. 'I think you'd better.'

Master Wentworth departed, his long legs crossing to the door in a couple of strides. He reappeared almost at once, paper in hand. 'Here's my copy. You can see for yourself.'

The paper he had brought was creased from folding, but he put it on the desk and smoothed it with a firm hand. He put the so-called original beside it. Walsingham and I almost bumped heads as we leant to compare them.

Master Wentworth was right. The texts were not the same. In fact, the copy that the clerks had tried to interpret was shorter by four lines.

I said, 'But . . .' And stopped.

'I gave the original to Roland Wyse to work on as you say,' said Walsingham slowly. 'I can't say I examined it in detail or memorized any part of it. He brought back what he said was the same original, along with the clear version. He must have switched a false original for the real one. It's the only explanation. I don't think he knew there were copies. I don't recall ever mentioning them to him; I just said some of my clerks had each tried to decode the letter and failed. In which case . . .'

I said, 'If the code turns out to be the same, may I have the privilege of deciphering a copy of the genuine original?'

I sat in the clerks' room, where a space had been made for me at the end of a table and stared in disbelief at the text I had uncovered. The result was making my head spin. When I rose to take it to Walsingham, I found that my limbs moved stiffly, as though I were a puppet, pulled by strings.

The helpful Wentworth knocked on Walsingham's door for me and said through it that Mistress Stannard had finished her task and wished to present it. Walsingham called me in.

'You've managed the decoding?' he said as I entered.

'Yes. But . . .'

'But?'

'You're going to find it unbelievable,' I said, looking at the papers in my hand. 'You're going to think I'm playing some mysterious and horrible game, but I'm not. Please check my work, or have it checked, if you so wish. If the cipher letter

I've been working on is a true copy of what was found on Jarvis's body, then it really does say what my translation says.'

'Give them both to me,' said Walsingham.

I walked over to his desk and handed my work over to him. He studied it in silence, while I waited. Humphrey Johnson was still busy at his desk. Walsingham called to him. 'Come and look at this.'

Humphrey obeyed. And then looked up, eyes wide with shock. 'This is beyond reason,' he said.

'Quite,' Walsingham agreed.'

'I know,' I told them. 'But that's what it *says*.'

'This,' said Walsingham, staring at the decoded letter once more, 'is apparently addressed to the Principal of the Jesuit seminary at Rheims. It thanks him for a recent payment, which has been safely received. The writer is happy with this generous reward and prays that the information he has provided will be of value. He hopes to be even more useful in the future.

'The letter then goes on to say that when, as the writer devoutly hopes, a full-scale Jesuit mission to England is finally mounted, he recommends that the missionaries should avoid Dover and come in by way of other ports – Norwich, Hull, or Bristol. It states that details of safe houses close to those ports will be supplied in good time. These are already being assembled but this has to be done with great caution and secrecy as no breath of suspicion must attach to the writer. The letter is then signed. With my name.'

There was a moment of appalled silence, and then Walsingham said: 'Ursula, did you let any of my clerks see this?'

'No, sir.'

'I'm relieved to hear it. There were three copies made of the original cipher, I believe. You have been working with one of them – this one. There are two others, presumably somewhere in the clerks' room. Humphrey, please go and collect them and bring them here. And not a word to any of the clerks about this monstrous translation.'

Humphrey went out. Walsingham said, 'If this were to become common knowledge, it would be the scandal of the century. I would never live it down. It could ruin me. You realize that?'

'Yes, I do.'

He twisted round in his chair and looked at me directly. His dark eyes were hard and piercing but he had gone pale, for all that. 'Do you believe that this is a forgery? Or not?'

'Of course it is.' I fumbled for the right words. 'My lord Burghley has known you; the queen has known you; I myself have been acquainted with you for many years. If you had Catholic leanings, they would have been noticed. It's almost impossible for a man in the positions you have held to hide these things. And I'm sure that all your income, from whatever source, is properly accounted for.'

'I could still have a strongbox hidden under my bed,' said Walsingham dryly. 'I haven't, of course, but that's what would be said. Ah, Humphrey. Thank you.' His secretary had brought the other two copies of the cipher. He held out a hand for them. 'I shall destroy all these copies, personally. I imagine Wyse himself has disposed of the original. Humphrey, may I assume that you, like Mistress Stannard here, feel certain that this outrageous piece of correspondence did not emanate from me?'

'You certainly may, sir.'

'Why?'

'I've known you too long, sir. If you did wish to . . . encourage . . . er . . . Catholic missionaries, you would go about it quite differently. You wouldn't be arresting them quite so enthusiastically, for one thing. And think of the plots there have been, where you could have given secret encouragement! Instead, you did all you could to bring the conspirators to justice. This' – Humphrey put out a thick forefinger and flicked my translation disdainfully – 'is crude. The work of a most unskilled conspirator, I would say. Your own name, put blatantly at the end, instead of using a code name! Acknowledgement of a payment, but no amount is mentioned. A poor sort of receipt! Talk of safe houses but only a vague promise of details.'

'Thank you. My own feelings entirely. But,' said Walsingham, 'where in the world does Roland Wyse come into all this? Why did he replace the genuine original with a tarradiddle about an illicit loom?'

'Trying to protect you, sir?' suggested Humphrey.

'Even though he loathes me?' said Walsingham. 'I'd have expected him to pounce on a letter like this with positive joy.'

'So . . . none of this,' I said wearily, 'makes any sense at all.'

'No. Although . . .' Walsingham was frowning. 'He *did* exchange the real original for a false one. Why? I do begin to think that the fact that Mistress Cobbold, Jarvis and Wyse all met in Jarvis's cottage, just before two of them were murdered, may have some significance, though I can't guess what. I can only say, Ursula, that I now agree that there are questions needing answers.'

'Where would Wyse be by now?' I asked. 'Well on his way to Dover, surely.'

'Yes. With John Ryder as his superior officer.' For once, I saw Walsingham look confused. 'I can hardly put a man under arrest for *not* seizing an opportunity to damage me! I will send word to Ryder and tell him to put Wyse under surveillance. Though not, as I said, arrest. I'll question him when he is back in London.'

'Do you now feel that my doctored wine could have significance?' I asked.

'*If* it was doctored. Dead mice don't prove that. But the tinkering with that letter . . . I'll get a queen's messenger on the road to Dover immediately, with word to Ryder. He'll be easy to find – he's on official business and his party is being accommodated at the castle. I can then leave it to him to decide whether he tells Wyse that he is wanted for questioning, or whether just to keep a discreet eye on him until they're all back here in London. I shall instruct Ryder to finish the business in Dover, though. He might as well, after taking my men all that way.'

'I can take the message to Ryder!' I said. 'I'd like to. Until all this is resolved, Roger Brockley is in danger.'

'You will do nothing of the kind. This is work for a queen's messenger. I am aware of your care for your servants,' said Walsingham, 'but I have never approved of involving women in affairs of state. Women have emotions that are too volatile.'

No wonder, I thought, Queen Elizabeth had sometimes thrown

things at Walsingham. 'Where is Roger Brockley now?' Walsingham enquired.

'Not in London,' I said.

Walsingham produced his disconcerting smile. 'You travelled alone?'

'I've done so before,' I told him.

'You fear that I might send men to apprehend him. I do know that the warrant has been re-issued. I will let Brockley alone for the moment. I'll try to get some sense out of Roland first. I suggest that you simply go home.'

'Yes, sir,' I said.

NINETEEN
A Trace of Fragrance

'We're going to Dover,' I said to the Brockleys when I rejoined them at The Boar. 'I am certainly not going home. I want to talk to Ryder myself. Walsingham's leaving it to him to decide whether he tells Wyse of the position he's in straightaway, or merely keeps a watch on him until they're all back in Whitehall. I want him to question Wyse at once – because I want to hear the replies! And if he manages to present us with a believable explanation of the extraordinary things he did with that cipher letter, something that will convince Walsingham, something that makes Wyse look like an innocent and put-upon victim of circumstances, well, Dover is a port. You two can get away. And you will, at once. I'll brook no argument.'

'Oh, ma'am!' said Dale, miserably.

'I think madam is right, Fran. Though I must say,' said Brockley, 'that I'm finding it harder and harder to imagine any kind of reasonable explanation! Wyse will be hard put to it to invent one! We seem to have got into the realms of madness. Every new thing we discover makes the muddle worse.'

'I know,' I said. 'Yet somewhere there *has* to be an explanation! Two dead bodies need some accounting for!'

'Mistress Cobbold could just have been murdered by a prowler,' said Brockley slowly, 'and Jarvis by footpads.'

'A prowler?' I said. 'In broad daylight, in her own garden, where people could have been wandering out to find her, or looking out of windows, or gardeners walking in? And just footpads to account for Jarvis's death? He met Wyse *and* Mistress Cobbold, on the day of her death, and then Wyse tinkered with a cipher letter found on Jarvis's body. No, there really is some thread connecting all these things but what it is, heaven knows. Heaven and, I think, Master Wyse.'

Brockley said, 'Queen's messengers ride fast. We may meet them all coming back. Then Fran and I will never get to Dover at all.'

'I expect the enquiries into Ballanger's loom may take a few days,' I said. 'Walsingham said he'd instruct Ryder to finish them before turning for home. But you're right all the same, Brockley. We should set off forthwith.'

We worked out that by riding steadily, we could be almost halfway to Dover before dusk. The queen's messenger, of course, would use the royal remounts provided on every main route and could travel much faster. He might even ride through the night, though I didn't think the urgency was great enough to justify that. Wyse wasn't fleeing. The messenger could have a night's sleep and arrive in Dover next day in good time for dinner. We were taking our own horses all the way and couldn't hope to catch up, but we need not be that far behind, just the same.

We reached Dover during the afternoon of the following day and pulled up on the outskirts, to consider what to do next.

We were hot and tired. It was a beautiful day but the sun was too warm for comfort, and we were all, people and horses alike, dusted over with the pale chalk of the track. Around us were grassy hills where sheep were grazing, and high on one of the hills were the mighty walls and towers of the castle. In the distance, the Channel was a sparkling blue, dotted here and there with shipping.

'Ryder and the rest are staying at the castle,' I said. 'But if they're poking their noses into Ballanger's weaving sheds, we're more likely to find them there. We'd better find out where Ballanger works. Well, we do the usual thing, I suppose. We ask a vicar or an innkeeper.'

'Try an innkeeper,' said Brockley. 'We're all hungry and thirsty. We haven't had any dinner or anything to drink for hours, and nor have the horses. Besides, we need an inn for the night. We're not expected at the castle. We're not official.'

We had been to Dover before and could remember where

to find the inn where we had stayed. It was called the Safe Harbour and we had found it satisfactory. We made for it, and Brockley was pleased to find the same ostler there. He was easily recognizable because of the gaps in his front teeth and the droop in his left eyelid. He remembered us as well. We knew he was a reliable man and, for once, Brockley was happy about leaving our horses in his care. Then we all gathered up our saddlebags and made our way round to the front entrance and into the vestibule.

'Well, here we are,' Brockley said. 'Will you bespeak some ale and things to eat for us, madam? I'll do the enquiring about Ballanger.'

The innkeeper came hastening down the stairs as soon as he heard us arriving in the vestibule, and he didn't disappoint us. The inn could provide rooms for the night; there was a cool parlour where we could partake of refreshments; and yes, the landlord did know of Ballanger's establishment and could direct us there. In fact, the place was only a hundred yards away; we had passed it as we rode in. Standing in his front doorway, the landlord pointed it out to us.

An hour later, our parched throats slaked with ale and our hunger pangs assuaged with cold pigeon pie and fresh bread, we set forth on foot for the Ballanger weaving shed. The horses, their hides now wisped clean of chalk dust, were left in peace in their comfortable stalls, with filled managers and buckets of well water.

There was nothing secretive about the weaving sheds. Ballanger's was a long timber building with a slate roof and a row of windows running, as far as we could see, right round the front and side walls. A wide double door opened on to the street and a cart, with a big grey horse between the shafts, stood in front of them. Bales of raw wool were being unloaded and carried inside.

Though not quite in the businesslike fashion one might have expected, for the men with the bales all seemed to have heads cocked towards sounds from within, and we noticed raised eyebrows and the exchanging of meaningful glances.

'I think we're in luck,' Brockley said. 'Something's going on – maybe Ryder and the rest are in there.'

No one took any notice of us. We edged past a skinny youth clutching a bale nearly as big as himself and slipped inside to find ourselves in a place like a big, untidy cave. It had a flag-stone floor and a door at the rear had the look of an internal door and presumably led into a further extension of the building. Above us, the ceiling was high, a criss-cross of beams supporting the slate roof and there were three glazed skylights, which amplified the light from the numerous windows. One could understand why natural light was so important. Fire would always be a danger in such a place, for one side of the cavernous room was full of piled up wool bales, to which the new delivery was being added, and the air was full of wool fibres, floating in the shafts of light from the windows. The naked flame of torch or candle would be perilous here.

The centre of the floor was occupied by two big looms, though at the moment they were silent. The weavers were at their posts but giving all their attention to what was happening on the side of the room opposite to the bales. This was open space, except that half a dozen men were standing in it, involved in an intense discussion. Ryder and his squad were not, however, among them. We stepped out of the way of the bale carriers, and moved to stand by the wall and assess the scene before us. Still, no one seemed to have realized we were there. We were able to listen unchallenged.

It took only a moment or two to identify Julius Ballanger, because just as we entered, someone addressed him by name. In any case, his well-fed frame and his smooth face, his confi-dent stance and his broad, plausible smile would have marked him out as the man in charge, even though he was in working clothes: boots, breeches, loose shirt and sleeveless jerkin, with a round cap on his head, no doubt to keep wool fibres out of his hair. Beside him was a leaner man who had the air of a chief assistant. The others, who formed a group facing Ballanger and his companion, were dressed more formally, with ruffs and doublets and slashed hosiery. Ballanger was now refuting something that had been said to him. We cocked our ears.

'. . . you have yourselves agreed that where there is a demand, a growing crowd of would-be customers, then a supply will be forthcoming from somebody. People like the worsted cloth. If they can't get enough of it, at a reasonable price, in England, they'll buy from abroad, and pay more. They'll still buy from somewhere. So why should we in England not provide it for them, yes, and sell some of it abroad ourselves? It will bring in money, help to make England prosperous! You accept all this – you've said so, here, this afternoon, under this very roof. So why, now, are you trying to attach strings to it? Why on earth should I have to pay Danegeld to you, in return for a licence to make my loom official?'

'Danegeld?' said the foremost of the be-ruffed gentlemen, a dignified figure with a neatly trimmed fair beard and a hat with a definitely expensive brooch in it.

'More money than education, that one,' muttered Brockley in my ear.

'Before the Norman Conquest,' said Ballanger's presumed assistant, 'a king called Ethelred the Unready bribed the Danish Vikings not to raid English shores. The bribe was called Danegeld. It didn't work. The Vikings took the money and went on raiding. Or so my schoolmaster told me, when I was a boy.'

'We are not talking about bribes!' said the fair-bearded gentleman indignantly. 'We are representatives of the Wool Weavers' Guild in this district and we have the interests of our members at heart. If some of the trades we represent, Master Ballanger, are to be curtailed because worsted cloth doesn't need them, then there must be recompense in some way. That's only right. There will be men put out of work. We recognize that licensed worsted looms are going to increase in number, because of public demand. We have said so. But . . .'

'This is ridiculous!' said Ballanger, also indignantly. 'We are going round in circles. First you agree, then you ask for a bribe . . .'

'It is *not* a bribe!'

'It most certainly is and it would bring my profit margin down to poverty level! I applied in good faith for a proper licence and this is the result!'

He stopped as a sudden uproar broke out in the street. All heads turned that way. Then the skinny youth I had noticed

as we came in burst through the door, almost tripping over
the bale he was clutching, and behind him, thrusting him ahead
of them like a bow wave, came another half-dozen men. John
Ryder and his associates were not among these either. These
men, like Ballanger himself, were dressed in working clothes.
They were also carrying axes and, by their angry shouts, had
a purpose for them.

'What is this?' Ballanger demanded, stepping immediately,
and courageously, into their path. Brockley seized Dale's hand
and my arm, and pulled us both further away, into a shadowy
corner.

'You . . . you . . . ask *that*?' The leader was a big man with
the beefy shoulders of an ox and the axe he was carrying had
a short handle but a dangerously glittering edge to its blade.
He was red with rage and barely coherent. 'We've just got to
know of this here . . . this *deputation,* this *treacherous deputation,* coming here to make terms with you and back up your
demand for a license. You've got away with running this illegal
place too long. We let you get away with it because we're
peaceable folk . . .'

'You look peaceable, I must say,' Ballanger said, or rather
boomed. He had a powerful voice. 'You'd sound more
convincing if you weren't waving axes.'

'That's quite right.' The Weavers' Guild spokesman bustled
forward. 'By what right do you come bursting in here, brandishing weapons and without an appointment . . .?'

He stopped, because at that point, the intruders laughed and
he probably noticed that his words were more than a little
ridiculous. The axe-wielding leader broke in.

'Peaceable we've been, for too long. Because just one
illegal loom don't make so much difference. But give you
a licence, and there'll be ten more like you, springing up,
and saying if you can be legal, why can't they, and snatching
our work away out of our very hands. We're carders and
fullers, we are. We get our living carding wool ready for
the looms and fulling the cloth in our mills, but worsted
yarn isn't carded and worsted cloth isn't fulled and if your
looms start sprouting up like mushrooms, where are our
livelihoods?'

'That's right!' shouted an excited voice from behind him. 'Taking bread out of the mouths of our wives and children, you are, Ballanger, and we're not going to have it.'

'No, we ain't!' The rest of the newcomers joined in.

'We won't stand for it!'

'No, that we won't! We'll make firewood of your looms, and we're going to do it now! Come on, lads!'

Dale let out a scared whimper. 'Keep huddled in this corner,' said Brockley. 'We'll get out when we can. This is going to be nasty.'

It was nasty already. Ballanger's assistant had sprung to his side and so had his weavers, forming a line between the intruders and the looms. Axes were flourished menacingly. After an uncertain moment, the Guild representatives moved to join the defenders, two of them drawing daggers.

And then, at last, came the familiar voice of John Ryder, bellowing: '*Stop!*' in a more stentorian tone than I had ever heard him use before, and in through the door, striding purposefully, came Ryder himself and ten liveried men behind him, all with swords out. The angry intruders swung round to be confronted with a row of sword points. From the defenders, a cheer broke out. The invaders started to expostulate but Ryder raised his voice again.

'An end to this unseemly business! Everyone who is not part of this establishment – leave now!' A jerk of his head and his men moved to leave the way out clear. 'Or you'll be taken up for causing a public affray.'

'Now see here!' The leader of the carders and fullers was truculent, standing with feet apart and gripping the handle of his axe in a determined fashion. 'We're here with a right good grievance and you can't—'

'I can. You leave these premises, or I can send to the castle and have a squad down here big enough to take every man of you to its dungeons. I'd have brought them with me if I'd known this was happening. I only found out on the way here! All Dover is buzzing with rumours about angry carders and fullers getting together to attack Ballangers. But it was still a disagreeable shock to find a lot of deliverymen clustered round the street door, scared out of their wits, and saying that there

were madmen inside, threatening people with axes! I represent
law and order and mean to have it respected. I repeat, everyone
who doesn't belong here – go!'

They were going, the carders and fullers first, pushing axes
into belts, melting past him, slipping off through the entrance.
Their leader snarled at them to stay but only a couple lingered
beside him, until Ryder walked towards them, sword in hand,
whereupon they gave in and trailed out after the rest of their
friends. They were all, I thought, essentially honest tradesmen
who had been stirred up by rabble-rousing speeches, but were
not really in the habit of marching about in gangs, brandishing
weapons. The gentlemen from the Weavers' Guild followed
them out, though in a more dignified manner.

'We were here on proper business, at the invitation of Master
Julius Ballanger,' their leader said as he came level with Ryder.

'I also have proper business, though *not* at Master Ballanger's
invitation,' Ryder said dryly. 'Mine, however, is on behalf of
Her Majesty the Queen. You may pursue your own business
some other time.'

He nodded in satisfaction as the last of them went out and
then, turning, found himself looking straight at me and the
Brockleys, as, indeed, the Ballangers and their weavers were
now doing.

A familiar figure emerged from the party of men with Ryder.
'Mistress Stannard? Whatever are you doing here?' said Roland
Wyse.

He sounded astonished. As well he might, I thought, if he
really had doctored my wine that evening in The Boar.
He had probably believed that I was dead or at least seriously
indisposed. Finding me here must be quite a shock.

'Who are these people?' Master Ballanger said. 'When did
they come in? I never noticed them!'

'You were much engaged with the leader of the deputation
from the Weavers' Guild,' I said. 'You didn't see us. Captain
John Ryder knows who we are, though.'

'Yes, although how you come to be here is a mystery,' said
Ryder. 'But we'll discuss that later. I won't order you out though
I must ask you to keep back and not interfere.' He turned to
his men. 'You have your orders,' he said. 'Search these premises.

Don't miss one single cranny. Test every floorboard, every panel, every keyhole. Proceed! You.' He pointed his sword at the Ballangers and their employees. 'Stay where you are. Wyse, bring in the fellows who were delivering the wool. I'll keep them all together.'

'What are you looking for?' demanded Ballanger. 'What do you mean, *search* these premises? Who are you? What do you expect to find?'

'Priests, possibly,' said Ryder. 'My name is Captain John Ryder, and I am here on the orders of one Francis Walsingham. You may have heard of him.'

Ballanger stood with his mouth open, struck speechless. Ryder's men scattered about their tasks and Ryder himself came over to us. I said, 'Has a queen's messenger found you?'

'Yes. He reached the castle just as we were about to set out for this place. He delayed us. I've read the message.' Wyse had gone out to fetch the deliverymen, but Ryder dropped his voice all the same. 'Roland Wyse has apparently been doing very odd things with the cipher letter found on Jarvis's body, and Walsingham wants an explanation. Wyse knows nothing of this, by the way. I take it that you do, however. I assume that it's the reason why you're here.'

Wyse reappeared, herding the deliverymen in front of him and pushed them to stand by the looms with the Ballangers and their people.

'Leave them there and join the search,' said Ryder. 'I'll stand guard.' He ran a finger suggestively along the blade of his sword. The group by the looms looked nervous. Wyse gave me a further puzzled glance, but obeyed, disappearing through the door at the rear of the room. I watched him go and then turned back to Ryder.

'On Brockley's behalf,' I said, 'I have been searching out facts. They made me suspicious of Wyse. When we came across him at The Boar, I set a trap. I don't know whether the message from Walsingham mentioned it, but . . .'

Ryder listened attentively while I described my trick with the wine, the discovery of the dead mice and the details of my conversation with Walsingham. 'He doesn't know we're in Dover,' I finished.

'I daresay! No, his message didn't tell me about it. It's been left to me to decide whether to question Wyse at once or take him back to London first. I suspect you would like me to do some questioning myself, forthwith?'

'Yes.' I looked at Brockley and Dale. 'All three of us have a stake in this.'

His brow creased. 'This is a serious matter. I must consider it carefully. I must also finish my task here, as well. I have orders to do that.'

I said, 'How is it that you didn't get here – to these works, I mean – before? You say the queen's messenger delayed you this morning, but you surely reached Dover yesterday!'

'The hazards of travel. One horse cast a shoe, miles from a forge, of course. Miles from anywhere! It was open common, all around. We had to lead the horse slowly for two hours to find any habitations, with its rider perched behind a friend. Then we found a village with a smithy and had the new shoe put on – *after* a long wait while the customer ahead of us had two plough horses and a pony shod. All round, four shoes for each of them. Then next day, one of the other horses stumbled in a pothole, came down and cut its off foreleg badly. Again, we were miles from anywhere, though we did find a farm where we could leave the animal to be looked after. But then we had to carry on with another man riding double, until we found a hiring stables where we could get a replacement. We didn't get to Dover till last night. I'd begun to think we never would! Where are you putting up?'

'The Safe Harbour,' said Brockley.

Ryder looked at him seriously. 'I wish with all my heart, old friend, that you were indeed in a safe harbour. If it was a shock when we arrived here to find that a dangerous mob was ahead of us, it was just as big a shock to find you inside!'

Brockley said, 'Wyse is coming back. I think they've found something.'

Wyse was hurrying towards us from the rear door. 'Captain, there's something you should see!'

'A priest in hiding?' asked Ryder hopefully.

'No, sir. But perhaps a place where one might have hidden. It's through there.' He pointed to the door.

'Show us,' said Ryder.

I and the Brockleys were not exactly invited to accompany Ryder and Wyse, but we went anyway and no one objected. The rear door, it turned out, led into living quarters. Unlike the weaving shed, they were built of stone and were probably older. We found ourselves first of all in a passageway that stretched from left to right. A door immediately opposite to us, however, was open and we followed Wyse through, to find ourselves in a dining chamber, big enough to seat twelve, with pewter and silverware displayed on a walnut sideboard. The left-hand wall had panelling; the others were of bare stone except for one *mille fleurs* tapestry.

In a corner to our right, a twisting stone staircase led up to what presumably were bedchambers overhead, and a door by the side of the stairs was evidence that there were other downstairs rooms, perhaps a parlour and no doubt a kitchen. In the panelled wall, there was an aperture, about five feet high by four feet wide, the foot of it one panel up from the floor. Within, we could see vague movements and a gleam of light.

'There,' said Wyse, pointing, and as he did so, two of Ryder's men, the younger one carrying what looked like one of Ballanger's own silver candlesticks, complete with a lit candle, emerged from the aperture, stepping over the awkward panel and crouching to avoid bumping their heads.

'We tapped the panelling,' said Wyse, 'to see if any sounded hollow and a section there did. Then Robin there' – he pointed to the young man with the candle – 'started pushing and pulling, and all of a sudden, there was a grating noise and a whole patch of panelling just slid.'

'There's a room in there,' said Robin, grinning. He was no more than eighteen by the look of him, and was boyishly pleased with himself. 'Not big, but it is a room, not a cupboard. It's got a grating, high up – must be set in an outside wall, because there's daylight coming in, kind of greenish, as though it's overhung by a creeper. It lets in air, anyway. There's no musty smell. Will you come and see, sir?'

'Yes,' said Ryder, leading the way. 'Wyse, fetch Julius Ballanger.'

The room was as Robin had described it. It was a stone cell, perhaps eight feet square inside and quite lofty. It was clean, as though it had been recently swept. It was also completely empty. As Robin had said, the air was fresh, although I thought I could detect a faint, aromatic smell which seemed vaguely familiar though I couldn't identify it. I wondered if the place had been used to store spices.

There were sounds of indignation from outside and Julius Ballanger was thrust roughly through the entrance to join us. He had to catch at the side of it to keep himself from tripping over the low panel. 'What is all this? Why am I being hustled about in my own house? And why have I been brought *here*?'

'Oh, come, Master Ballanger. This is a secret room,' said Ryder. 'Just the place to hide a priest, newly arrived in England and needing a place of safety. Wouldn't you say?'

'No, sir, I would not. I took these premises over three years ago and found this room already here. Since then, I've used it as an extra store, although I have no need to do that just now. What my predecessors used it for, I neither know nor care.'

'I see,' said Ryder pacifically, and signalled that we should all move out, which we did with some relief. With so many people in there, the place had felt uncomfortably crowded.

Back in the dining chamber, we found some more of Ryder's men, ready to report on what they had found, or not found, in other parts of the building. They had upset some womenfolk, who were clustered at the foot of the staircase and muttering indignantly together, but they had discovered nothing of significance. Only the enigmatic little space behind the sliding panel suggested anything untoward.

Ryder turned to Ballanger. 'You may continue your business for the time being. But I advise you not to attempt to leave Dover. We may well want to talk to you again.'

Our visit seemed to be over. We found ourselves trooping back through the loom chamber, watched by the nervous but resentful eyes of the weavers and the presumed Ballanger assistant, and then we were out in the warm late August afternoon. It seemed that Ryder and his men, like us, had arrived on foot. We began to walk along the street together.

The youthful Robin suddenly observed: 'Captain Ryder, I did notice something in that funny little room. At least, I think I did.'

Ryder stopped short. 'Noticed something? Why didn't you say so before? What did you notice?'

'I wasn't sure. I've kept thinking it over. But I don't think I imagined it. I keep remembering it. It was very faint, but . . .'

'*What* did you notice, young Robin?' I was a little amused to notice that even though Ryder was here in charge of a semi-military group, he still had his old fatherly way of speaking to juniors. He did not address the lad as *soldier*, or *trooper*, or use any other military term. It was *young Robin*, as though he were a father speaking to a son or at least a schoolmaster addressing a pupil.

'It was a smell, sir,' said Robin. 'A . . . a fragrance. Just a trace, but I thought I recognized it.'

I said, 'I thought I smelt it, too, but I couldn't put a name to it.'

'Two sharp noses are better than one, perhaps,' said Ryder. 'Robin evidently does think he could put a name to it. Well, Robin, what did you think it was?'

'Incense,' said Robin.

TWENTY
Untimely Sunset

We walked on in silence through the warm afternoon until we reached the Safe Harbour. Before parting from me and the Brockleys, Ryder drew me aside.

'I do realize, Ursula, that you want me to question Roland Wyse at once, and I know why. The Brockleys have so much to lose – Roger's freedom and perhaps his life. I know.'

'You have discretion,' I said.

'I know. But I am no skilled questioner. There is something to be said for carrying Wyse back to London for interrogation.'

'Isn't there anyone in Dover Castle who could undertake that?'

'Perhaps. I will give you my decision tomorrow. I need to think. We shall remain in Dover for a while. We'll probably do another swoop on the Ballanger household, just on the off chance that we find the hidden room occupied this time. Then we'd have a catch, and they're hard to come by.'

He made a wry face. 'The Dover port authorities do investigate the baggage of any likely suspects in case they find Popish vestments or other things of that sort, but we suspect that incoming priests get their regalia supplied by sympathizers here. And, of course, arriving passengers always have convincing documents with them and good reasons for coming to England. No, we're by no means finished with Julius Ballanger. I trust young Robin's nose; he's shown its worth before and this time, he has you to back him up.'

'How did Robin's keen nose help you before?' I asked, intrigued.

'Oh, when we were in Hertfordshire and making our stealthy approach to the house where we caught the household at Mass, we nearly blundered into a sentry. We'd silenced the dogs but they'd posted someone on watch instead. Robin stopped us just as we were creeping along a path towards a side door, which we hoped our obliging strolling player had unbolted for us. Robin whispered that he could smell something. So we all froze into the bushes alongside the path, and after a moment, sure enough, a man came pacing past, holding a pike. He'd eaten onions for supper and as he went by, I smelt his breath myself. But what Robin smelt must have been a trace he'd left when he went along the path before. We watched till we understood that he was on a beat between the side and front doors. Then, when he was at the front door end of it, we dodged out of the bushes, found the side door open, went in and made our catch. Robin has a nose like a bloodhound!'

'A useful man,' I said. I gave Ryder my hand. 'Till tomorrow, then. But I do hope . . .'

'I know. I will tell you then. Promise.'

'Thank you.' I thought it best not to explain that the real reason why I wanted Wyse questioned while we were all still in Dover, was because Dover was a port, from which the Brockleys might escape from England.

We passed a pleasant enough evening, walking down to the harbour to look at the shipping and watch a beautiful vessel bearing the name of *La Topaze* glide into port under oars. Then we sauntered back to the inn to rest and tidy ourselves and take some supper.

After supper, we went to bed, tired from our long ride, the exciting nature of our visit to the weaving shed, and the sea air. It was a stuffy night and I left my window unshuttered and partly open, wanting coolness. It looked to the west and when I suddenly awoke from my first sleep, I thought at first that the glow outside was a magnificent sunset. Then as I shook the sleep from my brain, I realized that a hubbub had aroused me. And also, the sunset was flickering oddly, and I could smell smoke.

I threw myself out of bed and ran to the window. A moment later I was flinging off my night-rail, hauling on some clothes and pulling on a pair of shoes. Having done so, I rushed out, intending to rouse the Brockleys, but met them on the gallery that linked our rooms. They, too, had flung on some clothes and were coming to find me.

'It looks like the weaving shed,' Brockley said. 'No danger to us here, I'd say, but we'd best see what's happening. I think Ryder's out there; I'm sure I heard his voice.'

Downstairs, doors were banging, people were shouting to each other or exclaiming in alarm. The whole inn seemed to be awake. We raced down and joined a crowd of inn servants and guests as they were jostling out into the street. Brockley was right; it was the weaving shed. Timber-built, full of wool and cloth and floating fibres, it was burning briskly and though the Safe Harbour was still at a good distance, the houses to either side of the blaze were in danger. Our landlord, who had his own well, was organizing a bucket chain, and was bellowing for extra hands and buckets, and against the dreadful glow, I could see men scrambling up ladders to the roofs of the houses adjacent to Ballanger's, and throwing water on to them to protect them from windblown sparks.

Brockley went at once to join the bucket chain. Dale and I stood anxiously in the midst of a murmuring crowd, knowing there was nothing we could do. Suddenly, Ryder was beside us, hastily dressed, just as we were, his face smudged with smoke. 'I thought you'd come out. We saw it from the castle and Captain Yarrow ordered his men out to help. I brought mine as well.'

'Captain Yarrow?' I asked.

'Deputy Constable. The constable's not here – paying a visit to his estates, I understand. Things always happen when the top man isn't there; I think it's called the Devil's law. Yarrow and some of the men we brought are round at the back of the shed; the fire hasn't got there yet or it hadn't just now. The living quarters are mostly stone and the wind's blowing the flames towards the street, which is a mercy.' He stopped to cough as a billow of smoke swept towards us. Through the coughing and with streaming eyes, he said: 'I sent Wyse to look for another well and start a second chain but . . . oh, there you are, Wyse! Christ, this smoke! What luck?'

Roland Wyse, grimy and out of breath, waved smoke out of his eyes and panted: 'I've got another chain going and I think the houses on either side will be saved, but there won't be much left of that weaving shed by the time this is over.'

'How did it happen?' I said.

'Arson!' snapped Ryder. 'And Yarrow's arrested two men – one of them is that hulking fellow that was brandishing an axe this afternoon. He's a carder. The other's a fuller. We saw them in the street, laughing and slapping each other on the back and we've not much doubt that it was those two who set light to the place. Dear God, if there's anyone killed tonight, they'll be for the rope! What's this?'

A small group of people were coming towards us. Three or four were women, clutching shawls round them and mostly in tears. With them were men in castle livery, who were dragging a couple of captives, though they were not the arsonists, since one was Ballanger himself, shouting and protesting. I didn't recognize the other, who was small and slight and not resisting, but marching stiff-backed in the grip of two burly soldiers. But when he caught sight of Wyse, he shouted: 'Roland! Roland! It's me, Gilles Lebrun! Make them let me go! Roland, help me!'

Gilles Lebrun. I had heard that name before. I was still wondering when and where, when the man in charge of the group, a dark, wiry fellow carrying a drawn sword, snapped at Lebrun to be quiet and strode up to Wyse. 'I shouldn't try to help him, my friend.'

Of course. The wine merchant's agent and Wyse's friend, who had comforted him when Norfolk died. Wyse, sounding frightened, was saying: 'Why not? What's wrong? How did he get here?'

'We were in time to rouse the household,' said the dark man. 'They didn't even know there *was* a fire! Wind was blowing it away from the house and they were all fast asleep in bed! They'd have been roasted in the end, though, but for us. Only, this Gilles Lebrun wasn't fast asleep in any proper bedchamber!'

He sheathed his sword and rubbed his hands together in a pleased manner. It was somehow a distasteful gesture. 'We woke him up with all our racket,' he said gleefully. He had a high-pitched voice for a man. 'We caught him climbing out from behind a sliding panel in the dining room. And when we had a look in there . . . well, guess what we found!'

'You found the secret room, Captain Yarrow,' said Ryder.

'Indeed we did, but not just that. Lebrun's a Catholic priest,' said Yarrow happily. 'In fact, from a Jesuit seminary. And in that room was all his paraphernalia. So I wouldn't recommend anyone to speak for him, Mr Wyse. Straight to London and the Tower, that's where he's bound.'

Wyse was now gaping. 'Gilles . . . a *Jesuit*? I don't believe it. I can't believe it! Gilles! When did you arrive?' Lebrun's captors had brought him up to us by now and Wyse was able to speak to him without shouting. 'What were you doing in that hidden room? You weren't a Jesuit when I last saw you, the day my brother died!'

'I came in this evening on *La Topaze*,' said Lebrun. He was using English though with a strong French accent. 'As for the last time I saw you, I was in training then for the Jesuit ministry but I knew you wouldn't sympathize! Though I sympathized with you, if you recall, over the death of the duke. I wasn't ready then to take up my duties. I am now and that's why I'm here.'

He flung his head back in an attempt at defiance but I could see that he was trembling. 'I haven't come to harm anyone! Only to bring comfort to people not allowed to take their sacraments openly; only to offer salvation to people lost in darkness. Roland, old friend, you must speak for me! You work for Walsingham! You—'

'*Quiet!*' barked Captain Yarrow, and one of Lebrun's captors struck him, a backhanded blow to the face. Lebrun's head jerked back from the blow and he let out a whimper.

'There's no need for that,' said Yarrow reprovingly to the soldier. He then added to Lebrun: 'Not that you've much to complain about yet. You'll whine louder than that in the Tower.'

'I can't help you!' Wyse was looking Lebrun as though his friend had turned before his eyes into something repulsive and not human, such as a giant slug.

'Why not?' Lebrun was angry as well as afraid. 'I helped you when you wanted me to! Didn't I give you the idea you said you were grateful for? Though I gather it hasn't done you much good. Did you ever put it into practice or did you lose your nerve?'

'It was too dangerous!' said Wyse. 'And this is no place to discuss it!'

'You always were timid, under the surface.'

'No more timid than you are now!' Wyse snarled back.

'That's enough!' said Yarrow, stepping in between them. 'You two will be taken to the castle and . . . yes?'

Ryder had stepped forward and laid a hand on Captain Yarrow's arm. He spoke rapidly into the captain's ear. We waited, noticing that the flames were at last dying down, as the fire ran out of fuel. The bucket chains were still at work, but had more than enough men to keep them going. Brockley rejoined us.

'There'll be nothing left of that weaving shed,' he said, 'but it looks as if the house behind it hasn't come to much harm. The Ballangers will still have a home. If they're left free to live in it!'

The colloquy between Ryder and Yarrow ended, and Yarrow barked out some orders. Lebrun's captors marched him and Ballanger away and two more men stepped forward to take hold of Wyse, who tried to resist but was also marched off, shouting a demand to know why he had been seized and where he was being taken. Ryder came over to us.

'I've put Wyse under restraint. He evidently knows Lebrun well and, by the sound of it, there's been something going on between them. I can't leave him free – even if he did protect Walsingham's reputation! You three should go back to the inn and rest. Tomorrow, I will fetch you to the castle. I think we may learn something. Have your horses ready by nine of the clock.'

Ryder fetched us as he had promised. Soberly, we rode with him along the sunlit street which nevertheless held the smoky smell of last night's catastrophe. I asked Ryder whether Ballanger had remained under arrest.

'He's being held for questioning, like Wyse. His chief assistant is, as well. We let the women and their maidservants go. They've gone back to the house to see what sort of a house it still is.'

'Who are we to see at the castle?' Brockley asked. His voice was wary. 'Are we being brought there for some sort of questioning, as well?'

Ryder laughed. 'No. You're witnesses. I've confided fully in Captain Yarrow and so has the queen's messenger – a good man, that; he was in a bucket chain last night. Captain Yarrow is very interested in the – shall I call it the fog? – of vague suspicion surrounding Roland Wyse.'

'He tried to marry me,' I said thoughtfully.

'That's suspicious, too. Once married to him, you would have been largely under his control.'

'And at his mercy,' I said grimly.

'Precisely. And now, of course, we find that he and Lebrun know each other and Lebrun seems to have advised Wyse to take what Wyse appears to think was a dangerous course, though we don't know what it was . . . There's a lot that needs clarifying. We are setting out now to clarify it. I think we may be in for an interesting morning.'

It took some time to reach the castle. There was a long winding chalk track up a green hill, towards the fortress at the top. As we neared it, we felt that it was looming over us. We passed under first one arch and then another, leading through walls so massive that they made me shiver. I think they made Brockley shiver, too, and Dale said to me: 'I'm glad we aren't staying here. I couldn't abide that. I'd never sleep, in a place like this. It's frightening.'

Once through the second arch, we dismounted and our horses were led away, while we were met by a butler with a gold chain of office, who showed us into the building. There were steps and passages and then, at last, we were brought into a small study where we found Captain Yarrow. There were some stools and the usual ledger-laden shelves and a desk strewn with papers, but Yarrow was not at his desk. He was perched on the window seat beyond it. He was clad in soldierly fashion, with well-polished boots, hose striped in sombre brown and black, and a black jacket with a wide leather collar. A white linen collar on top of this protected his neck from chafing. His hair was short and his beard trimmed. A small crossbow lay beside him, with a bolt placed ready for use.

And his strong, square hands were busy with an embroidery frame.

We all stopped short in astonishment but Captain Yarrow merely put down his improbable occupation and gave us good morning. The window was partly open and outside, we could hear someone barking orders. I moved nearer and saw that down below was an open space covered with sand, where a dozen or so young men appeared to be receiving a lesson in musketry.

'New recruits,' said Yarrow, jerking his head towards the window. 'This lot are unusually raw and useless but before Sergeant Burke has finished with them they'll be well-trained soldiers. He never fails. He's a hard taskmaster but his methods work . . . Good God!'

He had glanced out as he spoke and his body had stiffened. 'What is that idiot doing? Why hasn't Burke noticed? Does the stupid boy want to blow the sergeant's head off? He probably does, Burke being Burke, but it can't be allowed, no, really, it can't.'

He leant forward, snatched up the crossbow, wound it with a couple of swift and expert movements, shoved the window wider, leant out and discharged the bolt. I saw it strike just in front of a lad who was indeed holding his musket awkwardly, with its muzzle pointing towards the instructor, who was engaged just then in shouting at somebody else. The boy sprang back in fright and Yarrow, leaning out of the window, shouted: 'Never point a musket at anyone unless you're willing to kill him!'

I saw the sergeant swing round, and the boy's pale face turn to look up at the window, but Yarrow simply slammed it shut and put down the crossbow.

'He won't make that mistake again,' he said calmly. 'Of course, there's no gunpowder in those muskets and the lads at this stage have no means of firing them. They're just learning to aim straight and obey orders. But they have to grasp first principles. Now, my friends, to business. Everything is prepared.'

He rubbed his hands in that oddly disagreeable gesture of his, and emitted a laugh that was nearly a giggle. 'I daresay you are surprised at my choice of a pastime.' He patted the embroidery frame. 'I learned this art when I was laid up with a broken leg, after an accident during an exercise. I find it most relaxing. Also creative and even remunerative. I sell my embroideries to be used as cushion covers and dress trimmings and the like.' His voice altered suddenly. It was still high-pitched, but it had acquired authority. 'I also give instruction in accurate shooting, muskets or crossbows. People who make mistaken judgements about me, usually change their minds in the end.'

No one said anything. After the demonstration of the captain's skill with his weapon, no one would have dared to suggest that his liking for needlework was peculiar.

'In fact,' he said, quietly now, 'I somewhat dislike the use of force when questioning people. It's unpleasant to watch, and produces lies as often as the truth. That's why I've devised the method that you're about to witness. It isn't always suit-able, of course. One needs to be questioning two people at a time, not just one. But I have found it useful. Come with me.'

I had a hollow feeling in my stomach as we followed him out of the room. Dale, who had not uttered a word, looked pale and Brockley was uneasy, glancing from side to side as we were taken through a tangle of passages. In my ear, he said softly: 'I wish I knew what was going to happen. This place makes me nervous. I feel as if we'd all been arrested. Just suppose . . .'

He didn't finish the sentence. I put a hand on his arm, trying to offer reassurance, but I, too, wished I knew what was going to happen.

We were eventually shown through a heavy oak door with squeaky hinges, and into a cramped stone room, smaller than Yarrow's office, and shadowy, for the candles in the sconces weren't lit and the three small windows let in little daylight. The room was poorly furnished. There was an empty hearth, and against one wall was a settle, above which hung a small tapestry, with what looked like a geometric pattern, though in the bad light, I couldn't be sure. There was nothing else.

Yarrow, however, led us straight across to a low door on the far side and let us into a bigger, less gloomy chamber. The windows were no better but the candles were lit and the walls were panelled. There seemed to be some kind of cupboard door in the wall between this and the dismal stone room. Yarrow beckoned us towards it and we crowded round to see that we were looking into the adjacent room through a kind of window, or would have been, except that the tapestry had been hung over it, presumably to hide it.

'You'll find,' said Yarrow, 'that if we all stand here in a row, we'll be able to hear any conversation in the next room quite well. Its height is convenient enough for all of us.'

'Conversation?' I asked.

'Between Roland Wyse and Gilles Lebrun,' said Yarrow, rubbing his hands again. 'I feel sure they've a lot to talk about. Don't you feel that? Hush. Here they come.'

TWENTY-ONE
The Living Tool

We heard the door hinges squeak as someone came into the adjoining room. A man's voice said curtly: 'You wait in here till we're ready to interrogate you. You'll have company in a moment. We have quite a few of you to get through this morning.'

Wyse's voice, shakily, said: 'Who else?'

'Ballanger and his chief assistant,' said his escort. 'A carder and a fuller, suspected of arson. And here's Master Lebrun. He's on the list as well.'

Feet shuffled. A different man said: 'Just get in there and wait.' Then came the slam and squeak of the far door being closed, and the thud of a bolt being shot. Wyse said venomously: '*You!*'

'Yes, me. We seem to be in deep water together,' said Lebrun.

There was a rustling sound close by. The two of them had probably sat down on the bench below the tapestry. There was nowhere else to sit. Lebrun's voice said: 'The sun's bright enough outside but it's cold in here.'

'Fear,' said Wyse. 'That's what it is. What's going to happen to us? I curse the day I ever listened to you. And now I find that you – *you!* – are one of those damned Jesuits. How could you, Gilles? How *could* you?'

'God called me.'

'Phooey!'

'I was at a church service, in France, a simple country service, but the priest was a knowledgeable man and he gave a homily about the Jesuits, and their sacred task, the task of bringing true faith to all lost souls, and then I knew. It was like St Paul as he went towards Damascus. I *knew*. I heard God's voice calling. I went afterwards to talk to the priest and everything followed from there.'

'You poor, deluded *idiot!*'

'You don't understand, though I wish you would. It is wonderful! The yielding up of oneself, the passing through into a great, wide, marvellous world of light and faith! We swear utter obedience to the Pope, you know. If he were to declare that the night sky is white and the stars specks of black, we would believe it.'

'Even if you could see perfectly clearly that the truth is the opposite?'

'We would know our eyes had been deceived by the Devil.'

'I heard from my guards that you were caught with all your vestments and a silver chalice and a phial of incense. How did you get them past the Dover authorities?'

'I packed my ordinary clothes in a box with a false bottom, of course. What a silly question. And I would have been safe away at cockcrow, but for those fools setting fire to the weaving shed! More of the devil's work, I fear.'

'You're frightened now, for all your fine talk of light and faith,' said Wyse. 'I can hear it in your voice.'

'The flesh is frail. I shall pray for strength. Strength will be needed, and endurance. When enough Jesuit priests are ready, they will set forth on a major mission. The few priests that are here now are mostly from other Orders, and are mostly here as individuals – because they yearn to bring light into darkness and show lost souls the true way, whatever laws that man Walsingham may pass against them. I am here as an individual myself. I asked permission to come. But the priests that have come to England so far are but a trickle compared to the flood that the Jesuits will let loose when at last they sally forth officially! Oh, if only you had taken my advice and carried it through! Our hopes would be that much greater. Walsingham is dangerous – exceptionally so. Few can match him. My guards let something fall just as yours did – there's suspicion clinging round you, something to do with two deaths, and a cipher letter. It sounds as if you tried, but something went amiss. What was it?'

They were silent for a moment, during which Captain Yarrow breathed: '*Talkative guards. My idea.*'

Then Wyse said, 'I did try. God's death, I tried! I hate

Walsingham as much as it's possible for any man to hate another. He murdered my brother. Thomas Howard was not only my brother; he was my best friend. I only found him when I was fully grown and it was as though heaven had given me a marvellous gift. And then Walsingham took him away. Thomas could be foolish – he'd heard of Mary Stuart's charm; he'd fallen in love with her by hearsay, built absurd hopes round her, made her the centre of an imaginary world – but for all that, he wasn't wicked. Just . . . a dreamer. And my kin. But Walsingham destroyed him. I saw it done. I saw my brother die. I wanted to see Walsingham discredited, disgraced, charged with treason himself! I wanted to see him executed! With all my heart I wanted it.'

'So what went wrong?' said Lebrun.

There was a pause. Then: 'I lost my nerve,' said Wyse.

After another pause, Lebrun said, without expression: 'You poor wretch. Well? Just what did happen?'

'I took your advice. I picked a man who was poor and not very clever, and willing enough, if paid well, to carry what I called privy letters to Dover and not ask what was in them. Not the sort of man who's any loss. His name was Jack Jarvis. He was a cottager – a tenant of a man called Cobbold. I know Cobbold well and call on him sometimes. But things started going wrong from the very beginning. Cobbold's wife, Jane, a stupid, garrulous woman if ever there was one, had to butt in! She turned up at Jarvis's cottage while I was talking to him and overheard me from outside. It was a fine day and we had a window open. Then in she comes and starts talking about what she's heard! God's teeth, I nearly had a seizure, listening to her.'

'I heard something about this from my guards,' Lebrun said. 'She was murdered, wasn't she? By you? Because she'd overheard too much?'

'Well, what else could I do? *What's all this about you taking secret messages to Dover, Jack?* Jack was Jarvis's first name. *Why you? What's it all about? Well, make sure your chickens and garden are looked after while you're away. I won't try to stop you – I heard just now how well you're going to be paid and I don't grudge it to you, but my, it must*

*be important. Ah, well, I can see that neither of you are going
to tell me anything. How unkind of you, when you can see I
long to know all about it!'*

'She sounds like a silly woman,' said Lebrun.

'She was! Arch, silly, and I knew she'd never hold her tongue
and when Jarvis disappeared, she'd talk all the more and someone
somewhere might link a dead man, carrying an enciphered letter
and found on the Dover Road, with the Cobbolds' missing tenant
who was going to Dover with a mysterious message. I told her
it was a confidential matter and not something for ladies to concern
themselves with, but from that moment on . . . My God, I was
petrified. I couldn't leave her alive! I nearly put a stop to the
whole scheme then and there.'

'I see. Well, I understand that this Jane Cobbold had to be
dealt with . . . By the way, did Jarvis know what you'd done?'

'Good God, no. I said, he wasn't clever. When Mrs Cobbold
left us, he asked if it mattered, what she'd heard, and I laughed
and said oh, no, she's of no importance. Then I left, saying I
was on my way to London and so I was but I dealt with silly
Mrs Cobbold first. I don't think Jarvis dreamed I had anything
to do with that, though, not until the last moment. I met him
at an inn just outside London, as we'd planned. In the London
office, I was thought to be visiting my mother in Norfolk. I
gave him the letter, and then I intercepted him on the Dover
Road and said I had something else to give him – let's just
dismount and sit in the shade under that tree there while I
explain, I said. He trusted me until I pulled out my dagger.
What he guessed then, I wouldn't know, but he only had a
few seconds to do any guessing, anyway. Then the blade was
in his heart and that was that.'

'Poor sod,' said Lebrun cynically. 'Ah well. You'd got rid
of Mrs Cobbold and you'd carried out the Dover Road plan.
So why, after all that, did you lose your nerve, as you put it?

'Because I thought when Jarvis was found he'd be just an
unknown corpse. Mrs Cobbold was safely out of the way and
I hoped the cipher letter would start the ruin of Walsingham!
But Jarvis was recognized all the same! Of all the appalling
bad luck! The last thing I expected. A rotten, hateful
coincidence!'

'Or the work of the Devil,' said Lebrun.

'I felt as if Fate was conspiring against me,' said Wyse, aggrievedly. 'One of the men who found him had met him before! He'd been with me once or twice when I visited the Cobbold household. He thought he recognized the body. He wasn't certain but then the Stannard woman turned up in London and identified him for sure and that's when I knew that it was all going wrong. I didn't dare to go on. She has a reputation!'

'You should have got rid of her as well.'

'I tried, in the end. Not willingly. I'd already killed one woman. I made a good clean job of it but I didn't say I liked it. Besides, as it happens, I find Mrs Stannard attractive. Perverse of me, for she's one of those women who don't know their place, but who can explain these things? Her manservant Roger Brockley was arrested at first for murdering Jane Cobbold. That should have settled that problem, but Mrs Stannard interfered. She got him freed on bail! Then she arrives in Walsingham's office, wanting to talk to me, or so I heard later. I wasn't there when she came. But she'd been to Norfolk and talked to my mother. Obviously, she meant to go on and on, prying and probing, trying to clear Brockley, I suppose. So I tried to marry her, to get control of her. I could have made her love me, I know I could, if she'd only given me the chance, and then I'd keep her in order and she'd lick my hand for it, and keep my counsel. Women are like that. But she'd have none of me. And as I said, she has a reputation.'

'I know,' said Lebrun dryly. 'I've heard about her. I once met her husband – Matthew de la Roche. He greatly admires her intellect.'

'Women shouldn't be encouraged to develop their intellects, even if they have them,' said Wyse irritably. 'Which they mostly haven't. In my opinion, Mrs Stannard's intellect is mostly that of the manservant Brockley. But what of it? She somehow got Brockley out of prison, so she had his help again. I got away to meet Jarvis – and kill him – by saying I had to go to Norfolk because my mother was ill. By the grace of God, none of Walsingham's other clerks managed to decipher the letter I'd planted on Jarvis and when I came back, it was handed to me to decode. I thankfully snatched at the chance to stop the whole thing. I made up another letter, with something in it about an illicit loom I knew there was in Dover. Fairly harmless, I thought – a mystery that no one would solve. But . . .'

'You should have been the one to go on and on! You should have finished the work! Think of the gain!'

'Haven't you understood what I'm saying? It was too bloody dangerous once Jarvis was recognized. I was known to be acquainted with him, known to be a visitor at Cobbold Hall, known to dislike Walsingham. People might start making connections! I wanted to keep in the shadows and I felt as though someone carrying a bright torch was searching those shadows, to shine a light on my face!'

'I suppose you did have some reason to panic,' agreed Lebrun thoughtfully.

'I'd made further plans in case that one letter wasn't enough,' said Wyse glumly. 'I'd thought, if I could get invited into Walsingham's house, or go there on some pretext – with a message, something like that – I could plant some more damaging cipher letters, from and to Walsingham. I quite enjoyed planning what they might say, if decoded.'

'Brilliant! Oh, why *didn't* you go on?'

'I dared not. Oh, dear God, first that stupid Cobbold woman, and then Ursula Stannard! She wouldn't let things drop, she just *wouldn't*. I thought of trying to get Brockley out of the way – to make it look as if he'd killed himself from guilt or fear – but that was foiled, too . . .'

Beside me, Brockley moved sharply, and I saw Ryder's hand come out and press down, hard, on his shoulder, to keep him silent.

'And after that,' Wyse was saying, 'urged no doubt by Brockley, she *still kept on probing*. I met her by chance in an inn, and she told me she'd found out things about me. She'd found out that Thomas Howard was my brother. She was getting so near, so near. That was when I tried to be rid of her. I thought I'd poisoned her bedtime wine – and then I come here, to Ballanger's and there she is! Alive and well! *Nothing* went right for me!'

'They'll make you confess once you're in the Tower; you can be sure of that,' said Lebrun brutally. 'So if you had gone on, you wouldn't be in a much worse position than you are now and you would have avenged your brother's death. And Walsingham might have been brought down. Walsingham, who urged the queen into signing your brother's death warrant.'

'Dear Thomas. He was good to me, kind to me, he helped me. I loved him.'

'And you want Walsingham discredited, executed if possible. Of course you do! You can still do it!' There was excitement now in Lebrun's voice. 'You can! Tell them you've a statement to make! Be eager to make it! They'll want to know why you substituted a false cipher letter for the original! You can say you were protecting Walsingham, being loyal to your employer, that you didn't believe he could possibly be a traitor! But now you've had time to think and you've changed your mind! You can declare that the letter that damages him was genuine! Footpads killed Jarvis! The letter may still achieve its aim. You will have your satisfaction – and the true church will have a dangerous enemy made harmless. Do it, Roland! It's your golden opportunity, and ours, and it's still there! Why, it could save your life!'

The silence that followed this was lengthy. Then Wyse said: 'Are you telling me that when you advised me how to get rid of Walsingham, you were pursuing a motive of your own? That you wanted to use me to get Walsingham destroyed? That you were trying to make me a tool?'

'We both wanted him dead. I said, it was our chance. What's wrong with that? With him discredited, the usurper queen—'

'Elizabeth is not a usurper!'

'To us she is. It was a bitter thing for her to order Norfolk's execution; we know that. He was a kinsman and she thought him a friend and yet he betrayed her twice. Discrediting Walsingham would weaken her further. If she believed that Walsingham, too, had betrayed her, who, after that, could she trust? She would falter, lose faith in her own judgement, be vulnerable as never before, liable to make the wrong decisions, suspicious of her best men . . . alienating even those who have so far supported her. Driving some of them into the arms of those they once called enemies. She would become a much easier target for those who love the true queen and want to bring her to the throne.'

'You mean Mary Stuart?'

'Yes, of course.'

'That damnable woman, who had her husband murdered, married his murderer and would like to bring a Spanish army to England to put her on Elizabeth's throne and force England back to the Catholic faith with the help of the Inquisition? You made me a living tool not only for getting rid of Walsingham, but also to benefit *her*? You were conspiring against Elizabeth and tricking me into helping you? Helping you to destroy her as well as Walsingham?'

Wyse's voice had risen to a falsetto. I felt Captain Yarrow move sharply. In a tiny whisper, he said: 'We didn't expect this!'

'Of course,' Lebrun was saying, quite coolly. 'It is how we work. To achieve our ends, any means will do. All are sanctified by their purpose. They—'

'My God, I'll kill you!'

'What are you . . .?'

Lebrun's protest broke off in a shriek and a gurgle. We could not see but we could guess that Wyse's hands were round the throat of his one-time friend. Yarrow and Ryder sprang for the door and plunged through into the next room. Brockley went after them and I followed with Dale. She and I huddled in the doorway and watched as Wyse was dragged away from the choking Lebrun, who fell to the floor, clutching at his throat, his face congested.

'Two splendid confessions,' said Captain Yarrow happily, standing back and once more rubbing his hands together. 'Perfect!' He turned and gave Brockley a cheerful smile. 'I think your name will be cleared now, sir. I feel you have little in future to worry about.'

I didn't want to be there. I didn't want to watch as Lebrun, still gasping and choking, and Wyse, who had broken down in tears of mingled rage and fear, were manacled and taken away. But as he was being hauled towards the door, Wyse did momentarily drive his feet in hard enough to force his guards to a halt. He looked at me.

'I would have made you a good husband, Mistress Stannard. You've thrown away the chance of a lifetime. I'm a generous man. I give to charity; I am chivalrous towards women who are truly womanly. I could have made you happy. But women are so foolish!'

The guards tugged at him, but Yarrow signalled to them to wait. Brockley said sharply: 'But you don't mind pretending to care about them – when it suits you. You took leave from your work, didn't you, because you said your mother was ill and needed you, when all the time you were planning to meet Jack Jarvis and kill him. *Was* your mother ill, by the way? We know you went on to see her. She didn't deny she'd been ill when we visited her. But the timing of her sickness was convenient, wasn't it? What's the truth? I was nearly hanged because of you. I want an answer! You'll have to give one to Francis Walsingham anyway. Why not to me?'

'Oh, I invented the tale that she'd sent for me, but when I reached her, I told her she must back my story up, that it was part of a matter of state and that she must not ask questions. She did as I asked.' Astonishingly, he smirked. 'As I said, women are foolish. It can be useful, sometimes.'

I stared at him. 'I can't make sense of you. I think you loved your brother of Norfolk but you could never have loved me, or any woman, including your mother. You hold us in contempt and that sits ill with love.'

Then I turned my back, and when eventually I did turn round again, Wyse and Lebrun were gone.

'What will happen to them?' Dale asked timidly. Brockley had come to her and was holding her close to him, his arm round her shoulders.

'Those two?' said Yarrow. 'Better not to know. They'll hang at the least. They'll be fortunate if it's no worse.'

I shuddered, and was thankful that this time he didn't rub his hands together.

'The Ballangers may get away with fines and a stay in a gaol,' Ryder said, amplifying. 'As for the two we took in for arson, unless someone saw them setting light to the weaving shed, it may be hard to convict. They may well get away with it. And now, let us leave these little stone rooms, Captain Yarrow, for we all want light and air. Indeed we do.'

TWENTY-TWO
Queen of the Hive

'Wyse talked freely enough when he knew we'd overheard every word,' Ryder told us, arriving at the Safe Harbour that evening to join us for supper. 'He confirmed everything and added details. His orders to Jarvis were to meet him – in The Boar inn, as it happened – to receive a confidential letter to be taken to Dover. Then he waylaid Jarvis on the road, killed him and let the letter – the real original, that pointed such a shocking finger at Mr Walsingham – be found on him, to be deciphered, whether by Wyse or someone else.'

'Doing terrible damage to Walsingham,' I said.

'Indeed it would! Jarvis I think was a simple man in many ways. He was flattered and not suspicious. The scheme might have worked – except for Mistress Cobbold and you! Jane Cobbold had heard too much and he was right to think she'd never keep quiet. He followed her home, on foot, leaving his horse tied in the woods. The gardeners who arrived just then to climb their tree could see most of the track and he noticed them and knew he couldn't attack her there. But he saw her go into the garden. He ran round to where the shrubbery is, keeping out of sight of any windows, and slipped through that little door between garden and shrubbery. No one was about. When she came round to the back of the house, which isn't overlooked by any of the main rooms, well, you saw what he did.'

'It's horrible,' said Dale. 'Poor woman. We didn't like her but to have a thing like that happen to her! She must have been terrified, in those last moments when she realized what he was going to do.'

'We can only hope that she had no more than seconds to realize,' Brockley said. 'No one heard a scream, and screams carry. I know – I've been a soldier. I hope she had no time.'

'And then, Mistress Stannard,' said Ryder, 'you went and identified Jarvis's body. And Wyse panicked.'

'And he did intend to murder me when he broke into Hawkswood?' Brockley asked.

'Yes. He had a worrying time with your dogs,' said Ryder. 'He really wanted to poison them both, for safety's sake, but he intended Brockley's death to be taken for suicide. Two poisoned dogs would have suggested an intruder. So he trusted that Hero would just bark softly at him once or twice in her usual way, so that he need only kill Sandy. He hoped you'd think Sandy had got at something noxious while running in the woods.'

'And he intended it to look as though my husband had killed me as well,' said Dale bitterly. 'He'd have had to kill me too, after all.'

'It would have been said that I wanted to save you from disgrace – or that you tried to stop me and I struck at you in a rage,' said Brockley. 'We had a narrow escape.'

I said, 'And now we can go home.'

'By way of London,' Ryder said. 'A report must go to Walsingham. He will have to issue instructions to Heron, to get him off your scent!'

We came home to Hawkswood on an early September day. It was cloudy, but with the high, marbley, pale grey cloud that doesn't bring rain. The air was mild, the visibility good. The horse chestnuts were beginning to change colour but all the other trees were still in heavy, dark green leaf. I was more thankful than I can say to be back. I had also been thankful to get away from Dover and that looming, menacing castle with its eccentric deputy constable. Captain Yarrow was obviously highly competent and a loyal servant of the crown, but he made my skin crawl just the same.

As we drew near the house, Brockley said: 'There are the chimneys. A happy sight. There have been times, this year, when I thought I would never see them again.'

'It's Roland Wyse who won't,' I said. 'God knows what's happening to him now. He was a strange mixture. He really was charitable and generous in his way, you know, even if he *was* trying to buy popularity. Oh well, I've met other people who were strange mixtures, too.'

'I'd say you were that yourself, madam,' Brockley said, amused. 'So fond of your home and your son, and yet, with that longing for adventure that has got us into so many dangers. We've all feared for you, often.'

'None of us need be frightened now,' I said.

We rode on, our horses beginning to jog because they had recognized their surroundings and knew they were returning to familiar stables. Walsingham had sent an escort with us, including a queen's messenger with a letter for Sir Edward Heron. At my invitation, he was to dine at Hawkswood before riding on to find Heron. They all good-naturedly let their horses jog as well, to keep up with ours.

Adam Wilder and Sybil Jester met us in the courtyard. Adam had no cap and his grey hair was blowing about his head and both of them looked harassed. 'Madam! Everyone!' Wilder sounded quite distracted. 'I am so sorry, but I have to tell you that Sir Edward Heron is here!'

'He's been here for days,' said Sybil. 'We couldn't say no to the Sheriff of the county. But he has a warrant to arrest Master Brockley and . . .'

Sir Edward Heron himself now came marching out of the house, with four liveried men at his heels. 'Welcome home, Mrs Stannard. Wherever you have been.' He looked, I thought, more like a tall, predatory bird than ever. His long, faintly yellow nose seemed to be quivering with the desire to stab home. 'You, Roger Brockley, don't trouble to get off your horse. We'll be taking you off straight away. We've waited long enough! There'll be no more shilly-shallying. There's no doubt in my mind that you are the murderer of Mrs Jane Cobbold and you'll answer for it.' He stepped aside to let his companions advance on Brockley. 'Secure him!'

'But you can't! It isn't true! We've proved it isn't true!' Dale was terrified, and Brockley had gone so white that I thought he was actually about to fall from his saddle in a faint. It was for a moment as though everything we had heard and seen in Dover had been wiped out of existence.

Then the queen's messenger, who was a cheerful,

wind-reddened young man with a most engaging smile, rode forward, whisked his feet out of his stirrups, swung a negligent right leg over his horse's mane and slid to the ground. He put hand inside his doublet and produced the letter that Walsingham had provided.

'Let us not be hasty. This is for you, Sir Edward. It is important. Observe the seal. Please read it at once.'

Heron stared at him, but took the letter, examined the seal and tore the missive open.

I have to say that I much enjoyed the expression on his face, as he absorbed the information that there was no case against Roger Brockley, but that Roland Wyse had been arrested for the murders of both Jane Cobbold and Jack Jarvis, and also for conspiring with a Jesuit to blacken, falsely, the name of Walsingham.

Gracious things were said on both sides. We could afford to be gracious, after all, and Sir Edward Heron could not gainsay Walsingham's letter. Brockley and Dale magnanimously forgave Heron for his suspicions. I invited him to join us for dinner. He congratulated Brockley on his deliverance from a mistaken suspicion. He declined my invitation. He then ordered his men to saddle up and mount, and soon after that, he and they were gone. We all went inside and I went straight to the nursery to renew my acquaintance with Harry. We were home, and at peace.

It was not, in the end, as simple as that. I had not known, and I don't think even Dale knew, just how deeply fear and hopelessness had seared into Brockley. He was clearly thankful to be home and free of dread, but for the next few days he was nevertheless very quiet, not happy and serene as I – and probably Dale, too – had expected. Dale told me he was sleeping badly again.

Then one morning, he woke with a fever.

It was bewildering, because we had never known Brockley to be ill before. Dale looked after him, leaving his side only to fetch fresh sheets, or the medicines that Gladys brewed for him. For a long, unhappy week, he was constantly delirious and kept talking wildly of Lewes gaol and the horrors of imprisonment there, and sometimes cried out in protest as though he were having hallucinations of men coming to hang him. He did have lucid intervals but during these he seemed utterly listless and as if he were turning away from the world, even from Dale.

We kept Harry away from him, of course, for fear of contagion, but finally, it was Harry who turned the tide. He was becoming lively and extremely mobile and more than once evaded both me and Tessie and slipped into Brockley's room when Dale was absent.

The second time he did this, he got into the room during one of Brockley's lucid patches. He somehow climbed on to the bed and sat there, attempting in his infant's manner to talk to Brockley. Dale, coming in with a bottle of herb medicine, exclaimed in horror and went to lift him down, but Brockley gave her a faint smile and raised a hand to check her. 'Let him stay. I like him here. He's nice. Wish he was ours, don't you, Fran?'

'Roger always said he didn't mind us not having children,' Dale said to me after she had told me of finding Harry on the bed. 'But I think he did, perhaps. Under the surface, though he'd never say as much to me.'

'You're welcome to share Harry,' I said. 'But I don't like him going in there while Brockley's still ill.'

'No one else has got it, ma'am. I don't think it's catching. And Roger does seem to like the little boy being there.'

After that, we let Harry go into the room whenever Brockley was in his right mind, and within two days, his fever had dropped and the delirium was gone. A week later, he was back on his feet. Then he asked to speak with me alone.

I saw him in the Little Parlour. He had lost a great deal of weight but that, I hoped, would soon be put right. I told him to be seated. 'You shouldn't do too much too fast, after such an illness,' I said.

Brockley said abruptly: 'I was ill partly because I had been afraid for so long and when the fear was taken away, I felt as if something inside me had crumbled. But it wasn't only fear that caused it. I was so ashamed.'

'Ashamed? What in the world were you ashamed of?' I said, astonished.

'When we talked in the courtyard of the White Hart, in the moonlight, madam, and you wanted to leave me and Fran behind and I said no . . . Do you remember?'

'Of course I remember – and why ever should you be ashamed of that? You insisted on doing your duty even though it was dangerous for you. I can only admire you for it.'

'But I agreed that Fran and I should stay outside London while you finished the journey alone. I knew that to enter London would be to ride into danger, but it was my duty to escort you all the way to Walsingham's presence and I . . . couldn't face it. I dared not. I was too afraid. What would your husband, Master Stannard, have thought of me, letting you go on alone like that? I am sorry. I have told Fran all this, of course, and she says I was right, because staying behind at The Boar was what you had ordered us to do, but I can't agree. I did wrong.'

'I was never in the slightest danger in London! I've ridden alone many times – and done other, more risky things, alone as well! Brockley, put all thought of being ashamed out of your mind *now*! And forever.'

'I won't be able to do that,' said Brockley. 'But I will do my best never to fail you in such a way again.'

'You won't have the opportunity,' I said. 'I have finished with wild adventures. Now, find Dale, and let us all walk out into the rose garden. It will hardly be at its best, but the fresh air will be good for you.'

In the garden, the roses did indeed look sad, as they often did at summer's end, when there were few blooms left and the topmost twigs looked stringy. Dale considered them with obvious regret and said: 'It's been an unhappy year altogether.'

'One of the worst,' said Brockley with feeling.

'It's odd,' said Dale thoughtfully. And then, taking me by surprise as usual, she had one of her perceptive moments. 'I mean,' she said, 'it's odd how it all began. It all started, didn't it, with that woman in Norfolk, Agnes Wyse, taking Henry Howard away from her maidservant – that's Cat Spinner now. I think she was born that kind of woman, you know. She wasn't made that way by a harsh husband; if you ask me,

she made *him* harsh because of her queen of the hive ways.
Didn't that sensible young man Gilbert Shore call her that? If
Mistress Wyse hadn't insisted on being queen of the hive over
Cat and Henry Howard, the way she tried to be with Blanche
and Gilbert and probably was with Blanche's first suitor – that
farmer, Goodbody – then Roland would never have been born
and none of this would have happened.'

Brockley looked at her with respect. 'I never thought of it
that way. But yes, you are perfectly right. That *was* where it
started.'

I thought, though silently, of where it had led. To Jane
Cobbold, stabbed to death in her own garden; Jack Jarvis,
dead on the Dover Road. And Roland himself . . . where was
he now?

I didn't want to know the answer to that, nor did I want to
know the fate of Gilles Lebrun. I had even written to Sir
William Cecil, Lord Burghley, who I knew would understand,
to say as much.

Tessie appeared, carrying Harry. 'Madam, he's becoming
that heavy. Soon he'll have to do all his own walking, so he
will.'

'Give him to me,' said Brockley. 'I'm not too frail to carry
a lad his age. He fairly called me back to life again and I've
got fond of him.'

We walked on, with Harry seated on Brockley's shoulders.
There was a sense of closeness. Harry, by helping Brockley
back to health, had in some way bonded us together. From now
on, I thought, we would be a family, happy and united, without
dubious undercurrents of desire. And without danger or dread.
For I would have no more to do with crimes or plots or perilous
assignments. Not ever.